Tough Guys Don't Dance

Tough Guys Don't Dance

□

Norman Mailer

Random House
New York

A signed first edition of this book has been privately printed by the Franklin Library.

Grateful acknowledgment is made to Lord John Press for permission to reprint "One's
Neighbor's Wife," by John Updike. First published by Lord John Press.

Library of Congress Cataloging in Publication Data
Mailer, Norman.
Tough guys don't dance.
I. Title.
PS3525.A4152T6 1984   813'.54   84-42514
ISBN 0-394-53786-6

Manufactured in the United States of America
4689753

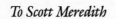

To Scott Meredith

Is it the mist or the dead leaves?
Or the dead men—November eves?

—JAMES ELROY FLECKER

There are mistakes too monstrous for remorse . . .

—EDWIN ARLINGTON ROBINSON

Tough Guys Don't Dance

One

At dawn, if it was low tide on the flats, I would awaken to the chatter of gulls. On a bad morning, I used to feel as if I had died and the birds were feeding on my heart. Later, after I had dozed for a while, the tide would come up over the sand as swiftly as a shadow descends on the hills when the sun lowers behind the ridge, and before long the first swells would pound on the bulkhead of the deck below my bedroom window, the shock rising in one fine fragment of time from the sea wall to the innermost passages of my flesh. *Boom!* the waves would go against the wall, and I could have been alone on a freighter on a dark sea.

In fact, I was awakening alone in bed, on the twenty-fourth drear morning after my wife had decamped. That evening, still alone, I would celebrate the twenty-fourth night. It must have proved quite an occasion. Over days to come, when I would be searching for a clue to my several horrors, I would attempt to peer through the fogbanks of memory to recall just what acts I might or might not have committed on all of that twenty-fourth night.

Little came back to me, however, of what I did after I got out of bed. It may have been a day like all the others. There is a joke about a man who is asked on his first visit to a new doctor to describe his daily routine. He promptly offers: "I get up, I brush my teeth, I vomit, I wash my face . . ." at which point the doctor inquires, "You vomit every day?"

"Oh, yes, Doctor," replies the patient. "Doesn't everyone?"

I was that man. Each morning, after breakfast, I could not light a cigarette. I had no more than to put one in my mouth and was ready to retch. The foul plenitude of losing a wife was embracing me.

For twelve years I had been trying to give up smoking. As Mark Twain said—and who does not know the remark?—"It's nothing to stop. I've quit a hundred times." I used to feel I had said it myself, for certainly I had tried on ten times ten occasions, once for a year, once for nine months, once for four months. Over and over again I gave them up, a hundred times over the years, but always I went back. For in my dreams, sooner or later, I struck a match, brought flame to the tip, then took in all my hunger for existence with the first puff. I felt impaled on desire itself—those fiends trapped in my chest and screaming for one drag. Change the given!

So I learned what addiction is. A beast had me by the throat and its vitals were in my lungs. I wrestled that devil for twelve years and sometimes I beat him back. Usually it was at great loss to myself, and great loss to others. For when I did not smoke, I grew violent. My reflexes lived in the place where the match used to strike, and my mind would lose those bits of knowledge that keep us serene (at least if we are American). In the throes of not smoking, I might rent a car and never notice whether it was a Ford or a Chrysler. That can be seen as the beginning of the end. On one occasion, when I did not smoke, I went on a long trip with a girl I loved named Madeleine to meet up with a married couple who wanted to have a weekend of wife-swapping. We indulged them. Driving back, Madeleine and I had a quarrel, and I wrecked the car. Madeleine's insides were badly hurt. I went back to smoking.

I used to say: "It's easier to give up the love of your life than to kick cigarettes," and suspect I was right in such a remark. But then last month, twenty-four days ago, my wife took off. Twenty-four days ago. I learned a little more about addiction. It may be simpler to give up love than dispense with your smokes, but when it comes to saying goodbye to love-and-hate—ah, that reliable standby of the head shrinkers, the love-hate relationship!—why, ending your marriage is easily as difficult as relinquishing your nicotine, and much the same, for I can tell you that after twelve years, I had gotten to hate the filthy stuff just so much as a bitter wife. Even the first inhale of the morning (whose sure bliss once seemed the ineradicable reason I could never give up tobacco) had now become a convulsion of coughing. No more might remain than the addiction itself, but addiction is still a signature on the bottom line of your psyche.

That is how it was with my marriage, now that Patty Lareine was gone. If I had loved her once while knowing her frightful faults—even as we smoke like happy fiends and shrug away the thought of a lung cancer still decades away, so did I always perceive that Patty Lareine could be my doom around the bend of some treacherous evening—yet, so be it, I adored her. Who knew? Love might inspire us to transcend our dire fevers. That was years ago. Now, for the last year and more, we had been trying to kick the habit of each other. Intimate detestations had grown each season until they rooted out all the old pockets of good humor. I had come to dislike her as much as my morning cigarette. Which, indeed, I had at last given up. After twelve years, I felt finally free of the largest addiction of my life. That is, until the night she left. That was the night I discovered that losing my wife was a heavier trip.

Before her departure, I had not had a cigarette for all of a year. Patty Lareine and I might, on the consequence, fight ferociously, but I was quits at last with my Camels. Small hope. Two hours after she drove off, I took up one coffin nail from a half-empty pack Patty left behind, and was, in two days of battling myself, hooked once again. Now that she was gone, I began each day with the most horrendous convulsion of my spirit. God, I choked in cataracts of misery. For with the return of this bummer habit came back every bit of the old longing for Patty Lareine. Each cigarette smelled in my mouth like an ashtray, but it was not tar I sniffed, rather my own charring flesh. Such is the odor of funk and loss.

Well, as I indicated, I do not remember how I spent my Twenty-fourth Day. My clearest recollection is yawping over that first cigarette, strangling the smoke down. Later, after four or five, I was sometimes able to inhale in peace, thereby cauterizing what I had come to decide (with no great respect for myself) must be the wound of my life. How much more I longed for Patty Lareine than I wished to. In those twenty-four days I did my best to see no one, I stayed at home, I did not always wash, I drank as if the great river of our blood is carried by bourbon, not water, I was—to put a four-letter word on it—a mess.

In summer it might have been more obvious to others what a sorry hour I was in, but this was late in the fall, the days were gray, the town deserted, and on many a shortening November afternoon you could have taken a bowling ball and rolled it down the long one-way lane of our narrow main street (a true New England alley) without striking a pedestrian or a car. The town withdrew into itself, and the cold, which was nothing remarkable when measured with a thermometer (since the seacoast off Massachusetts is, by Fahrenheit, less frigid than the stony hills west of Boston) was nonetheless a cold sea air filled with the bottomless chill that lies at the cloistered heart of ghost stories. Or, indeed, at many a séance. In truth, there had been a séance Patty and I attended at the end of September with disconcerting results: short and dreadful, it ended with a shriek. I suspect that part of the reason I was now bereft of Patty Lareine was that something intangible but indisputably repulsive had attached itself to our marriage in that moment.

After she left, there was a week when the weather never shifted. One chill morose November sky went into another. The place turned gray before one's eyes. Back in summer, the population had been thirty thousand and doubled on weekends. It seemed as if every vehicle on Cape Cod chose to drive down the four-lane state highway that ended at our beach. Provincetown was as colorful then as St. Tropez, and as dirty by Sunday evening as Coney Island. In the fall, however, with everyone gone, the town revealed its other presence. Now the population did not boil up daily from thirty thousand to sixty, but settled down to its honest sediment, three thousand souls, and on empty weekday afternoons you might have said the true number of inhabitants must be thirty men and women, all hiding.

There could be no other town like it. If you were sensitive to crowds, you might expire in summer from human propinquity. On the other hand, if you were unable to endure loneliness, the vessel of your person could fill with dread during the long winter. Martha's Vineyard, not fifty miles to the south and west, had lived through the upsurge of mountains and their erosion, through the rise and fall of oceans, the life and death of great forests and swamps. Dinosaurs had passed over Martha's Vineyard, and their bones were compacted into the bedrock. Glaciers had come and gone, sucking the island to the north, pushing it like a ferry to the south again. Martha's Vineyard had fossil deposits one million centuries old. The northern reach of Cape Cod, however, on which my house sat, the land I inhabited—that long curving spit of shrub and dune that curves in upon itself in a spiral at the tip of the

Cape—had only been formed by wind and sea over the last ten thousand years. That cannot amount to more than a night of geological time.

Perhaps this is why Provincetown is so beautiful. Conceived at night (for one would swear it was created in the course of one dark storm) its sand flats still glistened in the dawn with the moist primeval innocence of land exposing itself to the sun for the first time. Decade after decade, artists came to paint the light of Provincetown, and comparisons were made to the lagoons of Venice and the marshes of Holland, but then the summer ended and most of the painters left, and the long dingy undergarment of the gray New England winter, gray as the spirit of my mood, came down to visit. One remembered then that the land was only ten thousand years old, and one's ghosts had no roots. We did not have old Martha's Vineyard's fossil remains to subdue each spirit, no, there was nothing to domicile our specters who careened with the wind down the two long streets of our town which curved together around the bay like two spinsters on their promenade to church.

If this is a fair sample of how my mind worked on the Twenty-fourth Day, it is obvious I was feeling introspective, long-moldering, mournful and haunted. Twenty-four days of being without a wife you love and hate and certainly fear is guaranteed to leave you cleaving to her like the butt end of addiction itself. How I hated the taste of cigarettes now that I was smoking again.

It seems to me that I walked the length of the town that day and back again to my house—her house—it was Patty Lareine's money that had bought our home. Three miles along Commercial Street I walked, and back through all the shank of that gray afternoon, but I do not remember whom I spoke to, nor how many or few might have passed in a car and invited me to ride. No, I remember I walked to the very end of town, out to where the last house meets the place on the beach where the Pilgrims first landed in America. Yes, it was not at Plymouth but *here* that they landed.

I contemplate the event on many a day. Those Pilgrims, having crossed the Atlantic, encountered the cliffs of Cape Cod as their first sight of land. On that back shore the surf, at its worst, can break in waves ten feet high. On windless days the peril is worse; a sailing vessel can be driven in by the relentless tides to founder on the shoals. It is not the rocks but the shifting sands that sink you off Cape Cod. What fear those Pilgrims must have known on hearing the dull eternal boom of the surf. Who would dare come near that shore with boats such as theirs? They turned south, and the white deserted coast remained un-relenting—no hint of a cove. Just the long straight beach. So they tried going to the north and in a day saw the shore bend west, then continue to curve until it even turned to the south. What trick of the land was this? Now they were sailing to the east, three quarters of the way around from the north. Were they circumnavigating an ear of the sea? They came around the point, and dropped anchor in the lee. It was a natural harbor, as protected, indeed, as the inside of one's ear. From there, they put down small boats and rowed to shore. A plaque commemorates the landing. It is by the beginning of the breakwater that now protects our marshes at the end of town from the final ravages of the sea. There is where you come to the end of the road, to the farthest place a tourist can ride out toward the tip of Cape Cod and encounter the landing place of the Pilgrims. It was only weeks later, after much bad weather and the recognition that there was little game to hunt and few fields to till in these sandy lands, that the Pilgrims sailed west across the bay to Plymouth.

Here, however, was where they first landed with all the terror and exaltation of encountering the new land. New land it was, not ten thousand years old. A strew of sand. How many Indian ghosts must have howled through the first nights of their encampment.

I think of the Pilgrims whenever I walk to these emerald-green marshes at the end of town. Beyond, the coastal dunes are so low that one can see ships along the horizon even when the water is not visible. The flying bridges of sport-fishing boats seem to travel in caravans along the sand. If I have a drink in me, I begin to laugh, because across from the plaque to the Pilgrims, not fifty yards away, there where the United States began, stands the entrance to a huge motel. If it is no uglier than any other vast motel, it is certainly no prettier, and the only homage the Pilgrims get is that it is called an Inn. Its asphalt parking lot is as large as a football field. Pay homage to the Pilgrims.

No more than this, no matter how I press and force my mind, is what I remember of how I spent my Twenty-fourth afternoon. I went out, I walked across the town, I brooded on the geology of our shores, loaned my imagination to the Pilgrims, and laughed at the Provincetown Inn. Then I suppose I must have walked on home. The gloom in which I lay in the grasp of my sofa was timeless. I had spent many hours in these twenty-four days staring at the wall, but what I do recollect, what I cannot ignore, is that in the evening I got into my Porsche and drove up Commercial Street very slowly, as if afraid that this night I might run into a child—the evening was foggy—and I did not stop until I came to The Widow's Walk. There, not far from the Provincetown Inn, is a dark stained pine-paneled room whose foundations are gently slapped in the rising of the tide, for one of the charms of Provincetown I have neglected to pass along is that not only my house—her house!—but most of the buildings on the bay side of Commercial Street are kin to ships at high tide when the bulkheads on which they rest are half submerged by the sea.

It was such a tide tonight. The waters rose as languorously as if we were in the tropics, but I knew the sea was cold. Behind the good windows of this dark room, the fire on its wide hearth was worthy of a postcard, and my wooden chair was full of approaching winter, inasmuch as it had a shelf of the kind they used in study halls a hundred years ago: a large round platter of oak lifted on its hinges to enable you to sit down, after which it ensconced itself under your right elbow to serve as a table for your drink.

The Widow's Walk might as well have been created for me. On lonely fall evenings I liked to entertain the conceit that I was some modern tycoon-pirate of prodigious wealth who kept the place for his amusement. The large restaurant at the other end might be rarely entered by me, but the small bar of this paneled lounge equipped with its barmaid was all for myself. Secretly I must have believed that no one else had a right to enter. By November, the illusion was not difficult to protect. On quiet weekday nights most of the diners, good senior Wasps from Brewster and Dennis and Orleans, out for a smack of excitement, found their thrills in the sheer audacity of daring to drive all of thirty or forty miles to Provincetown itself. The echo of summer kept our evil reputation intact. Those fine Scotch studies in silver—which is to say, each Wasp professor emeritus and retired corporate executive—did not look to tarry in a bar. They headed for the Dining Room. Besides, one look at me in my dungaree jacket was enough to steer them to the food. "No, dear," their wives would say, "let's have our drinks at the table. We're starved!"

"Yeah, baby," I would murmur to myself, "starved."

Over these twenty-four days, the Lounge at The Widow's Walk had become my castle keep. I would sit by the window, study the fire, and watch the changes in the tide, feeling after four bourbons, ten cigarettes, and a dozen crackers with cheese (my dinner!) that I was, at least, a wounded lord living by the sea.

The compensation for misery, self-pity, and despair is that fed enough drinks, the powers of imagination return with force. No matter that they are lopsided under such auspices; they return. In this room my drinks were well stoked by a submissive bar girl doubtless terrified of me although I never said anything more provocative than "Another bourbon, please." Yet, since she worked in a bar, I understood her fear. I had worked in a bar myself for many years. I could respect her conviction that I was dangerous. That was apparent in the concentration of my good manners. In the days when I used to be a bartender, I had watched over a few customers like myself. They never bothered you until they did. Then the room could get smashed.

I did not see myself as belonging to such a category. But how could I say that the waitress' dire expectation did not serve me well? I received no more attention than I wanted and every bit I might need. The manager, a young and pleasant fellow, much set on maintaining the tone of the establishment, had now known me for more than a few years, and as long as I had been accompanied by my rich wife, considered me a rare example of local gentry no matter how obstreperous Patty Lareine might get on drink: Wealth is worth that much! Now that I was by myself, he greeted me when I came in, said goodbye when I went out, and had obviously made the proprietorial decision to leave me strictly alone. As a corollary, few visitors were steered into the Lounge. Night after night, I could get drunk in the manner I chose.

Not until now have I been ready to confess that I am a writer. From Day One, however, no new writing had been done, not in more than three weeks. To see one's situation as ironic is, we may agree, no joy, but irony becomes a dungeon when the circle is closed. The cigarettes I gave up at such cost to my ability to write had, on this last return to the domain of nicotine—it is no less than a domain—cut off all ability to come forth with even one new paragraph. In order not to smoke, I had had to learn to write all over again. Now that I could manage such a feat, the return to cigarettes seemed to have tamped out every literary spark. Or was it the departure of Patty Lareine?

These days I would take my notebook with me to The Widow's Walk, and when drunk enough, would succeed in adding a line or two to words I had set down in less desperate hours. On those random occasions, therefore, when visitors were actually sharing a predinner drink in the same public room with me, my small sounds of appreciation at some felicity of syntax or my bored grunts before a phrase that now seemed as dead as an old drinking friend's repetitions must have sounded strange and animal, as unsettling (given the paneled gentility of this Lounge) as cries made by a hound absolutely indifferent to any nearby human presence.

Can I claim I was not playing to the house when I would frown over a drunken note I could hardly read, and then chuckle in pleasure as soon as these alcoholic squiggles metamorphosed into a legible text? "There," I would mutter to myself, "studies!"

I had just made out part of a title, a bona-fide title, sufficiently resonant for a book: *In Our Wild—Studies among the Sane* by Timothy Madden.

Now, an exegesis commenced on my name. *In Our Wild—Studies among the Sane* by Mac Madden? By Tim Mac Madden? By Two-Mac Madden? I began to giggle. My waitress, poor overalerted mouse, was able to flick a look at me only by setting herself resolutely in profile.

Yet I was giggling truly. Old jokes about my name were returning. I felt one rush of love for my father. Ah, the sweet sorrow of loving a parent. It is as pure as the taste of a sourball when you are five. Douglas "Dougy" Madden—Big Mac to his friends and to his only child, myself, once called Little Mac, or Mac-Mac, then Two-Mac and Toomey and back to Tim. Following the morphology of my name through the coils of booze, I giggled. Each change of name had been an event in my life—if I could only recover the events.

In my heart I was now trying to launch a first set of phrases for the initial essay. (What a title! *In Our Wild—Studies among the Sane* by Tim Madden.) I might speak of the Irish and the reason they drink so much. Could it be the testosterone? The Irish presumably had more than other men, my father did for certain, and it made them unmanageable. Maybe the hormone asked to be dissolved in some liquor.

I sat with pencil poised, my sip of bourbon near to scorching my tongue. I was not ready to swallow. This title was about all that had come to me since Day One. I could merely ponder the waves. The waves outside the lounge-room window on this chill November night had become equal in some manner to the waves in my mind. My thoughts came to a halt and I felt the disappointment of profound drunken vision. Just as you waddle up to the true relations of the cosmos, your vocabulary blurs.

It was then I grew aware that I was no longer alone in my realm of The Widow's Walk. A blonde remarkably like Patty Lareine was sitting with her escort not ten feet away. If I had no other clue to the profound submersions of my conscious state, it was enough that she had entered with her bucko, a nicely tailored country-tweed-and-flannels, silver-winged-pompadour, suntanned-lawyer–type fellow, yes, the lady had sat down with her sheik, and since they now had drinks in front of them, must have been talking (and in unabashed voices, hers at least) for a considerable period. Five minutes? Ten minutes? I realized that they had sized me up, and for whatever reason, had the confidence, call it the gall, to ignore me. Whether this insularity derived from some not easily visible proficiency the man might call upon in the martial arts— Tweed-and-Flannels looked more like a tennis player than a Black Belt— or whether they were so wealthy a couple that nothing unpleasant ever walked up to them in the way of strangers (unless it was burglary of the mansion) or whether they were exhibiting simple insensitivity to the charged torso, head and limbs sitting so near them, I do not know, but the woman, at least, was talking loudly, and as if I did not exist. What an insult at this beleaguered hour!

Then I understood. From their conversation I could soon divine that they were Californians, just as loose and unselfconscious in deportment as tourists from New Jersey visiting a bar in Munich. What could they know of how they were degrading me?

As my attention went through those ponderous maneuvers of which only a human in deep depression can speak—the brain lurches like an elephant backed into its stall—I climbed at last out of the dungeon of my massive self-absorption to take a look at them, and thereby came to realize that their indifference to me was neither arrogance, confidence, nor innocence but, to the contrary, theatrical to the hilt. A set of poses. The man was highly keyed to the likelihood that a glowering presence such as mine was hardly to be ignored as a source of real trouble, and the woman, true to my premise that blondes believe it obscene not to comport themselves as angels or bitches—each option must be equally available—was stampeding along. She wished to provoke me. She wanted to test her beau's courage. No mean surrogate was this lady for my own Patty Lareine.

But let me describe the woman. It's worth the look. She must have been fifteen years older than my wife, and thereby, not far from fifty, but what a splendid approach! There used to be a porny star named Jennifer Welles who had the same appearance. She had large, well-turned promiscuous breasts—one nipple tilted to the east, one stared out to the west—a deep navel, a woman's round belly, a sweet buoyant spread of buttocks, and *dark* pubic hair. That was what encouraged the prurience to stir in those who bought a ticket to watch Jennifer Welles. Any lady who chooses to become a blonde is truly blonde.

Now, the face of my new neighbor was, like the porny star, Jennifer Welles, undeniably appealing. She had a charming upturned nose and a full pout on the mouth, as spoiled and imperious as the breath of sex. Her nostrils flared, her fingernails—the Liberation could go screw itself!—were scandalously well-manicured with a silver varnish to catch the silver-blue toning above her eyes. What a piece! An anachronism. The most complacent kind of West Coast money. Santa Barbara? La Jolla? Pasadena? Wherever it was, she must certainly come from an enclave of bridge players. Perfectly groomed blondes remain as quintessential to such places as mustard on pastrami. Corporate California had moved right into my psyche.

I can hardly describe what an outrage this seemed. As well paste a swastika outside the office of the United Jewish Appeal. This blonde reminded me so directly of Patty Lareine that I felt obliged to strike. Do what? I could hardly say. At the very least, gore their mood.

So I listened. She was one immaculately dressed full-bodied lady who liked to drink. She could take them back to back. Scotch, of course. Chivas Regal. "Chivvies," she called them. "Miss," she told the waitress, "give me another Chivvies. Lots of diamonds." That was her word for ice, ha, ha.

"Of course you're bored with me," she said to her man in a loud and most self-certain voice, as if she could measure to the drop just how much sex she might be sitting upon. A powerhouse. There are voices that resonate into one's secret strings like tuning forks. Hers was one. It is crude to say, but one would do much for such a voice. There was always the hope that its moist little relative below would offer something of the same for your preserves.

Patty Lareine had such a voice. She could be diabolical with her lip around a Very Dry Martini (which, of course, count on it, she would insist on calling a Marty Seco). "It was gin," she'd say in all the husky enthusiasm of her hot-to-trot larynx, "it was gin as done the old lady in. Yes, asshole," oh, and she would include you most tenderly in this jeer, as if, by God, even you, asshole, could feel all right if you were being kept around her. But then, Patty Lareine belonged to another kind of wealth, strictly derivative. Her second husband, Meeks Wardley Hilby III (whom once she most certainly tried to persuade me to murder) was *old* Tampa money and she drilled him good but not between the eyes, rather up his financial fundament thanks to her divorce lawyer, a whiz bomb (who, I used to assume to my pain, was probably massaging the back wall of her belly every night for a time, but then, one cannot expect less of a dedicated divorce lawyer—it pays off in presenting the witness). Although Patty Lareine was trim to bursting in her build, and in those days, peppy as a spice jar, he modulated the moxie of her personality down to more delicate herbs. With the aid of intense coaching (he was one of the first to use a video camera for rehearsal) he showed her how to be tremulous on the stand and thereby turn the judgmental eye into—forgive me!—one fat old judge melting away. Before they were done, her marital peccadilloes (and her husband had witnesses) came out as the maidenly mistakes of a desperately beleaguered and much abused fine lady. Each ex-lover appearing as witness against her was depicted as one more unhappy attempt to cure the heart that her husband had shattered. Patty may have begun life as one good high school cheerleader, just a little old redneck from a down-home North Carolina town, but by the time she was ready to divorce Wardley (and marry me) she had developed a few social graces. Hell, her lawyer and she grew equal to Lunt and Fontanne in the manner they could pass a bowl of soup back and forth on the witness stand. One scion of old Gulf Coast Florida money was certainly divested of a share of his principal. That was how Patty came to belong to wealth.

The more I listened to the lady in The Widow's Walk, however, the more I could discern that she was of other ilk. Patty's wits were true wit—that was all she had to stand between her and the crass and crude.

This new blonde lady now transforming my evening might be short on wit, but then, she had small need for it. Her manner came with her money. If all else was right, she would probably meet you at her hotel-room door attired in no more than white elbow-length gloves. (And high heels.)

"Go ahead, say you're bored," I now heard clearly. "It's to be expected when an attractive man and woman decide to go on a trip. To be thrown together for all these days creates the fear of disenchantment. Tell me if I'm wrong."

It was obvious that her interest in his reply was less than her pleasure in letting me know that they not only were not married, but were, by anyone's estimate, on a quick and limited fling. It could wrap itself up on any turn. Taken as a beast on the hoof, Tweed-and-Flannels shouldn't be too hard to replace for a one-night stand. This lady had a body language to suggest that you would be given one thoroughgoing welcome on first night—only later would difficulties arise. But the first night would be on the house.

No, I'm not bored, Tweed-and-Flannels was telling her now in the lowest voice, not bored at all, his voice droning into her ear like white noise put on the audio system to dull your synapses to sleep. Yes, I decided, he must be a lawyer. There was something in the confidential moderation of his manner. He was addressing the Bench on a point of law, helping the judge not to blow the case. Soothing!

Her text, however, was obstreperous! "No, no, no," she said, giving a light shake to her ice cubes, "it was my idea we come here. Your negotiations take you to Boston, well then, I said, my whim also takes me. Do you mind? Of course you don't. Daddy is mad about brand-new mama. Et cetera," she said, pausing for a sip of the Chivvies. "But, darling, I have this vice. I can't bear contentment. The moment I feel it, everything says 'Goodbye, my dear!' Moreover, I'm an avid map reader, as you have learned, Lonnie. They say women can't read directions. I can. At Kansas City, way back in—wait, it comes to me—in 1976, I was the only Jerry Ford woman in our delegation who could read a map well enough to drive from the hotel to his headquarters.

"So, there was your mistake. Showing me a map of Boston and its environs. When you hear that tone in my voice, when I say, 'Darling, I'd like to see a map of this region,' beware. It means my toes are itching. Lonnie, ever since I was in the fifth grade and started geography studies"—she squinted critically at the melting diamonds in her glass—"I used to stare at Cape Cod on the map of New England. It sticks out like a pinkie. You know how children are about pinkies? That's their *little* finger, the one close to them. So I wanted to see the tip of Cape Cod."

I must say I still didn't like her friend. He had that much-massaged look of a man whose money makes money while he sleeps. Not at all, not at all, he was telling her, laying his salad oil on her stirred-up little sorrows, we both wanted to come here, it's truly all right, and more of such, and more of such.

"No, Lonnie, I gave you no choice. I was a tyrant about it. I said, 'I want to go to this place, Provincetown.' I wouldn't allow you to demur. So here we are. It's a whim on top of a whim, and you're bored stiff. You want to drive back to Boston tonight. This place is *deserted*, right?"

At this point—make no mistake about it—she looked at me full out: full of welcome if I took it up, full of scorn in the event I did not reply.

I spoke. I said to her, "That's what you get for trusting a map."

It must have worked. For my next recollection is of sitting with them. I may as well confess that my memory is damnable. What I recall, I see clearly—sometimes!—but often I cannot connect the events of a night. So my next recollection is of sitting with them. I must have been invited over. I must, indeed, have been good company. Even he was laughing. Leonard Pangborn was his name, Lonnie Pangborn, a good family name in Republican California, doubtless—and hers was not Jennifer Welles but Jessica Pond. Pond and Pangborn—can you understand my animosity now? They had the patina that comes off a TV screen from characters in a soap opera.

Actually, I began to entertain her considerably. I think it is because I had not spoken to anyone for days. Now, depression or no, some buried good humor in me seemed well rested. I began to relate a few stories about the Cape, and my timing was vigorous. I must have been as energetic as a convict on a one-day pass outside the walls, but then, I was so well on my way to getting along with Pond that it came near to lifting me out of my doldrums. For one thing, I soon divined that she was drawn to substantial property. Fine mansions on good green lawns with high wrought-iron gates gave her the same glow a real estate agent derives from bringing the right client to the right house. Of course, I soon figured it out. To the money she was born with, Jessica had added her own pile. Back in California she was exactly that, a successful country real estate agent.

What a disappointment Provincetown must have been to her. We offer our indigenous architecture, but it is funky: old fish-shed with wooden-stairway-on-the-outside Cape Cod salt-box. We sell room-space to tourists. One hundred rented rooms can end up having one hundred outside stairways. Provincetown, to anyone looking for gracious living, is no more uncluttered than twenty telephone poles at a crossroads.

Maybe she was deceived by the delicacy of our site on the map: the fine filigree tip of the Cape curls around itself like the toe of a medieval slipper! Probably she had pictured swards of lawn. Instead, she had to look at honkytonk shops boarded up and a one-way main street so narrow that if a truck was parked at the curb, you held your breath and hoped nothing scratched your rented sedan as you went on through.

Naturally, she asked me about the most imposing house our town can point to. It sits on a hill, a five-story château—the only one in town—and is fenced about in high wrought iron. It is far removed from its gate. I couldn't say who lived there now, or whether he owned or rented. I had heard the name and forgot. It is not easy to explain to strangers, but in the winter, people choose to burrow down in Provincetown. Getting to know new arrivals is no simpler than traveling from island to island. Besides, none of my acquaintances, dressed as we were for winter (dungarees, boots and parkas) would ever get past a gate. I assumed that the present seigneur of our one imposing house had to be some kind of rich gink. So I drew on the rich man I knew best (who happened, indeed, to be Patty Lareine's ex-husband from Tampa) and I moved him all the way north to Provincetown and loaned him the château. I did not wish to lose momentum with Miss Jessica.

"Oh, that place belongs," I said, "to Meeks Wardley Hilby the Third. He lives all alone there." I paused. "I used to know him. We went to Exeter at the same time."

"Oh," said Jessica after quite a pause, "do you think we could pay him a visit?"

"He's not there now. He rarely stays in town any longer."

"Too bad," she said.

"You wouldn't like him," I told her. "He's a very odd fellow. At Exeter he used to drive all the deans crazy by tweaking the dress code. We had to wear jackets and ties to class, but old Wardley would get himself up like a prince of the Salvation Army."

There must have been some promise in my voice, for she began to laugh happily, but I remember that even as I began to tell her more I had the strongest feeling I should not go on—just as irrational as an unaccountable smell of smoke—do you know, I sometimes think we are all of us equal to broadcasting stations and some stories should not be put on the air. Let us leave it that I had an unmistakable injunction not to continue (which I knew I would ignore—that much is to be said for an attractive blonde!) and at the moment, even as I looked for the next words, an image came to me across the years, bright as a coin from the mint, of Meeks Wardley Hilby III, of *Wardley,* gangling along in his chinos, his patent-leather pumps and his old dinner jacket that he wore every day to class (to the consternation of half the faculty) his satin lapels faded and scuffed, his purple socks and heliotrope bow tie standing out like neon signs in Vegas.

"God," I said to Jessica, "we used to call him 'goon-child.' "

"You have to tell me all about him," she said. "Please."

"I don't know," I replied. "The story has its sordid touches."

"Oh, do tell us," said Pangborn.

I hardly needed encouragement. "Attribute it to the father," I said. "There has to be a powerful influence coming from the father. He's dead now. Meeks Wardley Hilby the Second."

"How do you tell them apart?" asked Pangborn.

"Well, they always called the father Meeks and the son Wardley. There was no confusion."

"Ah," he said. "Were they at all alike?"

"Not much. Meeks was a sportsman and Wardley was Wardley. In childhood, the nurses used to tie his hands to the bed. Meeks's orders. It was calculated to put a stop to Wardley's onanism." I looked at her as if to say, "This is the detail I was afraid of." She gave a smile, which I took to mean, "We're by the fire. Tell your tale."

I did. I worked at it with great care, and gave them a full account of the adolescence of Meeks Wardley Hilby III, never stopping to chide myself for this outrageous change of venue from the palace on the Gulf Coast to the northern estate here on the hill, but then, this was only

Pond and Pangborn I was telling it to. What would they care, I told myself, where it took place?

So I went on. Meeks's wife, Wardley's mother, was sickly, and Meeks took a mistress. Wardley's mother died when he was in his first year at Exeter, and soon after, the father married the mistress. Neither of them ever liked Wardley. He liked them no better. Since they kept a door locked on the third floor of their house, Wardley decided that was the room to get into. Not, however, until he was kicked out of Exeter in his last year was he ever home long enough to find his father and the new wife away for a night. On the first evening that that happened, he worked himself up sufficiently to inch along an exterior molding of the mansion's wall three stories up from the ground, and went in through the window.

"I love this," said Jessica. "What was in the room?"

He discovered, I told her, a large old-fashioned view camera with a black cloth, mounted on a heavy tripod in one corner, and on a library table, five red vellum scrapbooks. It was a special pornographic collection. The five scrapbooks contained large sepia photographs of Meeks making love to his mistress.

"The one who was now the wife?" asked Pangborn.

I nodded. As described by the son, the first pictures must have been taken in the year Wardley was born. Each successive volume of the scrapbooks showed the father and mistress getting older. A year or two after the death of Wardley's mother, not long after the new marriage, another man appeared in the photos. "He was the manager of the estate," I said. "Wardley told me that he dined with the family every day."

At this point Lonnie clapped his hands together. "Incredible," he said.

The later photographs showed the manager making love to the wife while the father sat five feet away reading a newspaper. The lovers would adopt different positions but Meeks kept reading the paper.

"Who was the photographer?" Jessica asked.

"Wardley said it was the butler."

"What a house!" Jessica exclaimed. "Only in New England could this occur." We all laughed a great deal at that.

I did not add that the butler seduced Wardley at the age of fourteen. Nor did I offer Wardley's statement on the matter: "I've spent the rest of my life trying to regain property rights to my rectum." There was probably a fine line of propriety to tread with Jessica. I had not found it yet, so I was cautious. "At nineteen," I said, "Wardley got married. I think it was to confound his father. Meeks was a confirmed anti-Semite and the bride was a Jewish girl. She also happened to have a large nose."

They enjoyed this so much that I felt a few regrets at going on, but no helping it now—I also had the ruthlessness of the storyteller and the next detail was crucial. "This nose," I said, "as Wardley described it, curled over her upper lip until she looked as if she were breathing the fumes of her mouth. For some reason, maybe because he was a gourmet, this was indescribably carnal to Wardley."

"Oh, I hope it turned out all right," remarked Jessica.

"Well, not exactly," I said. "Wardley's wife had been well brought up. So, woe to Wardley when she discovered that he, too, had a pornography collection. She destroyed it. Then she made it worse. She managed to charm the father. After five years of marriage she succeeded in pleasing Meeks enough for the old man to give a dinner party for his son and daughter-in-law. Wardley got very drunk, and later that night, brained his wife with a candlestick. She happened to die from the blow."

"Oh, no," said Jessica. "It all took place in that house on the hill?"

"Yes."

"What," asked Pangborn, "was the legal upshot?"

"Well, believe it if you will, they did not use insanity for a defense."

"Then he must have done some time."

"He did." I was not about to mention that we had not only gone to Exeter together but actually met each other again in the same prison at the same time.

"It sounds to me as if the father was directing his son's case," said Lonnie.

"I think you're right."

"Of course! With a plea of insanity, the defense would have had to bring the scrapbooks into court." Lonnie locked his fingers together and flexed them outward. "So," he said, "Wardley took the fall. What was going to jail worth to him?"

"One million dollars a year," I answered. "Put in a trust fund each year for each year he served, plus a split with his stepmother on the estate after the father's death."

"Do you know for a fact whether they paid it over to him?" Lonnie asked.

Jessica shook her head. "I don't see such people honoring their agreement."

I shrugged. "Meeks paid," I told them, "because Wardley had filched the scrapbooks. Believe me, when Meeks died, the stepmother kept the bargain. Meeks Wardley Hilby the Third came out of jail a wealthy man."

Jessica said, "I love how you tell a story."

Pangborn nodded. "Priceless," he said.

She was pleased. The trip to this strange place seemed to have come to a few good minutes, after all. "Does Wardley," she asked, "plan to live in the house again?"

I was hesitating what to say to this when Pangborn replied, "Of course not. Our new friend here has made it all up."

"Well, Leonard," I said, "remind me to hire you if I need a lawyer."

"*Did* you make it up?" she asked.

I was not about to give a small smile and say, "Some of it." Instead I said, "Yes. Every last drop," and emptied my drink. Leonard, doubtless, had already made his inquiries about who owned the estate.

My next recollection is that I was alone again. They had gone into the dining room.

I remember drinking, and writing, and watching the water. Some observations I would put in my pocket and some I would rip up. The sound of paper as it was being torn set off reverberations in me. I began to chortle within. I was thinking that surgeons had to be the happiest people on earth. To cut people up and get paid for it—that's happiness, I told myself. It made me wish Jessica Pond was next to me once more. She might have given a glad howl at the thought.

It comes back to me that I then wrote a longer note which I found in my pocket the next day. For some reason I gave it a title: Rec-ognition. "The perception of the possibility of greatness in myself has always been followed by desire to murder the nearest unworthy." Then I underlined the next sentence: *"It is better to keep a modest notion of oneself!"*

The more, however, that I read this note, the more I seemed to install myself in that impregnable hauteur which is, perhaps, the most satisfying aspect of solitary drinking. The knowledge that Jessica Pond and Leonard Pangborn were sitting at a table not a hundred feet away, oblivious to what might be their considerable peril, had an intoxicating effect on me, and I began to contemplate—I must say it was with no serious passion, rather as one more variety of amusing myself through another night—how easy it would be to do away with them. Consider it! After twenty-four days without Patty Lareine, this is the sort of man I had become!

Here was my reasoning. A clandestine couple, each of whom is obviously well-placed in whatever world they inhabit in California, decide to go to Boston together. They are discreet about their mutual plans. Perhaps they tell an intimate or two, perhaps no one, but since they drive off to Provincetown on a whim, and in a rented car, the perpetrator need only—should the deed be done—drive their car one hundred and twenty miles back to Boston and leave it on the street. Assuming the bodies have been well-buried, it would be weeks, if ever, before any concern for the man and woman as missing persons might stir newspaper publicity in these parts. By then, would anyone at The Widow's Walk remember their faces? Even in that event, the police would have to assume, given the location of the car, that they returned to Boston and met their end there. I lived within the logic of this fine scenario, enjoyed my drink a little more, enjoyed the power I possessed over them by thinking thoughts such as these, and there . . . it is precisely there . . . I lost the rest of the evening. In the morning I would no longer be able to put it together to satisfy myself.

What I can't recollect is whether or not I began to drink again with Pond and Pangborn. It is as likely, I should think, that I boozed by myself, got into my car and went home. If I did, I would have gone directly to sleep. Although that, by the evidence of what I found when I awakened, was not possible.

I also have another scenario, which is certainly clearer than a dream, although I could have dreamt it. It is that Patty Lareine returned and we had a terrible quarrel. I see her mouth. Yet I do not recollect a word. Could it have been a dream?

Then I also have the clearest impression that Jessica and Leonard did indeed join me after they ate, and I invited them to my home (to Patty Lareine's home). We sat in the living room while the man and woman listened to me with attention. I seem to remember that. Then we took a trip in a car, but if it was my Porsche, I could not have taken both of them. Perhaps we went in two cars.

I also remember returning home alone. The dog was in terror of me. He is a big Labrador, but he crept away as I came near. I sat down at the edge of my bed and jotted one more note before I lay down. That I recall. I dozed off sitting up and staring at the notebook. Then I woke up in a few seconds (or was it an hour?) and read what I had written: "Despair is the emotion we feel at the death of beings within us."

That was my last thought before I went to sleep. Yet none of these scenarios, nor very little of them, can be true—because when I woke in the morning, I had a tattoo on my arm that had not been there before.

Two

I have much to tell about this day, but it did not begin with any great rush to arise. The truth is that I stayed in bed for a long time and did not trust my eyes to the light. In that self-imposed darkness, I tried to decide on what I could remember of the night after I left The Widow's Walk.

The procedure was not strange to me. It did not matter how much I drank, I could always get my car home. I had returned my car safely on nights when others who had swallowed as much would have been slumbering at the bottom of the sea. I would enter the house, reach my bed, and come to in the morning with my brain feeling as if it had been split by an ax. I remembered nothing. Yet if that proved the only symptom, and I knew no other uneasiness than the debauch I had put upon my liver, it was all right. Others would tell me later what I had done. If I felt no dread, then I could have done nothing too terrible. Short-term amnesia is not the worst affliction if you have an Irish flair for the sauce.

Since Patty Lareine left, however, I had been encountering new phenomena, and they were curious. Did drink have me chasing for the root of the wound? I can only say that my memory would be clear to me in the morning, but shattered, that is to say, in pieces. Each fragment was sharp enough, yet like puzzles that have been thrown together, not all the pieces seemed to come out of the same box. Which is equal, I suppose, to saying my dreams were now as reasonable as my memory, or my memory was as untrustworthy as my dreams. In either event, I could not tell them apart. It is a frightful state. You wake up in pure confusion over what you might or might not have done. That is like entering a labyrinth of caves. Somewhere along the way, the fine long thread that is supposed to lead you back has been broken. Now at each turning it is possible to be certain that you have come this way, or, equally, that you have never been here before.

I speak of this because I awoke on Day Twenty-five and lay nearly still for an hour before I chose to open my eyes. I was feeling dread with an intimacy I had not known since I came out of prison. There were mornings in the penitentiary when you got up from sleep with the knowledge that somebody bad—far beyond your own measure of how to be bad—was looking for you. Those were the worst mornings in prison.

Now I had the conviction that something would happen to me before the day was done, and in this anticipation was my dread. Yet with it all, I had one surprise. Lying there with a ferocious headache, trying behind closed eyes to keep my memory in view—it was like following a film with numerous breaks—a weight of apprehension lying in my stomach mean as lead, I still had an erection, an honest-to-God all-out ram of an erection. I wanted to screw Jessica Pond.

I would be reminded of this little fact in the days ahead. But let us take it in order. When your mind is a book where pages are missing— no, worse, two books, each with its own gaps—well, order becomes as close a virtue as clean floors in a monastery. So I say only that it was because of this erection that I was saved the shock of opening my eyes on my tattoo, but remembered it instead. (However, at this instant, I could picture neither the parlor nor the face of the tattoo artist.) Some- where I had registered the fact. With all my distress, it was still curious. How many facets memory could utilize! To remember that an act had been undertaken (although one could visualize none of it) was like reading about someone in a newspaper. So-and-So embezzled $80,000. The headline is all one perceives; the fact, however, is registered. Ergo, I was noting this fact about myself. Tim Madden had a tattoo. I knew it with my eyes closed. The erection reminded me of it.

In prison I had always resisted acquiring one. I felt enough of a con. All the same, you cannot give three years to the slammer without pick- ing up a considerable amount of tattoo culture. I had heard about the rush. One man in four or five received a real rush of sexual excitement while the needle was being pricked into him. I also recollected how horny I had been for Ms. Pond. Had she been about while the artist was doing my watermark? Could she have been waiting in my car? Had we said goodbye to Lonnie Pangborn?

I opened my eyes. The tattoo was crusty, and sticky—some kind of glorified Band Aid had come loose during the night. Still, I could read it. *Laurel*, it said. *Laurel*, in a curlicue script of blue ink within a small red heart. Let no one say I had special taste when it came to engravings.

My humor broke like a rotten egg. Patty Lareine had also seen this tattoo. Last night! Abruptly I had the clearest vision of her. She was shrieking at me in our living room. "Laurel? Are you daring to inflict Laurel on me again?"

Yes, but how much of this had actually happened? It was obvious to me that I could conceive of conversations as easily as I could live them. Was I not a writer, after all? Patty Lareine disappeared twenty-five days ago with a black stud of her choice, a tall, sullen, beautifully put together dude who had been hanging around through the summer, ready to capitalize on that carnal affinity toward black men which lives in the hearts of certain blondes like lightning and thunder. Or, for all I know, smolders in the heart like oily rags behind a barn door. Whatever she felt, there was no mistaking the results. Once a year, give a season or two, she would have a fling with Mr. Black. Some big black. He could be heavy, or he could be as quick as a basketball player, but he was always big. The size put them out of my physical reach—I think it delighted her contempt for me that I was not man enough under such circumstances to load my pistol and do a down-home chase-off. "Just like your dad would in North Carolina?" I asked. "You bet!" she'd reply with all the sassy, spiteful, untrammeled mouth of an eighteen-year-old in cutoffs at some Dr Pepper gas station. God, she was unafraid of me. I was terrified I would indeed get my gun, but never to chase Mr. Black. He was just appropriating what I, too, would grab if I could fill his jockstrap and sweat properly in his black logic. No, I was afraid I would get my pistol and never leave the house before emptying a magazine into her all-superior fuck-you face.

Still! Why had I chosen to inflict the name Laurel on my wife? I knew she was the one lady Patty would never forgive. I was with Laurel, after all, when I met Patty, except that her name was Madeleine Falco. It was Patty who had insisted on calling her Laurel the day they met. I learned later that "Laurel" was short for Lorelei—Patty did not like Madeleine Falco. Had I chosen the tattoo to punish Patty? Had she truly been in the house? Or was I living with some fragment of last night's dream?

It occurred to me that if my wife had indeed come to visit, and then departed, some evidence must remain. Patty Lareine usually left half-consumed objects behind her. Her lipstick must be on our glasses. It was enough to get me dressed and down the stairs, but in the living room there were no traces of her. The ashtrays were clean. Why, then, was I now twice certain our conversation had taken place? Of what benefit were clues if one's mind was stimulated to believe the opposite of the evidence? It came upon me then that the only true test of the strength, the veritable muscle tone, so to speak, of one's sanity, was the ability to bear question upon question with not an answer in sight.

It is good I had such a perception, for I soon needed it. In the kitchen, during the night, the dog had been ill. The treasures of his belly befouled the linoleum. Worse, the jacket I had been wearing last night was hanging on a chair, crusted with blood. I felt of my nostrils. I suffered from nosebleeds. Yet the passages seemed clear. Now the dread with which I had awakened took a turn. A whistle of fear stirred in my lungs when I inhaled.

How could I ever clean the kitchen? I turned around, went back through the house and out the door. It was not until I reached the street and felt the damp air of November pass through my shirt that I realized I was still in my slippers. No great matter. I took five strides across Commercial Street and peered into the windows of my Porsche. (Her Porsche.) The passenger seat was covered with blood.

What a curious logic to these matters! I had a startling lack of reaction. But then, the worst hangovers are always like that—they are simply full of the most unaccountable spaces. So I did not feel frightened any longer but exhilarated as if none of this had anything to do with me. The rush from the tattoo came back.

I was also feeling very cold. I returned inside and brewed myself a cup of coffee. The dog, ashamed of the mess he had made, blundered about in every danger of compounding it until I let him out.

My good mood (which I treasured for its rarity the way a patient in a terminal illness is grateful for an hour without pain) lasted all the while I was cleaning up after the hound. With my hangover, there was gagging aplenty, but also the most thoroughgoing and satisfying expiation for the sins of my drinking. I might be only half-Catholic, and that all but untutored, since Big Mac never went near a church, and Julia, my mother (half-Protestant, half-Jewish—which is one reason I did not like anti-Semitic jokes) was prone to steer me to so many different cathedrals, synagogues, Quaker meeting houses and lectures at Ethical Culture that she was never much of a religious guide. I couldn't claim, therefore, to see myself as a Catholic. Yet I did. Give me a hangover, put me on my knees cleaning dog poop, and I would feel virtuous. (Indeed, I almost managed to forget how much blood had been spilled over the right seat of the car.) Then the phone rang. It was Regency, Alvin Luther Regency, our Acting Chief of Police, or rather, his secretary, asking me to wait until he came on the line, long enough to strip me of much good mood.

"Hello, Tim," he said, "you okay?"

"I'm fine. I'm hung-over, but I'm fine."

"That's nice. That's good. I woke up this morning feeling concerned about you." He was going to be a modern police chief, that was for certain.

"No," I told him, "I'm all right."

He paused. "Tim, would you drop in this afternoon?"

My father always told me that when in doubt, assume a confrontation is brewing. Next, get to it quickly. So I said, "Why don't I come over this morning?"

"It's lunchtime now," he said reprovingly.

"Well, lunch," I said. "That's all right."

"I'm having a cup of java with one of the Selectmen. Make it after."

"Fine."

"Tim?"

"Yeah."

"Are you okay?"

"I think I am."

"Will you clean your car?"

"Oh, Christ, I had a terrible nosebleed last night."

"Yes, well, some of your neighbors ought to belong to the Good Snoopers' Society. The way they phoned it in, I figured you lopped somebody's arm off."

"I resent that. Why don't you come over and get a sample? You can check my blood type."

"Hey, give me a break." He laughed. He had a real cop's laugh. A high-pitched soprano whinny that had nothing to do with the rest of him. His face, I can tell you, might as well have been made of granite.

"All right," I said, "it's funny. But how would you like to be a grown man with nosebleeds?"

"Oh," he said, "I would take good care of myself. After ten shots of bourbon, I would be punctilious about drinking a glass of water." *Punctilious* had just made his lunch hour. He gave a big whinny and signed off.

I cleaned the inside of my car. That did not feel nearly so unhazardous as the dog poop. Nor was my stomach taking the coffee well. I did not know whether to be agitated at the effrontery and/or paranoia of my neighbors—which ones?—or to live with the possibility that I had gotten sufficiently unhinged to break one or another blonde lady's nose. Or worse. How did you lop off an arm?

The difficulty is that my sardonic side, which had been designed, presumably, to carry me through most of a bad day, was, when all is said, not a true side, but only a facet—one stop on the roulette wheel. There are thirty-seven others. Nor was anything put to rest by my increasing conviction that the blood on this seat did not come from anyone's nose. It was much too abundant. So I was soon revolted by the task. Blood, like any force of nature, insists on speaking. It is always with the same message. "All that lives," I now heard, "clamors to live again."

I will spare you such details as the rinsing of the cloth and the trips with pails of water. I had friendly conversations about nosebleeds with two neighbors who passed while I was on the task, and by then I had decided to walk to the Police Station. Truth, if I brought the vehicle, Regency might be tempted to impound it.

There had been times over the three years I was in prison when I used to wake up in the middle of the night with no sense of where I was. That would not be unusual but for the fact that of course I knew exactly where I was, down to my cellblock and cell number, yet I would not accept it. The given was not permitted to be given. I would lie in bed and make plans to take a girl to lunch or decide to rent a catboat for a sail. It did no good to tell myself that I was not at home but within a cell in a medium-security prison in Florida. I saw such facts as part of the dream, and thereby at quite a remove from me. I could get off on my plans for the day if only the dream that I was in prison would not persist—"Man," I would say to myself, "shake these cobwebs." Sometimes it would take all of a morning for me to get back into the real day. Only then could I recognize that I would not be able to take the girl to lunch.

Something kin to this was being perpetrated on me now. I had a tattoo I could not account for, a good dog who was frightened of me, a car interior just washed of its blood, a missing wife whom I might or might not have seen late last night, and an ongoing, nicely simmering tumescence for a middle-aged blonde real estate lady from California, yet all I could think of as I took my walk to the center of town was that Alvin Luther Regency ought to have a reasonably serious purpose for interrupting a writer's working hours.

Now, the fact that I had done no writing in twenty-five days was not something I bothered to take into account. Rather, like those mornings in prison when I could not enter my day, so was I now like an empty pocket pulled out, and as much without myself as an actor who leaves his wife, his children, his debts, his mistakes, and even his ego in order to step into a role.

In fact, I was observing the new personality that walked into Regency's office in the basement of Town Hall, for I stepped through the door like a reporter, that is, I did my best to give an impression that the Police Chief's clothes, expression, office furniture, and words were all of equal import to me, as equal as the phrases that would go into a feature story of eight good paragraphs of approximately equal length. I entered, as I say, in the full concentration of such a role, and thereby noted like a good journalist that he was not accustomed to his new office. Not yet. His personal photographs, framed testimonials, professional licenses, paperweights and memorabilia might all be laid out or tacked to the walls, two file cabinets could flank his desk like posts at the gates of an ancient temple, and he might sit erect in his chair, like the military man he used to be, his close-to-the-scalp crew cut marking him as an old Green Beret, but still it stood out: he was not at home in his office. But then, which office would be at home with him? He had features that would ask a sculptor to use a jackhammer on the stone, all promontories, ledges and overhangs. In town, his nicknames abounded—Rockface, Target Shoot, Glint-eye—or, leave it to the old Portuguese fishermen: Twinkletoes. The townspeople were obviously not ready to buy

him yet. He may have been Acting Chief of Police for six months, but
the shadows of his predecessor hung over the office. The last Chief,
around for ten years, had been a local Portuguese who studied law at
night and moved up to the Attorney General's Office of the Common-
wealth of Massachusetts. Memories of the last Chief—considering it
was Provincetown, an unsentimental place—were now well-spoken.

I didn't know Regency well. In the old days, if he had come to my
bar, I would have been certain, doubtless, that I could read him on the
spot. He was large enough to play professional football, and there was
no mistaking the competitive gleam in his eye: God, the spirit of competition, and crazy mayhem had come together. Regency looked like
one Christian athlete who hated to lose.

I offer this much of a portrait because, in truth, I could not figure
him out. Just as I didn't always say hello to my day, so Regency didn't
always fit into the personality one knew him by. I will provide some
details by and by.

Now he pushed his chair straight back with military rectitude and
came out from behind his desk to draw up a chair near me. Then he
stared thoughtfully into my eyes. Like a General. He would have seemed
a total prick if somewhere along the way he had not been implanted
with the idea that compassion also belonged to the working police
officer's kit. The first thing he said, for instance, was "How is Patty
Lareine? Have you heard from her?"

"No," I said. Of course, by this one small remark he wiped out my
hard-held stance as a journalist.

"I wouldn't get into it," he said, "but I swear I saw her last night."

"Where?"

"At the West End. Near the breakwater."

That was not far from The Widow's Walk. "It's interesting," I said,
"to hear she's back in town, but I know nothing of that." I lit a cigarette.
My pulse had gone off on a race.

"It was just a glimpse of a blonde at the end range of my high beams.
Three hundred yards, probably. I could be wrong." His manner said he
was right.

Now he took out a cheroot and lit it, exhaling the smoke with panache enough for an old macho commercial.

"Your wife," he said, "is one attractive lady."

"Thank you."

On one of our drunken evenings this August past, in a week when we had in-the-water-at-dawn parties every night (Mr. Black already casing my home) we had made the acquaintance of Regency. Via a complaint about the noise. Alvin responded personally. I am sure he had heard of our parties.

Patty charmed him to the puttees. She told everyone—drunks, freaks, male and female models, half-nudes and premature Halloween types in costume—that she was turning down the stereo in Chief Regency's honor. Then she jibed at the sense of duty that restrained his hand from taking a glass. "Alvin Luther Regency," she said. "That's a hell of a name. You got to live up to it, boy."

He grinned like a Medal of Honor winner being commemoratorially kissed by Elizabeth Taylor.

"How did you ever get a name like Alvin Luther in Massachusetts? That's a Minnesota name," she said.

"Well," he said, "my paternal grandfather is from Minnesota."

"What did I tell you? Don't argue with Patty Lareine." She promptly invited him to the party we would be giving the following night. He came after duty. At the end, he told me at the door that he had had a fine time.

We started a conversation. He said he still kept his house in Barnstable and (Barnstable being fifty miles away) I asked if he didn't feel a bit out of place working here in all the melee of the summer frenzy. (Provincetown is the only town I know where you can ask such a question of the police.)

"No," he said, "I asked for this job. I wanted it."

"Why?" I asked. I'd heard rumors he was a narc.

He cut that off. "Well, they call Provincetown the Wild West of the East," he said, and gave his whinny.

After that, when we had a party, he'd drop in for a few minutes. If it continued from one night through to the next, we'd see him again. If it was after duty, he would have a drink, talk quietly to a couple of people, and leave. Just once did he give a clue—it was only after Labor Day—that he had taken on some booze. At the door he kissed Patty Lareine and shook hands formally with me. Then he said, "I worry about you."

"Why?" I did not like his eyes. He had the kind of warmth, when liking you, that reminds one most certainly of granite after it has been heated by the sun—the warmth is truly there, the rock likes you—but the eyes were two steel bolts drilled into the rock. "People have told me," he said, "that you have a great deal of potential."

Nobody would phrase things that way in Provincetown. "Yes, I fuck up with the best," I told him.

"I get the feeling," he remarked, "that you can stand up when the trouble is brightest."

"Brightest?"

"When it all slows down." Now his eyes at last showed light.

"Right," I said.

"Right. You know what I'm talking about. Damn right I'm right." And he walked out. If he had been the kind to weave, I would have seen it then.

He was more together when drinking at the VFW bar. I even saw him get into an arm-wrestling match with Barrels Costa, who got his name by flipping barrels of fish up from the hold to the deck, and at low tide, from the deck up to the wharf. When it came to arm wrestling, Barrels could defeat every fisherman in town, but Regency, to stake a claim, took Barrels on one night and was respected for not hiding behind his uniform. Barrels won, but had to work long enough to get a taste of the bitterness of old age, and Regency smoldered. I guess he wasn't in the habit of losing. "Madden, you are a fuckup," he told me that night. "You are a damn waste."

The next morning, however, as I was going down the street to get the newspaper, he stopped his squad car and said, "I hope I wasn't out of line last night."

"Forget it." He irritated me. I was beginning to fear the end result: a big-breasted mother with an enormous phallus.

Now, in his office, I said to him, "If the only reason you invited me here was to say you saw Patty Lareine, I wish you had told me on the phone."

"I want to talk to you."

"I'm not good at taking advice."

"Maybe *I* need some." He said the next with pride he could not conceal, as if the true heft of a man, the brand mark itself, was in the strength it took to maintain this sort of ignorance: "I don't know women very well."

"If you are coming to me for pointers, it is obvious you don't."

"Mac, let's get drunk one night soon."

"Sure."

"Whether you know it or not, you and me are the only philosophers in town."

"Alvin, that makes you the sole thinker the right wing has produced in years."

"Hey, let's not get testy before the bullets are fired." He started to show me to the door. "Come on," he said, "I'll walk you to your car."

"I didn't bring it."

"Were you afraid I'd impound your heap?" That gave him the sanction to guffaw all the way down the corridor and out to the street.

There, just before we parted, he said, "Do you still have that marijuana patch in Truro?"

"How do you know about it?"

He looked disgusted. "Man, what's the secret? Everybody talks about your home-grown. I sampled some myself. Why, Patty Lareine dropped a couple of rolled ones in my pocket. Your stuff is about as good as I used to get in Nam." He nodded. "See, I don't care whether you're a Left-Winger or a Right-Winger, I don't care what kind of fucking wing you fly. I love pot. And I will tell you. Conservatives aren't right in every last item of the inventory. They miss the point here. They think marijuana destroys souls, but I don't believe that—I believe the Lord gets in and wrestles the Devil."

"Hey," I said, "if you ever stop talking, we might have a conversation."

"One night soon. Let's get drunk."

"All right," I said.

"In the meantime, if I had placed my stash in a patch in Truro . . . " He paused.

"I don't keep a stash there," I said.

"I'm not saying you do. I don't want to know. I'm just saying if I did leave something there, I would contemplate getting it out."

"Why?"

"I can't tell you everything."

"Just want to tickle my stick?"

He took a good pause before he replied. "Look," he said, "I've been a State Trooper. You know that. And I know them. Most of those guys are all right. They're not high on humor and they never would be your kind, but they're all right."

I nodded. I waited. I thought he would go on. When he didn't, I said, "They are not nice about marijuana."

"They hate it," he said. "Keep your nose clean." He gave me a whale of a buffet on the back and disappeared down into the basement offices of Town Hall.

I found it hard to believe that our State Troopers, who considered it part of their job description to be lazy in fall, winter and spring so that they would be gung ho for a prodigious three months of suffering through summer traffic and its associated madness on Cape Cod, were now, in November, going to come pouring out of South Yarmouth Barracks in order to search Down-Cape through every petty field of marijuana in Orleans, Eastham, Wellfleet, and Truro. Still, they might be bored. They might also know about my plot. Sometimes I thought there were as many narcs as dopeheads on the Cape. Certainly in Provincetown the trade in dope information, disinformation, deals and double-crosses had to be the fourth largest industry right behind the polyester day tourists, the commercial fishing, and the congeries of gay enterprise.

If the State Troopers knew about my field—and maybe the proper question was, How could they not?—should I assume they were also well-disposed toward my wife and myself? One could doubt that. Our summer parties were too famous. Patty Lareine had large vices—madness of the heart and serious disloyalty being two I could name on the instant—but she also had the nice virtue of not being a snob. It might be said that she could hardly afford to be, given her redneck commencements, but who did that ever inhibit? If, after the trial, she had stayed in Tampa or made a daring move to Palm Beach, she would have had to play by the tactics that ambitious predecessors had perfected: slice, snip, soft-claw, and tenderize her way into marrying even higher respectability than Wardley—that was the only game with high stakes for the ego that a rich and notorious divorcée could play on the Gold Coast. An interesting life, if those are your talents.

Of course, I never pretended to understand Patty. She may even have been in love with me. It is hard to find a clearer explanation. I am a great believer in Occam's Razor, which states that the simplest explanation accounting for the facts is bound to be the correct explanation. Since I was no more than her chauffeur in the year before we got married, and since I had "crapped out" (those were her words) for deciding I did not care to murder her husband; since I was also an ex-con who could certainly assist her up no marble stairways in no mansions in Palm Beach, it was never comprehensible to me why she should desire my medium-attractive presence in marriage unless she did feel a salubrious melting in her heart. I don't know. We had something in bed for a while, but that can be taken for granted. Why else would a woman marry down? Later, when it all got bad, I began to wonder if her true passion was to reveal the abyss beneath my vanity. Devil's work.

No matter. Once we got to Provincetown, my only point is that she proved no snob. You couldn't move to Provincetown if you were a snob, not if social advancement was your goal. Some year I would like a sociologist to crack his teeth on the unique class system of our local society. The town, as I would probably have enjoyed explaining to Jessica Pond if I had had the chance, was once, a hundred and fifty years ago, a port for whalers. Cape Cod Yankee captains made up our establishment then, and they brought in Portuguese from the Azores to man the boats. Then the Yankees and Portuguese intermarried (just as the Scotch-Irish and Indians, Carolina cavaliers and slave women, Jews and Protestants were wont to do). By now, half the Portuguese had Yankee names like Cook and Snow, and by whatever name, owned the town. In winter the Portuguese dominated just about all of it, fishing fleet, Board of Selectmen, St. Peter's Church, the lower ranks of the police force, and most of the teachers and students in the grade school and high school. In summer the Portuguese also presided over nine tenths of the rooming houses and more than half of the bars and cabarets. Yet they were a down-in-the-grease up-to-the-elbows gearbox of an establishment. They kept to themselves, and enjoyed no high houses on any hills. The richest Portugee in town might, for all you knew, be living next to one of the poorest, and but for the new coat of paint, you could not tell the houses apart. No Portuguese son I heard of went to any great university. Maybe they were all too respectful of the wrath of the sea.

So if you wanted to look for some little splash of money, you waited for summer when enclaves of psychoanalysts and art-oriented well-to-do members of the liberal establishment came up from New York to be flanked by a wide panorama of gay society plus the narcs and dope dealers, and half of Greenwich Village and SoHo. Painters, presumptive painters, motorcycle gangs, fuckups, hippies, beatniks and all their children came in, plus tens of thousands of tourists a day driving in from every state of the Union to see for a few hours what Provincetown looked like, because there it was—on the extremity of the map. People have a tropism for the end of the road.

In such a stew, where the townsfolk were the only establishment we had, and the grandest summer houses (with one or two exceptions) were beach cottages, *medium* beach cottages; in a resort where there were no mansions (but one), no fine hotels, no boulevards!—Provincetown owned only two *long* streets (the rest were hardly more than connecting alleys)—in a bay village where our greatest avenue was a pier, and no pleasure yacht with deep draft could come in free of agitation at low tide; in a place where the measure of your dress was the logo on your T-shirt, how could you advance yourself socially? So you didn't give large parties to strike a note. You gave them, if you were Patty Lareine, because one hundred interesting-looking—that is to say, bizarre—strangers in her summer living room were the minimum she needed to offset the biles and jamborees of her heart. Patty Lareine may have read ten books in her life, but one of them was *The Great Gatsby*. Guess how she saw herself! Just as bewitching as Gatsby. When the parties went on long enough, she would, if the moon was late and full, get out her old cheerleader's bugle and there in the night blow a Retreat to the moon—don't try to tell her it was the wrong hour for Retreat.

No, the State Troopers would not like us. They were as stingy as airline pilots, and never was so much spent on parties where so little was accomplished. Such waste would irritate State Troopers. Besides— for the last two summers—cocaine was sitting on our table in an open bowl, and Patty Lareine, who liked to work the door, hand on hip, next to whoever was serving as bouncer (almost always some local lad built like two) was never the lady not to take a chance on a new face. Everybody crashed our portal. Narcs sniffed as much of our coke as any other inflamed septum.

I can't pretend, however, that I was privately cool about that open bowl. Patty Lareine and I fought over putting it on display. Patty, I decided, had hooked into cocaine more than she recognized, and I now hated the stuff. One of the worst years of my life had been spent buying and selling snow—I took my trip to the penitentiary for a cocaine bust.

No, State Troopers would not like me much. Yet to think of them arrayed in spiritual vengeance against my little marijuana plot was hard to believe this cold November afternoon. In the frenzy of summer, yes. The summer before this, in all the frantic August madness of a tip that a raid was near, I ran out to Truro in the heat of the day (when it's considered gross to harvest your crop—spiritually disruptive to the plant) and chopped it down, and spent an irrational night (what with having to explain my absence from a number of parties) wrapping the fresh-fallen stalks in newspaper and storing them. It was none of it done well, and so I didn't trust Regency's warm regard for the quality of that year-old product (maybe Patty Lareine had slipped him a couple of Thai nicely rolled and told him they were home-grown). All the same, my next crop, harvested just this last September, did have a flavor, call it a psychic distinction. Although it smelled a hint rank from the Truro woods and bogs, still I believe it offered something of the mist endemic to our shore. You can smoke a thousand sticks and never know what I'm talking about, but I did grow marijuana with a fine edge. If one wished to entertain the illusion that one could commune with the dead, or at least put up with the possibility that they were whispering to you, then my pot was fine. It was as spooky as any stuff I ever smoked. That I attribute to many factors, not least of which is that the Truro forests are haunted. Years ago—it is now more than a decade—a young Portugee in Provincetown killed four girls, dismembered their bodies, and buried them in several graves in these low woods. I was always immensely aware of the dead girls and their numb, mutilated, accusing presence. I remember that when I harvested my crop this year—and again I was in a great hurry, for a hurricane (which later wandered out to sea) was expected to strike us, indeed, the gusts were gale-force—on a hot, overcast, wind-inflamed mid-September day while a fearful surf was smashing on our bulkhead back in Provincetown, and townspeople were racing around to nail up storm windows, I was sweating like a swamp rat among the near-hysteria of the bugs in the Truro woods eight miles away. What an air of vengeance was about!

I remember I sliced each stem with a ceremonial patience, trying to feel the instant when the life of the plant passed through the knife into my arm and the plant was cut down to the half-life of its future. Now, its spiritual existence would depend on its ability to commune with whichever human—evil, wicked, contemplative, comic, sensual, inspired or plain disruptive—was ready to smoke it. I tried, in effect, to meditate while I performed the act of harvest, but (it may have been the rabid panic of the bugs or the bodeful imminence of the hurricane) I rushed the job. Despite myself, I began to slash at the roots and gathered the plants too quickly. In compensation, I tried to cure them with care, converting a large closet in our cellar, never used before, into an im-promptu drying room, and in the dark air (I had set up bowls of baking soda to keep the product dry) the Mary Jane was provided a real chance to rest over the next few weeks. After I stripped its leaves and buds, however, and packed them in small glass coffee jars with red rubber pressure-washers (I detested Saran-Wrap or plastic bags for stuff as fine as this) and actually began to smoke it, I found that something of the hour of its violent harvest was in each poke. Patty and I had fights to strike new notes of ugliness—we would pass from bouts of detestation to blood rage in the throat.

Moreover, that crop of marijuana (which I took to calling Hurricane Head) began to bring exaggerated effects down on Patty's head. It has to be understood that Patty Lareine believed she had psychic powers, which, speak of Occam's Razor, gives all the explanation one may need for why she chose Provincetown over Palm Beach inasmuch as the spiral of our shore and the curve of our sea contained, she claimed, a reso-nance to which she was sensitive. Once, in her cups, she said to me, "I've always been a swinger. When I was just a cheerleader in high school, I knew I was going to swing. I thought it would be a damn shame if I didn't get to fuck half the football team."

"Which half?" I asked.

"The Offense."

That was rote between us. It soothed the waters. She could give her large laugh, and I might offer two slightly widened lips.

"Why is your smile so evil?" she would ask.

"Maybe you should have fucked the other half."

She loved that. "Oh, Timmy Mac, you are nice at times." She took a deep puff of Hurricane. Never did the ravages of her hunger (for what, I cannot name—I wish I could) show so vividly as when she drew in smoke. Then her lips curled, her teeth showed, the smoke *seethed*—like a strong tide going through a narrow gate. "Yeah," she said, "I com-menced as a swinger, but as soon as I got divorced the first time, I decided to be a witch. I been one ever since. What are you going to do about it?"

"Pray," I said.

That broke her up. "I'm going to blow my bugle," she told me. "There's a real moon tonight."

"You'll wake up Hell-Town."

"That's the idea. Don't let those motherfuckers sleep. They get too powerful. Somebody's got to keep them down."

"You sound like a good witch."

"Well, honey, I am a white witch. Blondes are."

"You're no blonde. Your pussy hair says you're brunette."

"That's carnal taint. My pussy hair was bright gold until I went out and scorched it with the football team."

If she had always been like that, we could have kept drinking forever. But another toke put her on the promontory of Hurricane Head. Hell-Town began to stir.

Let me not pretend I was immune to her occult claims. I had never been able to make a philosophical peace with the notion of spirits, nor come to any conclusion. That you might die but still remain alive in some vale of our atmosphere seemed no more absurd to me than the notion that every part of your person ceased to exist after death. Indeed, given the spectrum of human response on any matter, I was ready to assume that some who died remained near, and others went far away, or were altogether extinct.

Hell-Town, however, was a phenomenon. When you smoked Hurricane Head, it became a presence. Over a hundred and fifty years ago when whaling was still active in these waters, a whore town sprang up on the other arm of Provincetown harbor, where now there was nothing but a long-deserted spit of sand. In the years after whaling ended, Hell-Town's warehouses and brothel cribs had been put on rafts and floated across the bay. Half the old houses in Provincetown had those sheds attached to them. So while much of what was most crazy in our moods on Hurricane Head may have come to us compliments of Patty Lareine, part of the manifestation emanated, I think, from our house itself. Half of our holding of sills, studs, joists, walls, and roof had been ferried over from Hell-Town more than a century ago, and thereby made us a most material part of that vanished place. Something of a perished Klondike of whores and smugglers, and whalers with wages hot in their pockets, lived in our walls. There had even been unspeakable cutthroats who, on moonless nights, would set a beach fire on the back shore to encourage a sailing vessel to believe it was rounding a light. Thereby the ship might come around for port too soon and run aground on a shoal. Whereupon these fiends would plunder the foundering vessel. Patty Lareine claimed she could hear the cries of the sailors who were slaughtered trying to fight off the marauders' long boats. What a Biblical scene Hell-Town must have offered of catamites and sodomites and whores passing the infections of the ages on to each pirate with blood in his beard. Provincetown, then, was just far enough away to be able to keep up the Yankee proprieties of widows' walks and white churches. What an intermingling of the spirits, therefore, when the whaling ended and the shacks in Hell-Town were floated over to us.

Some of that rut was added to our marriage during the first year we lived in our house. A bawdy force came down to us from one-night stands of whores and seamen more than one hundred years dead. I would, as I say, not enter into disputes about the real or unreal possibility that they lived in our walls—I only say our carnal life did not suffer. In truth, it thrived on the lusts of our unseen audience. It is nice when a marriage may feel like an orgy each night without having to pay the toll—that is, having to look on the face of the neighbor who is screwing your wife.

If the wisest rule of economy, however, is that you can't cheat life, it may as well be true that the most vigorous law of the spirit is: Do not exploit death. Now that Patty Lareine was gone, I had to live most mornings with the unseen presence of much of the population of Hell-Town. For if my wife was not with me, her much-vaunted sensitivity still seemed to be on loan to my psyche. One reason I could not open my eyes in the morning was for the voices I heard. Let no one say that a century-old New England whore does not snicker on a cold November dawn. There were nights when the dog and I slept together like children huddling before a fire that is out. Once in a while I would smoke Hurricane Head by myself, but the results lacked clarity. Of course, such a remark can hardly be understood unless marijuana is your guide. I was convinced it was the only nostrum to take when sailing the seas of an obsession—you could come back with answers to questions twenty years old.

Now that I was living alone, however, the Hurricane Head stirred no thoughts. Desires arose, instead, that I did not care to name. Serpents were laboring up from the murk. So, for the last ten days, I had not gone near my own reefer.

Can this explain why I acted with such reluctance to so generous a piece of advice from my Chief of Police?

While I did, so soon as I returned home, get into my car and drive out to the highway and there took the direction to Truro, I was still not at all certain that I would actually move my cache of Hurricane Head. I hated to disturb it. On the other hand, I most certainly did not want to be busted.

What a nose Regency had for my habits! I could not even say why I had chosen to keep the stash so near my marijuana field, but I had. Twenty glass coffee jars filled with carefully harvested crop were packed into a steel footlocker varnished and oiled against rust. That had all been placed in a hole in the ground beneath a most distinctive tree two hundred yards down an overgrown trail from a one-lane humped sandy road in the forest.

Yes, among all the hollows of the Truro woods to choose, I had nonetheless concealed my stash close to the stubble of my garden-size plot. That had to be the worst place to keep one's private store. Any hunter blundering through on the same trail (as they did a few times a year) might recognize the character of the agriculture practiced there, and so devote a little effort to examining the environs. I kept only an inch of soil and some much tamped-down moss over the rock that closed the burrow where I stowed the footlocker.

Yet this particular site was important to me. I wanted the product kept near its home. In prison, where the food we ate had been shipped to us out of the entrails of the largest food corporations in America, there was never a bite that did not come out of a plastic wrapping, cardboard package, or can. Taking into account the trip from the farm to the processing factory, and from there to us, I figure most of the food must have voyaged, on average, two thousand miles. So I saw a panacea to the world's ills: Let no one look to sup on food grown farther away from his home than the distance he can carry it on his back in a day's walk. An interesting idea. I soon ceased to look for ways to implement it. But it left me fierce about respecting the origins of my marijuana. Like wine that mellows in the shade of the vineyard where it grew, so would my Mary Jane be stored close to the earth out of which it sprouted.

I felt one good full dread, therefore, at shifting the stash, and it was close to the fear with which I had awakened this morning. Truth, I

needed to leave everything as it was. Nonetheless, I took the turn off
the highway to the country road that (by way of a crossroad or two)
would lead eventually to my sandy lane in the middle of the forest.
Driving slowly, I began to realize how much I had been calling upon
gifts of balance through this day. How else account for one's aplomb—
everything considered!—during the dialogue with Alvin Luther? After
all, where *had* the tattoo come from?

At that moment I was obliged to pull the car over. Where *had* the
tattoo come from? This thought might as well have come upon me for
the first time. With no warning, I was near to being as ill as the dog.

I can tell you that by the time I was able to move forward again, it
was with the absurd caution a poor driver brings to his wheel after a
missed collision. I crawled.

That way I passed through the back roads of Truro on this chill
afternoon—would the sun never appear again?—and I studied the lichen on tree trunks as if their yellow spores had much to tell me, and
stared at blue mailboxes on the road as though they were security itself,
even halted by a green-bronze sign at a crossroads to read the raised
metal letters commemorating a local boy who died in an old war. I
passed many a hedge in front of many a gray-shingled salt-box whose
white crushed-shell walks were still offering their whiff of the sea. In
the woods, the wind was strong on this afternoon, and whenever I
stopped the car, a murmur came to me like a high surf washing over
treetops. Then I was out of the woods again and drove up and down
abrupt little hills and passed by moors and quaking bogs and kettle
bowls. I came to a well I recognized by the side of the road, and stopped
and peered into its bottom where a green moss I knew would gleam
back at me. Soon I was in the woods again, and the paved road was
gone. Now I had to drive in low gear down the sandy lane, scratching
first one side of the Porsche, then the other, on thickets and briars, but
the hump in the middle was so high that I did not dare to ride the ruts.

Then I was not certain I would get through. Rivulets crossed the
road, and in several places I had to ford shallow pools where the trees
grew together overhead and formed a tunnel of leaves. On sunless afternoons I had always liked to drive through the mournful, modest lay of
these Truro hills and woods. Provincetown, even in winter, could seem
active as a mining town in comparison with such sparse offerings. Up
on any of these modest summits, if there was a high wind like today,

one could watch the seawater in the distance thrash through a millrace of light and whitecaps, while the color of the ponds in the hollows remained a dark and dirty bronze. All the palette of the woods seemed to accommodate itself between. I liked the dull green of the dune grass and the pale gold of the weeds, and in that late autumn panorama when the beef's blood and burnt orange are out of the leaves, the colors came down to gray and green and brown, but with what a play between! My eye used to find a dance of hues still left here between the field grays and the dove gray, the lilac gray and the smoke gray, the bracken brown and the acorn brown, fox brown and dun, mouse gray and meadowlark gray, and the bottle green of the moss, and sphagnum moss and fir green, holly green and seawater green at the horizon. My eye used to dart from lichen on a tree to heather in a field, in and out of the pond weeds and red maples (no longer red but wet-bark brown) and the scent of pitch pine and twist of scrub oak were in the still of the forest with the wind in the leaves overhead coming again in the high sound of the surf: "All that has lived clamors to live again" was the sound of the surf.

So I parked my car where I could look from the pond to the sea and tried to calm myself with these soft and wistful colors, but my heart was pounding now. I drove on until I came to my trail off this sand road, and there I stopped and got out of the car and tried to recover that immaculate sense of being alone which these woods had given me before. But I could not. People had been here in the last few days.

As soon as I stepped onto my trail, half hidden by shrubs from the road, this sense became more keen. I did not halt to look for traces, but doubtless some could be found. There are subtleties to a stale presence that only the woods can reflect, and as I walked the hundred steps from the road to my stashing box, I was sweating again in the way I had before on that hot September afternoon when the advance of the hurricane hung over us all.

I went by the marijuana field and its stubble had been beaten to the ground by rain. Some shame at the haste with which I had cut the stems this September left me now as uneasy as one feels on encountering an ill-used friend, and so I came to a stop as if to pay my respects, and indeed my little plot had the air of a cemetery ground. Yet I could hardly pause, a panic was too much on me, and therefore I hurried farther down the trail past the clearing and in and out of thicket and stunted pine, and there, another few steps along, was the most curious tree of all. A dwarf pine poked up from the crest of a small sandy ridge that had pushed through the loam of these woods, a fearfully twisted little force of a tree, its roots clinging to the uncertain rise, its limbs all contorted together on one side and trammeled down before the wind like a man kneeling, only, at the last, to thrust up his arms to the sky in prayer. That was my tree, and at the foot of it, under the roots, was a small cave not large enough to hold a bear cub, and my door to this burrow was a rock with its moss many times raised and patted back into place. Now I saw it was much disturbed, the edges as raw as a dirty bandage pushed up on end by the swelling of the wound. I removed the stone and felt into the hole in front of the footlocker, my fingers scraping and searching into this soft loam like field mice at the edge of food, and I felt something—it could be flesh or hair or some moist sponge—I didn't know what, but my hands, fiercer than myself, cleared the debris to pull forward a plastic garbage bag through which I poked and saw enough at once to give one frightful moan, pure as the vertigo of a long fall itself. I was looking at the back of a head. The color of its hair, despite all the stains of earth, was blonde. Then I tried to see the face, but when to my horror the head rolled in the bag without resistance—severed!—I knew I could not go on to search the features, no, I pushed back the bag and then the rock with hardly an attempt to replace the moss, and flew from those woods to my car, driving down the humpbacked road with speed to compensate for the caution with which I came in. And it was only after I was back in my house and deep in a chair trying to calm my shivering with bourbon neat that the realization came over me in all the burning woe of one wall of flame falling upon another that I did not even know whether it was the head of Patty Lareine or Jessica Pond lying in that grave. Of course, I also did not know whether I should be afraid of myself, or of another, and that, so soon as night was on me and I tried to sleep, became a terror to pass beyond all notions of measure.

Three

The voices came to me at dawn. I listened to Hell-Town in the hour between waking and sleep.

"Oh, Tim," the voices said, "you've burned your candle by both ends: the balls and the brain, prick and tongue, your bunghole and your mouth. Is any tallow left in your wick? As if the wicked could tell."

They said, "Oh, Tim, don't lick the thighs of whores. You come too fast tasting the old sperm whale. Give to us the dying salts. Give us back the scum of all who lost. Goodbye, sweet friend, I curse your house. I curse your house."

Let me speak of the little I could comprehend. Horror films do not prepare us for the hours lost in searching after one clear thought. Waking from nightmares and sleeping in terror, I climbed at last onto one conclusion. Assuming I was no part of this deed—and how could I be certain of that?—I still had to ask: Who was? It must be someone who knew my marijuana patch. That spoke directly of my wife—unless it was her hair I touched in the burrow. So I had my conclusion: I must go back to the woods and look again. As fixed in my memory, however, as the flash of light that is followed by the thunder of pain when your shoulder is pulled out of its socket, was the remembered glimpse of that dirtied blonde hair. I knew I could not go back. I was a jelly. I preferred to molder in the last suppurations of cowardice.

Is it evident why I do not care to describe my night? Nor why each logical step cost so much? Now I understood how the laboratory rat develops psychosis in a maze. There are shocks at too many of the turnings. What if Jessica was there? Would I know then that I had done it?

On the other hand—and I could have driven a hundred miles in the time it took me to go back to this alternative—if Pond and Pangborn had returned to Boston, or were by now even back in Santa Barbara, or back wherever their fling would chuck them—then it had to be Patty's head. That brought on a wholly unmanageable sorrow. Sorrow, and a surge of nasty vindication—which was only choked off by the onset of a new fear. Who could have killed Patty but Mr. Black? If that was true, how safe was I?

Do you feel a hint uncool around strange black dudes? Try such a thought in the night when you have come to the conclusion that the dude may be looking for you. Every wave that slapped on the shore, every gull that stirred, was an invader: I could hear windows raised and doors forced.

It was degrading. I had never seen myself as a hero. My father—with the best will in the world—had taken care of that. But I had usually been able to picture myself as not wholly un-macho. I could stand up for my friends; I could close a wound and keep the festering to myself. I tried to hold my own. Yet now, each time my mind was clear enough to bring forth a new thought, panic soiled me. I was like a puppy in a strange house. I began to fear my friends.

It had to be someone who knew where I kept my marijuana. That much was demanded by logic. In the false dawn, therefore, I realized that as I met my friends on the street in the day or two to come, I would distrust the look in every eye. I was like a man plummeting down a slippery slope who finds a little horn of ice to grasp, but so soon as he embraces it, the projection breaks loose. I saw that if I could not decide the first question, which was: Put it!—Was I the killer?—then I could not stop the slide, and madness would wait at the rim.

As dawn came up, however, and I had to listen to the solicitations of Hell-Town—why did these voices always call most loudly between waking and sleep, as if waking and sleep were a century apart?—I became aware at last of the chirks and cronks of the gulls, their gabble loud enough to chase the larvae of the night. But saying "larvae" now offered the minuscule pleasure that one word from Latin had come back in the midst of all this. You *larvae*, you ghosts! They taught Latin well at Exeter.

I clung to this thought. In prison, when one was at odds with another convict, and fear became as heavy as the leaden breath of eternity itself, then the smallest pleasure to reach your heart in such a state was, I learned, as valuable as a rope cast down into the abyss. Concentrate on the pleasure, whatever it was, and you could lash yourself to the edge. So, in this hour, I tried to embrace matters that were far away, and thought of Exeter and Latin, and by such means proceeded—not so much to calm myself as—to insulate the dread, and thereby manage to keep thinking about the little furnished room in a boardinghouse west of Tenth Avenue on Forty-fifth Street where my father now lived at the age of seventy. By the aid of such concentration I could see again the piece of paper he had tacked above his mirror and read again the words he had printed carefully on the paper. They said INTER FAECES ET URINAM NASCIMUR and beneath this, my father, with a flourish, had inscribed the name of the author: *St. Odon of Cluny*. My father's nickname (which I like to present in this context) still remained Big Mac in defiance of all McDonald hamburgers.

"Well, what do you want with that?" I said to Big Mac the first time I saw the note on the mirror.

"It's a reminder," my father replied.

"You never told me you knew Latin."

"Parochial school," he said. "They tried to teach us. Some of the droppings stuck."

"And how did you get this?"

"From a priest I know. Father Steve. He's usually in trouble with the Cardinal," remarked Big Mac in an agreeable tone, as if that were the first virtue to ask of a priest.

Well, I knew enough Latin to translate. "*Inter faeces et urinam nascimur*"—"Between shit and piss are we born." Even culture came to Big Mac at the edge of a longshoreman's hook.

But now the phone was ringing on the table by my bed, and I was ready to expect that it was my father. We had not called each other in a good while, yet I was sure it would be his voice. I had the faculty to be thinking of a friend even as he or she was picking up the phone to give me a call; this happened often enough not to surprise me any longer. On this morning, however, I took it as a sign.

"Hello, Tim?"

"Well, Dougy," I said. "Let us speak of the devil."

"Yeah," he said. That told me how hung-over he was. His "yeah" could offer you the devastated landscapes of the brain after sixty years of drinking. (This is, of course, on the assumption he did a little boozing when he was ten.)

"Tim," he said, "I'm in Hyannis."

"What are you doing on the Cape? I thought you hate to travel."

"I been here three days. Frankie Freeload retired up here. Did I tell you?"

"No," I said. "How is he?"

"He passed away. I been at his wake."

For my father, the death of an old friend would prove as awesome as a cliff by the side of your house crumbling into the sea.

"Well," I said, "why don't you come over to Provincetown?"

"I've been thinking of that."

"Do you have a car?"

"I can rent one," he said.

"No, I'll drive down and pick you up."

There was a long pause, but I could not tell if he were thinking of himself or of me. Then he said, "Let's wait a day or so. There's some loose ends here with the widow."

"All right," I said, "you come when you're ready." I thought I had offered no sign of my miserable condition, but Big Mac asked, "Are you all right?"

"My wife isn't here. She took off. That's okay."

There was a long pause. He said, "Yeah. I'll see you." And he hung up.

He had, however, given me some of the means to rise from my bed and go about the day.

Speak of hangovers, I was like a man on the edge of an epileptic attack. If I watched each move and never stubbed my toe or took a misstep, if I did not turn my head too suddenly, nor make any motion not prepared in advance, then I might be able to carry myself through the hours without a seizure. Here, it was not the convulsions of my body but the caterwaulings of the witches that I kept away by the singularity of my thoughts, which is to say I only allowed myself to think of particular matters and no others.

Since my immediate problems were as untouchable as a raw wound—even my tattoo began to throb if my mind cast a glance in its direction—so in compensation I discovered that to reminisce about my father was, on this morning, a palliative. I did not have to think pleasant thoughts, I could even dwell on old pains, but they were virtually agreeable to contemplate so long as they adhered to the past, old regrets serving as counterbalance to keep me from slipping back to where I was now.

For instance, I thought again of Meeks Wardley Hilby III. There had been a month in my life down in Tampa when I literally awakened each morning with the problem set before me: How were Patty and I to murder him successfully? Still that recollection caused no pain now. Indeed, it aided my concentration for two good reasons which served me like panniers carried on either side for balance. One was that I most certainly did not kill Wardley, even came to discover that there was no very determined assassin in me—not the worst thought to have on this morning! The other was that I was not thinking at this point of Mr. Hilby as I knew him in Tampa with Patty, but on the contrary, was remembering our curious bond at Exeter, and that had much to do with my father, indeed it brought back the best day I suppose I ever spent with Big Mac.

Meeks Wardley Hilby III, it may as well be repeated, was the only inmate I knew in prison who had also been in my class at Exeter. What always impressed me most about such a connection was the fact that we were also both kicked out of school on the same morning a month before graduation. Prior to that, I hardly knew him. Hilby had been a wimp and I had been a fair jock. He had gone to Exeter for four years like his father Meeks before him, and I put in one fall and spring as a Post Graduate on athletic scholarship after senior year at high school in Long Island. (My mother wanted me to go on to Harvard.) I had been trying to bring my promise as a Wide Receiver to an Exeter team that could not pass. (Have you ever seen Eastern prep schools play football?) We walked together out of the Headmaster's Office the day we got the boot, and Meeks Wardley Hilby III was crying. The scuffed satin on the lapels of his dinner jacket and the heliotrope bow tie were like a costume to wear to one's execution. I was sad. Even now, recalling the moment,

I can feel the sadness in my limbs. I had been caught smoking marijuana (which was no small matter twenty years ago). The Headmaster was truly shocked—and Hilby's case was worse. It was hard to believe, considering how slack he looked, but he had attempted to rape a town girl he took out on a petting date. I didn't hear about it then. Nobody concerned wished to speak (and the girl's parents were soon bought off) but Hilby gave me the story eleven years later. In prison, there was all the time to tell one's tale.

So, on this morning in Provincetown, when I wished to keep myself apart from all that was on me, it was, as I say, almost agreeable to return to the dolorous day I left Exeter. I remember it was a beautiful afternoon in May twenty years ago when I said goodbye to the school forever. I packed my gear into two duffel bags, dumped them and myself on a bus, and my father (whom I had already phoned—I could not bear to call my mother) took the shuttle to meet me in Boston. We got drunk. I would love him for that night alone. My father (as you may have gathered from our conversation on the phone) was not often a man to do any more talking than the exigencies of communication would re- quire, but he could soothe you by his silence. He was six-foot-three and at that time, in his fiftieth year, he weighed two-eighty. Forty of it he could have done without. It stood in front of him like the round rubber fender on an amusement-park car that bumps other cars, and he breathed heavily. With his prematurely white hair, boiled red face and blue eyes, he looked like the biggest, shrewdest and most corrupt old detective in town, but in fact he hated cops. His older brother, whom he never liked, lived and died on the police force.

This afternoon, as we stood side by side at an Irish bar (which stretched out so far into the interior darkness that it was long enough, my father commented, for the dogs to have a track) he put down his fourth drink—taken, like the first three, in shot glasses—and said, "Marijuana, huh?"

I nodded.

"How could you get caught?"

He meant: How could you be so dumb as to get nabbed by a bunch of Wasps? I knew his opinion of their wits. "What's wrong with certain people," he stated once in an argument with my mother, "is that they expect God to buy His clothes in the same store they do." So I always reacted to Wasps through his eyes. Big Mac saw them as well-knit, silver-haired, gray-suited and forever speaking in such swell accents that they had to believe God was using *them* to display His decency.

"Well," I told him, "I got careless. Maybe I was laughing too hard." And I described the morning of the night I was caught. I had been in a sailing race on a lake near Exeter whose name I no longer remember (the wages of pot!) and the boats were still. They almost called the race off. I knew nothing about sailing, but my roommate did, and had me crewing for an old history teacher who certainly managed to fit my father's idea of a Wasp. He was a good skipper, probably the best in school, and so contemptuous of his competition that he even took on an ignoramus like myself. In the race, however, we had light winds and bad luck. The wind would die, breathe us forward on a zephyr, then die again. At last we stood by the mast, our empty spinnaker hanging in the bow, and watched a boat creep ahead of us. At its helm was an old lady. She was much closer to land than we were, and had gambled that while there would not be wind anywhere this morning, she could count on a touch of current licking the lakeshore as it moved toward a stream. She counted well. She crept from three boat lengths back to eight ahead, while we, now down to second place, five hundred yards farther out from land, never moved at all. She had outfoxed our old fox.

After a while it grew boring and I began to banter with my roommate. The skipper stood it as long as he could, but the inert spinnaker finally did him in. He wheeled on me, and in his best master's voice said, "I wouldn't talk so much if I were you. It spills the wind out of the sails."

After I told this story my father and I laughed so hard we had to clutch each other and whirl around for balance.

"Yeah," Big Mac said, "with people like that, it's a favor to get caught."

That took away my need to tell him how I had come back to my room in a riot of laughter and fury. What retorts I had swallowed. One year at Exeter had obviously not been enough for me to learn the customs of the people who ran the works. (Oh, the English have airs in their nose and the Irish sprout hairs in their toes!)

"I'll try to explain it to your mother," Big Mac said.

"I appreciate that." I knew he and she had probably not spoken in a year, but I could not face her. She would never understand. From the time I was eleven until I turned thirteen (and was outdoors every evening) she managed to sit beside me long enough each night to read one poem from Louis Untermeyer's *Treasury of Great Poems*. To her credit (and Untermeyer's) I did not hate poetry when I was done. All the more reason I could not tell her now.

Of course, I had to listen to my father repeat through each drink to come, "It spills the wind out of the sails." Like many a good drinker before him, he was not above using the same remark for a different glass—but then, at this point, my recollections were shattered. The telephone began to ring for a second time this morning. I picked up the receiver with no sense of any good omen.

It proved to be the proprietor of The Widow's Walk. "Mr. Madden," he said, "I hate to bother you, but I couldn't help noticing the other night that you seemed to know the couple who sat in the lounge while you were there."

"Oh, yes," I said, "we had a nice drink together. Where were they from—the West, wasn't it?"

"During dinner," he replied, "they told me they were from California."

"Yes, I have some recollection of that," I said.

"The only reason I ask is that their car is still in our parking lot."

"Isn't that odd," I told him. "Are you certain it's their car?"

"Well," he answered, "I do think it's theirs. I happened to notice when they came in."

"Isn't that odd," I repeated. My tattoo had begun to smart fiercely.

"Frankly," he said, "I was hoping you might know where they are." Pause. "But I guess you don't." "No," I said, "I don't."

"The name on the man's credit card is Leonard Pangborn. If they don't pick up the car in another day or two, I suppose I could check with Visa."

"I would think you could."

"You didn't get the lady's name, did you?"

"She did tell me, but, you know, I'm just darned if I can remember it now. May I give you a ring if I do? I do remember, Pangborn was certainly *his* name."

"I'm sorry, Mr. Madden, to disturb your morning, but it's just so peculiar."

Count on it. After this call I could not recover my concentration. Every thought went rushing to the woods. Find out! But this loosed an unmanageable panic. I was like a man who is told he has a mortal illness, yet can cure it by jumping off a fifty-foot cliff into the water. "No," he says, "I'll stay in bed. I'd rather die." What is he protecting? What was I? Yet the panic carried everything before it. It was as if I had been told in my sleep that the worst malignancies of Hell-Town were gathered beneath my tree in the Truro woods. If I went back, would they enter me? Was that my logic?

Sitting beside the telephone with a panic as palpable as physical distress itself—my nostrils were colder than my feet, my lungs burned—I began the work, and it was equal to labor, of recomposing myself. How many mornings had I gone from a quarrel over breakfast into my small room on the top floor where I could look on the harbor and try to write, yet each morning I had learned how to separate out—and it was much like straining inedibles from a soup—all the wreckage of my life which might inhibit writing that day. So I had habits of concentration gained first in prison and gained again from learning to do my work each morning no matter how upsetting the fracas with my wife; I could keep my mind on a course. If the seas before me now pitched uncontrollably—well, I knew, if nothing else, that I must try at this point to think of my father and not ask any question that had no answer. "Do not attempt to recall what you cannot recall" was a rule I had long kept. Memory was equal to potency. To seek to remember what one could not bring back—no matter how urgent the need—was like calling for an erection when a girl was wide open before you, but your cock—that perverse cur!—was resolutely, obdurately, finally, refusing to stir. You had to give up. I would recall, or I would not recall what happened two nights ago—I would have to wait for that—but in the interim I had to build a wall around my panic. Every recollection of my father felt therefore like a good stone laid down properly.

So I went back to such thoughts, and knew the beginning of that peace which comes from contemplating the love, no matter how pinched, that one holds for a parent. Since I had poured myself a drink as the one legitimate sedative I could call upon this morning, and had gone to my *querencia*, that study on the third floor where I used to work looking out on the bay, so did I go back to the legend of Dougy "Big Mac" Madden and meditate on its great cost to him, and to my mother, and to me. Because for all his height and bulk we never had enough of him. A good deal of my father, I can tell you, was lost before he ever met my mother. That much knowledge I had already gained in child-hood listening to the talk of his old friends.

I remember that they used to come out to our house on Long Island to visit him for an afternoon before they all went over to his bar, and since they were longshoremen and former longshoremen like himself, and almost as large, my mother's modest living room would look, so soon as they all stood up, like an overloaded boat ready to capsize. How much I liked those occasions. I would already have heard, over and over, the story of my father's great hour.

Years later I was told by a lawyer that if separate accounts given by two witnesses agree in every detail, you are listening to a lie. In that case, my father's legend must have had a good deal of truth in it. All the versions varied. They could, however, agree this much: On a day back in the late thirties, at a time when the Italians were driving the Irish out of the leadership in the longshoremen's union, my father—one of the leaders in the ILA—was parking his car on a side street in Greenwich Village when a man darted out of a doorway and took six shots at him with a .45. (I also heard it was a .38.) How many struck him, I do not know. It is hard to believe, but most of the stories said six, and I could count four gunshot wounds on his torso when he showered.

He was renowned in those days for his strength. A strong man among longshoremen had to be a phenomenon, but he must have been as powerful as a Kodiak bear on this occasion because he looked at his assailant and took a step forward. The gunman (whose .45, I assume, was now empty) saw that his victim did not drop. So he began to run. I find it hard to believe, but my father chased him. For six blocks along Seventh Avenue in Greenwich Village he ran after his assailant (some say eight blocks, some say five, some say four) but it took all of such a distance before Dougy recognized that he could not catch him and came to a stop. Only then did he see blood oozing from his shoes and realize that he was dizzy. He turned around just before the street began to turn around on him and saw that he was outside the emergency entrance of St. Vincent's Hospital. So he knew he was in bad shape. He hated doctors and he hated hospitals, but he was going in.

The attendant at the desk must have decided the new arrival was a drunk. A huge distraught man with a considerable amount of blood on his clothing was teetering over the table.

"Please sit down," said the orderly. "Wait your turn."

While my father normally did no more than nod or frown as friends told the story, here he would sometimes speak up himself. When I was a child, the look of absolute murderous certainty that came into his eyes was so thrilling to my keyed-up young interior that once or twice I wet my pants a drop. (Although before such manly company, I kept the secret to myself.)

My father, in telling it, would seize an imaginary orderly by the shirt, his arm extended stiffly, his fingers clutching the collar as if his strength might be all but expired, yet what remained was enough to throw this specimen of unfeeling humanity through a wall.

"Take care of me," Dougy Madden said in a low, deadly voice in my mother's living room. "I'm hurt."

He was. They kept him in St. Vincent's for three months. When he came out, his hair was white, and he was done with the union. I don't know whether lying in bed for so long a time took away a part of his massive nerve or whether the Irish leaders had lost. Maybe, by now, his mind was in another place, that far-off place, full of unspoken sorrow, where he lived for the rest of his life. In this sense, he retired before I was born. Maybe he was mourning no more than his lost eminence, for he was a labor leader no longer, merely a barrel of a man. In any event, he borrowed money from his relatives, opened a bar on the Sunrise Highway forty miles out on the South Shore, and for eighteen years was the proprietor of a place that did not prosper and did not fail.

Most bars, given this description, figure to be managed with economy, since they are usually empty. My father, however, had a bar that was like himself, large, full of generosity and only half managed, even if Big Mac did look like the bartender out of whom the mold was made.

He was there for eighteen years in his white apron and his prematurely white hair, his blue eyes measuring the drinkers when they got obstreperous, and his skin so red from the steady inflow of drink ("It's my only medicine," he would tell my mother) that he looked an angrier man than he was, fierce as a lobster making one last lunge out of the pot.

He got a fair daily crowd, a good Saturday crowd, albeit beer drinkers, and a heavy summer crowd, full of weekend lovers out on Long Island and fishermen going or coming. He would have been a prosperous man, but he drank a bit of the profits, gave back more across the bar, sent scuds of them across on free drinks to the farthest reaches of the room, let people run up a tab so large they could have paid the funeral expenses of their fathers and mothers and uncles and aunts, and he loaned money at no interest and didn't always get it back, and gave it away, and gambled it away—so as the Irish say (or is it the Jews?), "It was a living."

Everyone loved him but my mother. She came to love him less over the years. I used to wonder how they ever got married and finally decided she had to be a virgin when they met. I would suspect that their short and most loving affair (for long after they divorced, my mother's voice would still be tremulous when she spoke of their first weeks together) was stimulated not only by how different they were but because she was also a liberal and wished to defy the prejudices of her parents against the Irish, the working classes and the smell of beer in bars. So they married. She was a small, modest, pleasant-looking woman, a schoolteacher from a nice town in Connecticut, as delicate as he was large, and she had nice manners and was a lady to him. I think she always remained a lady to him, and while he would never admit that his own great secret prejudice was just for that, for the high elegant splendor of a lady's hand in a long glove, nonetheless, he adored her. He was terribly impressed that he had married such a woman. Alas, they remained a sad couple. To use his expression, neither could move the other a cunt-hair to the left. If not for my presence, they would soon have foundered in frustration and boredom. I was there, however, and their marriage lasted through my fifteenth year.

Maybe it would have gone all the way, but my mother made one error. She won a fundamental argument with my father and got him to move from our floor-through apartment above his bar, to a town called Atlantic Lanes, and that was a quiet catastrophe. The shift proved equal, doubtless, to the shock his grandfather took on leaving Ireland. The one major concession given my mother was the one he should never have agreed to. Dougy distrusted Atlantic Lanes on sight. Although it sounds, I know, like a bowling alley, the developers bestowed the name on their brand-new town because we were no more than two miles from the ocean, and our streets had been designed to show a few bends. (Lanes.) The shape of our twisting roads came from the draftsmen laying it out on drawing paper with French curves. Since the land was as flat as a parking lot, our S-turns served no purpose I could see except to make it easier not to have to look at your neighbor's ranch house which was exactly like your own. It's a joke, but Dougy could not find his way back when drunk. It was no joke. Something was leached out of all of us who grew up there. I cannot name it, although in the eyes of my father, we kids were awfully civilized. We didn't hang out on a street corner—no right angles in Atlantic Lanes—we didn't run in gangs (we had best friends instead) and once when I was having a fist fight, my disputant said in the middle of it, "Okay, I quit." We stopped and shook hands. My mother was not displeased that (1) I won, since she had learned over the years that would make my father happy and (2) I had acted like a gentleman. I had shaken hands nicely. My father was intrigued. It was truly the suburbs. You could get into a fight and say "I quit," and the winner would not celebrate by banging your head on the pavement. "Boy, where I grew up," he told me (it happened to be Forty-eighth Street west of Tenth Avenue) "you never quit. You might just as well say 'I die!' "

Once, a few years before the end of their marriage, I overheard my mother and father in the living room on a rare night when he was home from the bar. I was trying not to listen, in fact was staying away by doing my homework in the kitchen. When, on these rare occasions, they would find themselves together, they could sit for hours without speaking, and their mutual gloom often got so intense that even the audio on the TV seemed to quaver. On this night, however, they may have been close, for I heard my mother say in a gentle voice, "Douglas, you never say that you love me."

That was true enough. For years I had hardly ever seen him give her a kiss and then only like a miser pulling out the one ducat he will spend this year. My poor mother. She was so affectionate she would kiss me all the time. (Out of his sight.) She never wanted him to think my habits were unmanly.

"Not once, Douglas," she now repeated, "do you ever say you love me."

He did not reply for a minute, but then he answered in an Irish street voice—it was his declaration of love—"I'm here, ain't I?"

Of course, he was famous among his friends for such an ascetic view. In longshoreman days, he had earned another legend for the number of women he could attract and the powerful number of times he could do it in a night. All the same, it was his manly pride that he was never obliged to kiss the girl. Who knows what ice room of the heart my skinny Irish grandmother raised him in? He never kissed. Once, not long after I was kicked out of Exeter, I went drinking with Dougy and his oldest buddies, and he was meat for the roast on this matter of a kiss. His friends might be scarred and half toothless and in their fifties, and since I was twenty, they looked ancient to me, but, God, they were filthy-minded. When they talked, they rolled around in sex like it was stuck to their pants.

My father was, by then, not only divorced from my mother, but had, in the general waste that followed, lost his bar. He lived in a rented room, had a lady friend once in a while, worked in a barroom for wages and saw a lot of his old friends.

Every one of these old friends, I soon discovered, had a quirk, and the rule of the game was to kick your old buddy on the quirk. Some were tight with a dollar, some had foolish habits like betting long shots, one of them always threw up when he was drunk ("I have a sensitive stomach," he would complain. "Yeah, we have sensitive noses," they would reply) and my father always got it about kissing.

"Oh, Dougy," his old friend Dynamite Heffernon would say, "last night I was with a nineteen-year-old who had the juiciest, sweetest, plumpest, loveliest mouth you ever saw. Could she kiss! Oh, the moist breath of her fine smile. Do you have any idea of what you're missing?"

"Yeah, Dougy," another would cry out, "give it a try. Break down. Give the broad a kiss!"

My father would sit there. It was the game, and he would suffer it, but his thin lips showed no pleasure.

Francis Frelagh, a.k.a. Frankie Freeload, took his swipes at the ball. "I had one widow with a tongue last week," he told us. "She put that tongue in my ears, down my mout', she licked my t'roat. If I let her, she would have swiped my nostrils."

At the look of disgust on my father's face, they laughed like choir boys, high-pitched and shrill, Irish tenors kicking Dougy Madden's quirk.

He took it all. When they were done, he shook his head. He did not like to be performed on while I was there—that was the measure of his fallen state—so he said, "I think you're all full of shit. None of you has been laid in the last ten years." When they whooped at his anger, he stuck out his palm. "I'll give you," he said, "the benefit of the doubt. Let's say you know a couple of girls. And they like to kiss. Maybe they even go down on you. All right. That's been known to happen. Only, ask yourself: The broad is taking care of you now, but whose joint did she cop last night? Where was her mouth then? Ask yourself that, you cocksuckers. Cause if she's able to kiss you, she can eat dog turds."

This speech put his old gang in heaven. "I wonder who's kissing her now," they would croon in Dougy's ear.

He never smiled. He knew he was right. It was his logic. I knew. I had grown up with it.

This was as much, however, as I could go on thinking about my father before the itch of my tattoo began to distract me out of measure. By a look at the clock, I saw it was nearly afternoon, and I stood up with the thought of taking a walk but had to sit down again beneath the sudden weight of fear that came upon me from no more than the thought of stepping outside.

Yet now I felt a whole decomposition of myself, a veritable descent from man to dog. I could no longer cower here. So I put on a jacket, and was through the house and into our damp November air with the jaunty sense that I had just performed a near-heroic act. Such are the warps of pure funk. It is a low comedy.

Once on the street, however, I began to comprehend my reason, at least, for the new fear. Before me, a mile away, was the Provincetown Monument, a pinnacle of stone over two hundred feet high, and not unlike the Tower of the Uffizi in Florence. It was the first sight of our town from the road or sea as one approached our harbor. It sat on a good hill back of the Town Wharf, indeed, so much in the middle of our existence that one saw it every day. There was no way not to. Nothing built by man was of such height until you got to Boston.

Of course, a native never needed to recognize it was there. I probably had not looked at it for a hundred days, but on this day, so soon as I turned to walk toward the center of town, my tattoo, like a meter to mark the pulsations of my anxiety, seemed to crawl over my skin. If normally I looked at our monument without seeing it, now I most certainly did. It was the same vertical tower that I had tried to climb on a drunken night almost twenty years ago, and I came so near to the summit as to reach the overhang of the parapet not thirty feet below. I had gone up the vertical, taking handholds and footholds where I found them in the granite blocks, enough at least for my fingertips and my toes. It was a climb to awaken me in the middle of many a night for years after, since in more than one place I had to lift myself by the strength of my arms alone, and in the worst places I ran into ledges wide as two fingers for my toes, but nothing for my hands—I could only mount palms flat against the wall—it is incredible, but I was drunk enough to keep going until I came to the overhang.

Now, I have talked to rock climbers since, and one or two have even looked at the monument with me, and when asked if they could manage the overhang, said, "A piece of cake," and meant it. One even explained the technique he would use, although I hardly understood. I was no rock climber myself. That night was the only hour in my life when I lived on a wall near to two hundred feet from the ground, but it came to so poor an end that I never had the moxie to try again.

For I locked myself up, as they say, in the overhang. It seems I should have trusted the holds I had, and leaned out backward until I got a hand on the parapet—it was only a small overhang!—but I could not figure how to surmount it, and so I pressed instead against an arch just beneath, my back on one supporting column, the soles of my feet on the other, and there I remained, my body stuffed in the small arch just under the parapet until my strength began to go, and after a while I knew I would fall. Let me say I thought it was not possible, given the position I was in, to descend, and I was right. It is easier, I was told later, to go up a wall than to go down if you do not have a rope. There I perched, then there I clung, while all the collected valor of the spirits I had drunk began to wane. Then I was sober, and so frightened that I began to shout, and soon, I suppose, to scream, and to cut such recollection to its shortest, I was rescued by the Volunteer Fire Department in the middle of the night by a huge fisherman in a bosun's swing (no less a person than Barrels himself) who was let down on a rope from the balcony above (having gone up the stairway within the tower) and he was able to grasp me finally while they hauled both of us up, but by then I was like a cat trapped for six days in a tree—I had smelled my death—and they say I fought him off, even tried to bite him when he came near. I suspect it is true, for in the morning I had a huge knot on the side of my head where he gave me one bang against the rock to chasten some of that lividity.

Well, I was also ready to take the bus that morning, and packed my suitcase and was going to leave Provincetown forever when some friends came by and treated me like a figure of valor. It seemed I was not looked upon as a fool. So I stayed, and came to realize why Provincetown might be the place for me, since no one ever thought I had done anything crazy or even particularly bizarre. We all had extraordinary stuff to get out of us, that was all. Do it the way you could.

Still, I kept that bag beneath my bed for all of the winter months I stayed that year, and I do not think there was an hour when I was not ready to decamp—one jeer at the wrong time would have been enough. It was, after all, the first time in my life I had to recognize I was not automatically sane.

Of course, I had some idea of what could be at the core of it. Years later, reading Jones's biography of Freud, I came across a reference Freud made to what was "doubtless, an unruly attack of latent homosexual panic in myself," and had to set the book down, for just so suddenly was I overcome with thinking of the night I tried to scale the monument. Now my tattoo throbbed. Was that *unruly attack* with me still?

Yes, was it not true that every place renowned for its colony of homosexuals invariably had such a monument? I thought of the men and boys who cruised the obelisk in Central Park, and the invitations with phallic measurements listed next to many a telephone number inscribed on the partitions of the public toilets at the foot of Washington Monument. What in me had I been attempting to extirpate on that lunatic climb? *In Our Wild—Studies among the Sane* by Timothy Madden.

There was one other man in town who could call himself my mate for he, too, had attempted to go up the Provincetown Monument. Like me, he had failed to solve the overhang and been rescued by the volunteer firemen, although this time (there are limits to symmetry) Barrels was not on the rescue rope.

His attempt took place only four years ago, but such are the number of freak-outs and flare-outs who bob in the churn of the great washing machine that is Provincetown in summer that no one remembers anything. My father's legend has been walking along with his life, but here, by the time Hank Nissen made his attempt, all had forgotten mine— too many people pass through!—and sometimes I think Nissen was the only one who remembered that I had also tried.

I regretted, however, that our exploits were privately wed, for I could not bear the guy. Will it help to explain that his nickname was Spider? Spider Nissen. Henry Nissen a.k.a. Hank Nissen, a.k.a. Spider Nissen, and the last clung to him like a bad smell. He had a touch of the hyena for that matter—the same we-eat-tainted-meat-together intimacy that burns out of a hyena's eyes behind the bars of his cage. So Spider Nissen would look at me and give a giggle as if we had both had a girl together, and each took turns sitting on her head.

He bothered me prodigiously. I do not know if it was our mingled glory and shame on the monument wall, but I could not see him in the street without having my mood altered for the day. I knew as much physical uneasiness around him as if he kept a knife in his pocket to use below your ribs, and indeed he did keep a knife. For that matter, he was the type to knowingly sell you pot ravaged with paraquat because he needed the bread to score for coke. A bad man, yet through the winter, winter after winter, one of my twenty friends in town. In winter we paid a toll not unlike living in Alaska—a friend was someone to pass an hour with against the Great Ice-Man of the North. In the silence of our winter, dull acquaintances, drunks, wretches and bores could be elevated to a species thought of as friend. Much as I disliked Spider, we were near, we had shared an hour no one else could comprehend even if our hour was sixteen years apart.

Besides, he was a writer. In winter we needed each other if only to be critical of our contemporaries together. One night we would look for the faults in McGuane, next came DeLillo. Robert Stone and Harry Crews were saved for special occasions. Our rage against the talent of those who were our age and successful made the marrow of many an evening, even if I suspected he didn't value my writing. I knew I didn't like his. My lips were sealed, however. He was my dirty, treacherous, raunchy neighbor-friend. Besides, one had to admire half his mind. He was trying to launch a series of novels about a private detective who never left his room, a paraplegic in a wheelchair who managed to solve all crime set before him through his computer. He would tap into giant networks, put knots in the CIA's internal communications, mess with the Russians, but Spider's man also took care of intimate deeds by peering into private computers. He'd locate the murderers through their shopping lists. Spider's protagonist was a true spider. Once I told him, "We've evolved from invertebrates to vertebrates. You'll take us on to the cerebrates." Saying that, I saw heads with tendrils substituting for torso and limbs, but his eye glittered as if I had made a direct hit in a video arcade.

I may as well describe his appearance—it was by now obvious to me that I was on my way to his house. He was tall and thin with very long limbs and long thin blond hair that was near to blue-green from dirt, even as his faded blue denims were almost a dirty yellow. He had a long nose that went nowhere—that is to say, it had no climax, merely ended with two functioning nostrils and a nondescript tip. He had a wide, flat, crablike mouth and dark gray eyes. The ceilings in his house were too low for him. The exposed beams were only eight feet from the floor— another fish-shed from Hell-Town!—and so the place consisted of four small rooms at the top of a narrow Cape Cod stairway above four small rooms below, all reeking of some sad, dank aroma, of cabbage, the faded scent of wine, diabetic sweat—I think his girl had diabetes—and old bones, an old dog, spoiled mayonnaise. It was like the poverty of an old lady's room.

But then in winter we huddled in our houses as if we belonged to the century behind us. His house was on one of the narrow lanes between our two long streets, and you could not even see its roof until you made your entrance through a gate in a high hedge. Then the door was on you. There was no yard, just the hedge encircling the house. On the ground floor, as you looked through each window, you saw nothing but that hedge.

I remember wondering on my walk why I was visiting him now, and soon recalled that the last time I had been at his house he had cut a plug from a melon, poured in vodka and later served it to all of us with hash cookies. There had been something in the way he cut the melon—a high surgical precision in the turning of the blade that excited me to the joys of using a knife, much as a man who is eating with a highly refined gusto can inspire your taste for the same food.

So it was that walking along the street, contemplating the monument and my tattoo, I thought not only of Spider Nissen but of the frightful scream he gave on the night of a séance over a month ago and the rare event that ensued: Patty Lareine had a most uncharacteristic fit of hysterics immediately afterward. With no more than this recollection of how he used a knife, and the quick but immaculate certainty (which came to me like an angel's gift) that he might know how I received my tattoo, I was suddenly possessed of the conviction it was Spider's knife that severed a blonde head from its neck.

All this at once. The most intolerable pressure in my head now released itself. It is agony to live without a clue when you are in peril whose depth cannot be measured. Now, I had a premise. It was to observe my friend Spider. I am afraid, after every bad remark I have just made about him, that I had still been generous enough to take him along on more than one trip to the marijuana patch. Our winter loneliness is, as I say, the source of half our actions.

Nissen's woman, Beth, opened the door to my rap on the knocker. I mentioned earlier that there was no snobbery in Provincetown, and none there was, but you could still find a good many people to be offended. For instance, most of my winter friends never locked their door when they were home. You did not ring or rap. You walked in on people. If the door was locked, it meant only one thing—your friends were screwing. Some of my friends, for that matter, liked to make love with the door unlocked. If you came in, there was the option to watch or, given the phase of the moon, to join. There is not that much to do in Provincetown in the winter.

Patty Lareine, however, considered this trashy. I never came close to understanding her mores, since I think she would have cohabited with an elephant—but only to win a bet, a very large bet. Where she came from, white trash were always wandering around in one another's bedding. So while my good wife could consider many a proposal, some touch of class had to accompany it. This Provincetown custom of one smelly joining two sleazos under dingy-gone blankets was revolting to her. They could go for it because they came from good middle-class families and were, as Patty Lareine once put it, "trying to get vengeance on their folks for giving them cancer!" Patty was having no part of that. Her body was her proud possession. She loved nude beach parties on the back shore and enjoyed standing (with her brown snatch limned in honey-gold by the sun) a foot away from the eyes of some potential lover on the sand who was eating a hot dog, one eye on the red meat covered with mustard coming up to his lips, the other on the copse between her thighs.

She could cavort bare-ass in the sea, her arms around two other naked women, her mean, pinching Southern fingers tweaking their nipples— nipple-pinching, tit-grabbing, ass-slapping being good girl sports in the waterholes she used to know, the splash-rope hanging from the big limb of the old tree up on the bluff.

She also liked to walk about our house in her high heels and nothing else, and it grated on her most sensitive tissues when some old parka with a man inside would fling our door open to ask, "Tim at home?"

"You stupid low crude son of a bitch," she would say, "did you ever hear of knocking?"

So a law was imposed on our friends: Ring the bell before you come in. And we—meaning her—enforced it. We were looked down on for being so uptight, but as I indicated, reverse snobbery occupied our town in winter.

Therefore I made a point of knocking on Spider's door and nodded at his woman, Beth, when she let me in. There was a submission in her so slavish to every one of Nissen's whims that even the most gung ho women in town gave up on her. The irony is that Beth supported Nissen's household; indeed, it was her little house and had been bought with money given by her well-to-do parents (corporation types, I was told, from Wisconsin). Yet Spider held the salt-box as his fief. The fact that it was her money that had bought his Honda 1200CC, his Trinitron TV, his Sony video camera, his Betamax recorder and his Apple computer seemed only to strengthen his power. Her poor sense of worth was kept dimly alive by surrendering funds to him: she was a quiet, pale, soft-spoken, furtive, dun-colored young woman with eyeglasses, and I always had the impression, even as Beth and I bobbed our heads and gave shy smiles to each other, that she had deliberately refused every small charm that could have attached itself to her. She looked like a weed. Yet she wrote good poetry. On reading what little she would show, I had discovered that she was cruel as a ghetto rapist in the brutality of her concepts, quick as an acrobat in her metaphors, and ready to slay your heart with an occasional vein of feeling as tender as the stem of honeysuckle on a child's mouth. Still, I was only surprised, not dumbfounded. She was one weed that had been fed on radium.

Let me warn you, however, that her sex life with Spider—no mystery to any friend—was sordid, even for us. Somewhere along the way, Nissen had hurt his back and now had a serious slipped disc. Every few months he would have to take to the floor for a couple of weeks, do his writing there, his eating, and his fornicating. I think the worse his back began to treat him, the more he went at it, which had to make his spine worse. First he ground the meat and then the bones, and finally the tripe and offal of their attraction for each other as if during the length of this incarceration on the floor—speak of flattening time!—he had to keep plucking the one banjo string left to him until either his back would break, his mind would go screaming into outer space or she would slit her wrists. He used to make video tapes of them fornicating. Maybe as many as a dozen of us had been shown them. She would sit among us like a nun, silent, while he demonstrated his slipped-disc techniques. They consisted mainly of Spider on his back while she (and he was proud of her bone-slender body when it undulated on him) did all sorts of turns. They usually ended with her mouth clamped on his joystick and the crimp in his back vibrating like a dog's tail as he gave it all to the video camera, coming at last in a flash, one spasm, no more, last thread of the last visible semen in a man who for want of other diversion had been screwing all day. It was awful to watch. He used to urinate on her, there also for us to see on the TV screen. He had grown a wispy light-brown D'Artagnan mustache which he would tweak like a villain while he hosed her down. You may ask why I watched, and I can tell you: I knew the great vaults of heaven were for the angels, but there were other conduits in the sky, and underground railways for the demons, and I used to feel as if Nissen's house (although the owner's name was hers, White, Beth Dietrich White) was one more station on the line. So I stayed to watch, not knowing if I was an acolyte or a spy, until at last his back, thank God, got a little better over the months, and he eased off from all that insane crossed-wires short-circuit fucking. Of course, in compensation, he now wrote long detailed descriptions of how he got it on with Beth, and he would lay this on you and you would read it and discuss the merits. It was the ultimate literary workshop.

I could have endured him, this Spider, this monster, who shared with me the feat of climbing seven eighths of the way up the stone phallus of the highest monument between here and Washington, D.C., if only he had believed in God, or the Devil, or both. If he had been a soul in torment, or wished to murder the Lord, or had kissed the Devil beneath his tail and was now a slave, I could have put up with heresy, fallacy, perjury, antinomianism, Arianism, emanatism, Gnosticism, Manichean-ism, even Monophysitism or Catharism, but not this damn atheist who believed in spirits that came in electronic streams. I think his theological view came to this: there might have been a god once, but now, for whatever reason, It was gone, and had left us a cosmic warehouse where we could rattle around and poke our fingers into the goods, tap into all the systems. Yes, he was in the vanguard of the cerebrates.

On this day, as I came in, their living room was dark, the shades were drawn. Spider and two other men, whose faces at first I could not see, were watching the Patriots try to score from the ten-yard line. It had to be Sunday, a sign of how far I was removed from all about me. I had not even known. On any other Sunday in November I would have made my bets after much consideration and would have been ensconced here from the kickoff since, I confess, that no matter how I disliked Nissen, and did not take to watching TV for hours inasmuch as it leached me out as thoroughly as a dose of salts, still, if you were going to, there was no place for watching television like Nissen's small parlor. The odor of stale socks and old spills of beer blended with the subtle scents of video equipment—scorched wires, plastic boxes. I could feel as if I were in a cave out there on the edge of the future civilization—out with the new cavemen of the cerebrates, anticipating the millennia to come. If Sunday afternoons were spent in the deep if much depressed peace of dissipating time, still the seasons could go by and I would know a dull happiness watching the Patriots, the Celtics, the Bruins and then, in April, the Red Sox. By May, the atmosphere changed. Our winter was over, the summer was in our minds, and Nissen's living room would no longer seem like a cave so much as an unaired den. Now, however, we were at the beginning of hibernation. If this had not been so unusual an autumn for me, I might have enjoyed (in a sort of gloom) bringing a six-pack or quart of bourbon as my contribution to the cave and would have flopped without another thought on one of his two couches or three broken-down stuffed chairs (all of this crammed into a living room not twelve by sixteen!) stretched out my brogans on his rug to make myself one with all the colors in the room—the walls, carpet and furniture having by now faded, darkened, been bleached by spills and turned by stains into the ubiquitous colorless color of them all which was neither ash-gray nor washed-out purple nor dulled-down green nor a wan brown, but the mixture of them all. Who cared about the color? The TV screen was our altar of light, and all of us watched it with an occasional grunt or sip of our beer.

I cannot tell you how soothing this felt to me now. To someone living like myself these days, it was honest relief to sit among Spider's guests, two dudes I could do without on better occasions, but today they were company. One was Pete the Polack, our bookie, who had a last name nobody including himself would pronounce twice in the exact same way (Peter Petrarciewisz may be the spelling) and I disliked him for being an unfair son of a bitch full of greed since he put a vigorish of 20 percent on all losing bets instead of the 10 percent you could get from the Boston books ("Make a phone call to Boston," he would say, knowing his clients could get no credit there) and besides, he shifted the line against you if he had a clue which way you'd bet, a big surly kid with a sour face, an all-purpose ethnic: you would have taken him for Italian, Irish, Polish, Hungarian, German or Ukrainian if that was what you were told. He disliked me as well. I was one of the few who could get credit in Boston.

That Pete the Polack was here today could only mean Nissen had bet a lot on the Patriots. It was disquieting. Nissen might be unsentimental enough to piss on his slave woman, but he'd lick the shoelaces of any athlete godlike enough to play for the Pats. His paraplegic detective might be able to penetrate CIA computers and roll up friend or foe with equal panache, but Nissen was so metaphysical about his allegiance that Pete could make the team a six-point favorite on a day when I only had to give three in Boston. How many times the Spider had been trapped in the middle! I assumed the bet today was so large that Pete was here to collect if he won, and after five minutes knew I was right; the Spider soon began to shout at the set. Before long I was convinced he must have bet at least the value of his motorcycle on the game, and Pete was here to wheel it away if Nissen lost.

It is also worth stating about Pete that he was perfectly capable of letting Spider run up his losses in return for promises—"Carry me another week and I'll take you out to where Madden keeps his product." The stash had to be worth a couple of thousand dollars and Nissen knew it: he would not be above offering it as collateral.

The other man in the room I hardly knew. You would have cast him for a greaser. He had tattoos of eagles and mermaids all over his arms, and straight black hair, a low brow, a dented nose, a mustache and a couple of missing teeth. Everybody called him Stoodie because he used, when an adolescent, to steal nothing but Studebakers all up and down the Cape. That was the legend, and it was untrue—he stole all kinds of cars—but they called him Stoodie because it was a Studebaker he had been busted on. Now he collected on losing bets for Pete, and, as I had heard, was a machinist and metalworker (all learned in the pen at Wal-pole) good enough to change the serial numbers on the engine blocks of cars other people had stolen. However, he, I assumed, would not know of my small part of the Truro woods.

I mention this because like John Foster Dulles, who—whatever his sins—gave us the phrase, I was going through an agonizing reappraisal. I liked to look upon myself as a writer searching for a somewhat larger view of man. It did not please me to reduce everyone I encountered to the ranks of those who knew and those who did not know where Timothy Madden might keep his stash.

Now, however, my mind was nothing but this list. Nissen knew, and by extension, Beth knew. Patty knew. Mr. Black knew. For all I knew, I had taken Jessica and Mr. Pangborn there. Regency seemed to have a clear notion. I could think of others. I could even add my father. He had made unsuccessful attempts over the years to cut out drinking by the substitution of marijuana. Once, over a year ago, on the last visit to Patty and me, I had taken him out to my clearing and tried to get him interested in the crop. I figured if he saw the plants, he might respect them as much as hops. So, yes, add my father to the list.

But that was like urinating on Beth. Abruptly, I recognized the mon-strousness of my new mental preoccupation. Everybody came out as items on a computer list. Was I becoming a cerebrate? So much had this activity taken over my head that I felt like a computer trembling on its foundations. I kept kicking my father's name on and off the list. Give me, in preference, a storm at sea.

I watched the football game for as long as I could. At last, on a time-out in the beginning of the second quarter, Nissen went to the refriger-ator for beers. I followed.

There was only one way to treat him and that was with no ceremony. Since he could show his wife and himself in a confetti of electronic dots, or ask you in the middle of biting a sandwich if you were constipated, I had no compunctions about injuring him with a quick question. There-fore I said, "Spider, remember the séance?"

"You forget it, man," he said. "I can't."

"It was weird."

"It was pure horrendous." He sloshed his beer around a missing molar in his mouth, gulped the fluid and added, "You and your wife can go for that shit. I won't. It's too disruptive."

"What did you see?"

"Same thing your wife saw."

"Well, I'm asking you."

"Hey, don't lay it on me. Everything's all right, right?"

"Couldn't be better."

"Sure," he said.

"So why don't you tell me?"

"I don't want to get into that place again."

"Listen," I said, "you got to keep yourself pure today. You have a big bet."

"So?"

"I'm asking a favor. Keep yourself pure with your buddies. Your team will cover the bet."

"Don't give me that mystical sauce. It went out with LSD. I don't have to fucking keep myself pure by telling you what you want to hear. That's desperate betting, man, that's degenerate. I pick the Patriots on their merits."

"You need my help today," I said, looking into his eyes as if I wouldn't relent.

"You're crazy," he said. "How many hundred thousand people betting on this game, two million probably, and I got to get myself pure with you—that puts the result where I want it? Madden, every one of you potheads is tipped. Cut yourself a little coke." He slammed the refrigerator door. He was ready to go back to the game.

"You're wrong," I said. "You and me can help them cover if I am able to put my mind right alongside of yours."

"I get no input whatsoever from you."

"Well," I said, "I hate to bring it up. But you and me have this one thing in common that two million other bettors don't have."

"All right."

"We've been one special place together."

As I said this, the most peculiar phenomenon occurred. I had never told it to anyone, not even quite to myself, but in that hour I was trapped beneath the overhang, the most terrible odor oozed out to me from—I do not know if it was the rocks or my own sweat—but a dreadful odor of corruption came up nonetheless, the way perhaps a battlefield of many dead would smell, or was it—and this was my fear— the nearness of the Devil waiting to receive me? It was, in all events, so terrible a smell that once I was down on the ground it remained the worst fear in days to come until I told myself, and for all I knew, this is true also, that I was sniffing no more than some old guano of the gulls magnified by my own terror into the stench of a satanic beast. But now, even as I said what should have remained unsaid, "We've been one special place together," so did a whiff of that incredible odor come off of Nissen, and I think we both knew that the experience had been equal for both of us.

"What did you see," I asked again, "at the séance?"

I could feel how he was on the edge of telling me, and had the good sense not to push further. I could feel the truth coming forth even as his tongue picked at his lips.

During the séance we had been six of us about a round oak table, our hands flattened out on the surface, our right thumb touching our left thumb, and the little finger of each hand in contact with the little finger of each person to left or right. We were trying to get the table to tap. Let me not even speak now of our purpose, but in that darkened room by the back shore (for we were all at a rich acquaintance's home in Truro and the ocean waves were tolling on the back shore not two hundred yards away) it seemed to me that with each question asked, the table was actually coming closer to some small quiver when, right then, our communal senses were shattered by Nissen's fearful scream. Having brought this much back for myself, I must have returned the memory to him as well, for now he said, "I saw her dead. I saw your wife dead and with her head cut off. The next fucking moment, she saw it too. We were looking at it together."

In this instant the smell that came off him was overpowering, and I could feel a reverberation of my fear beneath the overhang. So I knew that no matter how I might like to banish the impulse, I had no choice: I must go back to the tree on the sandy ridge and discover whose head was in the burrow below.

Yet in this moment a look of incredible spite came into Nissen's face and he reached over and squeezed my right arm beneath the shoulder with fingers that dug in like five spikes.

As I winced he laughed. "Yeah," he said, "you got a tattoo. Harpo told the truth."

"How does Harpo know?"

"How does he know? Man, you are so fucking spaced out that you need your wife. She better come back." He snorted as if some grains of coke were leaking out of his nose. "Hey," he said, "yeah," he said, "I'm pure. Now, you get yourself pure."

"How does Harpo know?" I repeated. Harpo was a friend of Nissen's and raced motorcycles with him.

"Well, mate," said Spider, "he gave you the fucking tattoo."

Sven "Harpo" Veriakis. He was a short blond Greek-Norwegian on his father's side, Portuguese by his mother, and built like a fireplug. He had been the third shortest man ever to play in the NFL (even if he only lasted for a season). Now, Harpo had moved to Wellfleet, and one didn't see him often, but he had conducted our séance, that I recalled. "What did he say?" I asked.

"Who knows," said Nissen. "I never can figure out what he's saying. He's a space cadet like you."

Cries came out of the living room then, and imprecations. The Patriots had just scored again. Spider whooped and led me back.

In the intermission at half time, Stoodie began to talk. I had never heard him say as much before.

"I like to lie awake at night and listen to the sounds in the street," he said to Beth. "There's a lot of significance then. You must provide yourself with the proper framing of mind, and that makes it all pregnant with space. Pregnant with grace," he amended, and nodded, and nipped on his beer. I was remembering something I had heard about Stoodie. He used to tie his wife by her ankles to hooks he had put in a ceiling beam. Then he would caress her. In his fashion.

"I admire the natural situation of the Cape," he now said to Beth. "I will take an Indian summer over all. Strolling among our dunes, I have had the privilege of seeing another someone, a male or female person on another dune as much as half a mile away, but the glow of the sun is on them. They are feeling just as full of love for all this golden goodness as we are in our own feelings. That's God's blessing right there. No escaping it. Beauty inexorable." He took a breath. "I mean beauty exalted."

It was here I made the decision to add Stoodie to my list.

Four

I did not learn that afternoon who won the game, for I left Nissen's house at half-time (the Patriots were ahead) and drove the fifteen miles to Wellfleet to see Harpo, who lived in a loft over a dry-goods store on one of the off-roads. I say "off-road," but then, no street in Wellfleet ever seemed to bear relation to any other, as if on founding day some two hundred and more years ago five sailors, each swigging his own keg of rum, had meandered out from the bay shore along the streams and around the bogs, and people followed to mark each road by the vagaries of each sailor's promenade. As a result, no one I knew in Provincetown could ever find anyone in Wellfleet, and indeed we did not often try. Wellfleet was by now a proper town, and none of us ever saw a Yankee there who did not have a nose long enough to serve as a rifle barrel siting you in his mean nostrils' cross hairs. Some of us, therefore, used to ask Harpo how he could ever have left Provincetown for Wellfleet and he replied, "I didn't like the warp. The warp was getting to me. I had to move."

So a few began to call him Warpo. Since he had, however, a tangle of curly blond hair over a face as rubbery as the great comedian (albeit considerably more scarred: after pro football, he played semipro without a helmet) Harpo it remained.

In any event, he was named for the harpoon, not Harpo Marx. Harpo Veriakis was famous for saying, "That's a beautiful girl over there. I wish I was man enough to harpoon her." So, some called him Poon for poon tang, some still called him Harpoon. I mention this as a way of indicating how hard it was to locate his place. On the Cape in winter, nothing ever came right to the point.

Well, I found his turning, and he was in, which made two surprises, but I still did not believe he had pricked the tattoo into me since I did not even know he practiced such an art, and besides, I could not understand how I would ever have found his place in the dark while drunk, but once I climbed the outside stairs to his loft, my doubts were gone. He looked up from feeding his cats (he lived with five such pets in lieu of one beautiful girl) and the first thing he said was "Is your arm infected?"

"It's itching."

He didn't say another word to me while spooning out the rest of the can, although he did speak to a couple of the creatures who were rubbing around his ankles like connubial little fur pieces, but as soon as he was done with that, he washed his hands, removed my bandage, got out a plastic bottle of some disinfectant and laved it over my upper bicep. "It don't look infected too much," he said, "and that's good. I was worried. I don't like to use the needles when the atmosphere is screwing me up."

"Was something wrong?" I asked.

"You were shit-face."

"All right. I drink and get shit-face. What's new about that?"

"Mac, you wanted to pick a fight with me."

"I must have been crazy." (He was strong enough to lift a car by its rear end.) "I didn't really try to pick a fight with you?" I asked.

"Well, you were showing off."

"Did I have a woman with me?"

"I don't know. She might have been downstairs in the car. You kept yelling out the window."

"What did I say?"

"You kept yelling out the window, 'You're going to lose your bet.' "

"Did you hear anyone answer?"

One of the virtues of the people I live among is that none of us is ever surprised by a friend's inability to remember a vivid hour.

"There was a lot of wind," said Harpo. "If it was a woman, she was laughing like a banshee."

"But you think there was a woman in my car?"

"I don't know," he said sepulchrally. "Sometimes the woods get to laughing at me. I hear lots of sounds." He put away the bottle of disinfectant and shook his head. "Mac, I begged you not to get a tattoo. Everything was in fearsome shape. Before you walked in, I almost went on the roof. If there had been lightning, I would have had to."

Some would argue that Harpo was psychic and some that he was punchy from playing without a helmet, and I always expected that he was both, and each reinforced the other. For that matter, he had been in Vietnam, and his best buddy, so went the story, had blown up on a land mine twenty yards from Harpo. "It deranged me" was what he told a few. Now he lived in the heavens, and the words of angels and demons were major events to him. Several times a year, when the clans that threatened existence massed among the cloud banks like medieval armies, and lightning came with great rain, Harpo would climb up on the ridgepole of his roof and dare the forces above. "If they know I'm standing there, they offer respect. They don't know whether I can exorcise them. But it makes me cry like a baby. It's awesome, Mac."

"I thought you only went up on the roof when it's raining."

"Never follow a law to its absolute," he said hoarsely.

I could rarely be certain what he was talking about. He had a deep and hollow voice with such groundswells of echo (as if his head were still ringing from collisions you could never bear) that he would ask for a cigarette and the request itself would sound gnomic. He could also make the most extraordinary confessions. He was like those athletes who talk about themselves in the third person. (" 'Hugo Blacktower is worth one million dollars playing center in the NBA,' says Hugo Blacktower.") So Harpo could make the first person nearly equal to the third person. "Your wife is most attractive," he said at one of our summer parties, "but she makes me afraid. I could never get it up with her. I respect you for being able to." Extraordinary stuff came out of him like a roll of the dice. Now he said, "The day of the hurricane, I stood on the ridgepole for three hours. That was why the hurricane didn't come."

"You held it off?"

"I know it's going to fuck me up. I had to take a vow."

"But you held off the hurricane?"

"To a degree."

Anyone else would have thought I was mocking him by my next

question. He knew I was not. "Are the Patriots," I asked, "going to win today?"

"Yes."

"Is this your professional opinion?"

He shook his head. "It is my impression. I heard it on the wind."

"How often is the wind mistaken?"

"In ordinary matters, one time in seven."

"And extraordinary matters?"

"One time in a thousand. It fixes on the problem then." He grasped my wrist. "Why," Harpo asked, as if we had not already spoken of this, "did you cut down your marijuana just before the storm?"

"Who told you?"

"Patty Lareine."

"What did you say to her?" I asked. He was like a child. If he was ready to tell, he would tell all.

"I said she should warn you," he replied in his gravest voice. "It would have been better to lose your crop than cut it down suddenly."

"What did she say?"

"She said you wouldn't listen. I believed her. That is why I didn't take offense when you came here two nights ago shit-face. I figured you'd been smoking your own stuff. Your stuff has *evil* in it." He said this word as if evil were a high-tension wire fallen to the ground and now writhing in sparks.

"Did I come here," I asked, "for a tattoo?"

"No." He shook his head vehemently. "People don't know I am able to do that. I only work for people I honor." He stared at me somberly. "I honor you," Harpo now said, "because you are man enough to fuck your wife. Beautiful women make me timid."

"You are saying," I replied, "that I didn't come here for a tattoo?"

"No," he repeated. "I would have shown you the door."

"Then what did I want?"

"You asked for a séance. You said you wanted to find out why your wife was hysterical during the last séance."

"And you wouldn't help me?"

"Oh, no," he said. "There could not have been a worse night."

"So you said no?"

"I said no. Then you said I was a phony. Terrible things. Then you saw my kit. My needles were on the table. You said you wanted a tattoo. 'I'm not leaving empty-handed,' you said."

"And you agreed?"

"Not at first. I told you that a tattoo must be respected. But you kept going to the window and shouting, 'Just a minute!' I thought you were talking to *them*, except it could have been a person. Then you started to cry."

"Oh, shit," I said.

"You told me that if you couldn't have the séance, I had to give you the tattoo. 'I owe it to her,' you said. 'I wronged her. I must carry her name.' " He nodded. "I understood that. You were asking someone for forgiveness. So I said I would do it. Right away you ran to the window and yelled out, 'You're going to lose your bet!' That provoked me. I doubted your sincerity. But you didn't seem to know I was angry. You said to me, 'Put on the name I gave you at the Truro séance.' 'What name is that?' I asked. Tim, you remembered."

"Didn't I say at the séance that I wanted to get in touch with Mary Hardwood—my mother's cousin?"

"That's what you said for the others, but to me you whispered, 'The real name is Laurel. Tell them it's Mary Hardwood, but think of Laurel.' "

"That's what I told you?"

"You also said, 'Laurel is dead. I want to reach her, and she is dead.' "

"I couldn't have said that," I told him now, "because I was hoping to find out where she is."

"If you thought she was alive, then you were trying to take advantage of the séance."

"I guess I was."

"That may be the reason for the chaos." He sighed at the weight of all human perversity. "Two nights ago just as I was starting your tattoo, you said, 'I can't fuck you over—the girl's real name is not Laurel. It's Madeleine.' That fouled me up very much. I'm trying to be in touch with the forces around me when I put in the first needle. That is basic protection for all. You injured my concentration. Then, next minute, you said, 'I changed my mind. Make it Laurel, after all.' You messed up your own tattoo. Two times you messed it up."

I was silent as if to respect his words. When I felt that enough time had gone by, I asked, "What else did I say?"

"Nothing. You fell asleep. When I was done with the tattoo you woke up. You went downstairs, got into your car and drove off."

"Did you come with me?"

"No."

"Did you look out the window?"

"I did not. But I believe people were with you. Because once you were outside, you got very loud. I think I heard a man and a woman trying to quiet you. Then you all drove off."

"All three of us in my Porsche?"

Harpo knew the sound of motors. "There was only your car."

"How did I get two people into one bucket seat?"

He shrugged.

I was about to leave when he said, "The girl you call Laurel may still be alive."

"Are you certain?"

"It feels like she is on the Cape. She is damaged, but she's not dead."

"Well, if you get it from the wind, that's six to one you're right."

Outside it was dark, and the highway back to Provincetown was being scourged by the last dead leaves to cross the hardtop from one part of the forest to the other. The wind was in a fury, as if indeed my last poor jest to Harpo had displeased it, and gusts that could have knocked over a sailboat slammed against the side of the car.

Once, a couple of years ago, I had been to another séance. A friend of Harpo's had been killed in an auto crash on this same highway, and Harpo had invited me together with two men and two women I did not know, and we sat in a dimly lit circle around a small end table with thin legs. Our palms were on the table, our extended fingers touched. Then Harpo gave the table its instructions. He spoke to the table as if there were no question that his voice would be heard, and he told it to tilt up on one side and then come down, thereby tapping the floor once for yes. If the table wished to say no, it would have to rise and fall twice. Two taps. "Do you understand me?" Harpo asked.

The table went up on two legs with the same obedience a trained dog will give to the command to beg. Then it tapped the floor. We proceeded from there. Harpo expounded a simple code. One tap would be for the letter A, two for B, on up to twenty-six taps for Z.

Since he had to be certain he was talking to the friend who had been killed the week before the séance, he began by inquiring, "Are you there,

Fred?" and the table, after a pause, tapped once. To verify this, Harpo asked, "What is the first letter of your name?" The table gave six slow taps to indicate the letter F.

We went on. That event also took place on a November night. We sat about in Harpo's small Wellfleet loft, not leaving the table from nine in the evening until two in the morning, and we were, all but for Harpo, strangers to each other. There was time to observe every likelihood of a trick. Yet, I could see none. Our knees were visible, and our hands rested lightly on the surface, too lightly for anyone to tip the table by himself. We sat so closely that one could not fail to detect physical exertion in the others. No, the table tipped in response to our questions as naturally as water may be poured from one glass to another. It did not seem spooky. Rather, it was tedious. It took a long time to spell each word.

"How does it feel," Harpo asked, "where you are?"

Seven taps came back. We had a G. A pause, and a new series of slow taps began, the table tilting two of its legs a clear foot off the floor, but slowly, rising slowly like one half of a drawbridge, and then, as leisurely, descending for the tap. The next sequence took eighteen taps and several minutes. We now had an R. That made GR . . .

"Great?" asked Harpo.

The table tapped twice: "No!"

"I'm sorry," said Harpo. "Continue."

Now we received fifteen taps. We had a G, an R and an O.

It was only when we arrived at G-R-O-O-V that Harpo said "Groovy?" and the table replied with a single tap.

"Fred, is it really groovy?" asked Harpo.

Again the table went up, again it came down. It was not unlike conversing with a computer.

So we continued for five hours and heard a bit of small talk about Fred's new state on the other side. No information came to us that would shake the foundations of eschatology or of karma. It was only past two in the morning, driving home through a wind like this, that I realized how a common end table, in defiance of many laws of physics, had been able to rise and fall hundreds of times in order to send a word or two across a divide whose gulf I could no longer measure. It was then, alone on the highway, that the hair stiffened on the back of my neck, and I knew I had been present at an eerie and incomprehensible evening. Whatever had made it possible might still be in the air around me. I was alone with *it* on a windswept highway not far from the depths of the sea—no, I had never felt so alone in my life. The awe I had hardly experienced while it was happening was now all about me on the road.

Next day, however, I was as apathetic as if my liver had been pounded against a cement wall, indeed, was left in such depression that I had not gone again to a séance until the night in Truro when we embarked on our fiasco. I was ready to believe that one could communicate with the dead. It was just that I could not afford the funds it required.

Arriving back at my house, I started a fire, poured a drink, and was just beginning to search for any recollections I could recover of a trip out to Wellfleet two nights ago, carrying two other people in one small Porsche, when there was a thump on the door knocker, or so I would swear, and the door blew open.

I do not know what entered, or whether it left when I bolted the door, but I heard that clapper as a summons. I had a sniff again of the intolerable odor of corruption I had breathed beneath the overhang, and could have cried out at the inexorable logic of the demand on me. For with all the weight of a decree I could not refuse came the bidding to go back to that wood in Truro.

I held out for as long as I could. I finished my drink and made another, and knew that whether it took an hour or three days, whether I finally went forward sober or became so drunk I could live in flames, I must indeed go out and search the burrow. There could be no release until I did. That force which went into the tapping of the table had now seized me—by my entrails and my heart. I had no choice. Nothing could prove worse than to remain here and live through the hours of the night ahead.

I knew. Once before I had been held in the grip of an imperative larger than myself, and that was the week twenty years ago when I walked each day to the Provincetown Monument with cold oil in my lungs and sick worms in my belly, stared up at the climb and saw, with a gloom equal to losing all reason itself, that the ascent could be attempted. As high as I could see, handhold by handhold, there were indentations in the mortar and small ledgelike irregularities in the granite blocks. It could be done, and I could do it, and I stared so hard at the base that—can you believe me?—I never contemplated the overhang. All I knew was that I must climb it. If I did not make the attempt, something worse than panic would befall me. Maybe I learned nothing else from those old seizures of terror in the middle of the night when I used to sit bolt upright in bed, but, at least, I gained (could I term it that?) some small measure of compassion for all who are afflicted by the compulsion to go out and do what is absolutely not to be done—whether it is the seduction of little boys or the rape of adolescent girls—at least I knew the nightmare that blazes beneath the stupefaction of those who never dare to come near to themselves, or disaster will ensue. So in all of that week when I wrestled with this strange will so external to myself, trying to convince this foreign presence that I did not have to climb the Monument, I also learned about the varieties of human insulation. For to keep from encountering that fiend who dwells in the sweet Kundalini of our spine, so do we take on our booze, our pot, our coke, our nicotine, our tranks and sleeping pills, our habits and our churches, our prejudices and our bigotries, our ideology, our stupidity itself—that most vital of the insulations!—and I encountered nearly all of them in the week before I tried to climb the Monument and conquer the unmanageable in myself. Then, with a brain inflamed by speed, tilted one way by pot and the other by drink, squealing within like an unborn child in terror of suffocation before it finds the light, feeling as murderous as a Samurai, I tackled that wall and found, no matter how absurd the outcome, that I was better afterward, if by no more than the reduction of my terror in sleep.

So it had been worth it. I knew that must be true now. I had to go back and look upon the face of the blonde who was dead. Indeed, I must do it not knowing whether her end came from my hands or belonged to others. Will you ever comprehend me if I say that such knowledge, while crucial to my self-preservation—was I in danger of the law, or of all that was outside the law?—was still not what called me forth so much as the bare impulse to go: that came from the deepest sign I could recognize—the importance of the journey must be estimated by my dread of doing it.

I will spare you those hours while I vacillated in my will. I can only say that it was near to midnight before I had conquered my terror sufficiently to begin the voyage in my mind, and so was ready, in my imagination at least, to leave the house, enter the car and set out over the reaches of a highway whose wind-whipped leaves were at this hour like an onslaught of spirits. Yet, with each detail of this journey foreseen, composing the trip in my thoughts before it was ever undertaken, I now found at the center of my terror the calm of composition itself. So I was finally armed to set out, and was at the door and ready to step into the real air of the night when the knock resounded again, just as powerfully as a hammer on my tomb.

Some interruptions are too profound to disturb your composure. One's limbs do not have to shake as one encounters the hangman. I pulled the bolt and drew open the door.

Regency stepped in. For the first moment, seeing the strain upon his face and the bright light of anger in his eyes, I had the idea he was there to arrest me. He stood in the foyer and stared at the furniture in the living room and shook his head from side to side, but for so long that I finally comprehended he was revolving his neck against the grind of his own tension.

"I'm not here for a drink, buddy," he said at last.

"Well, you can have one."

"Later. We talk first." He poked the light of his angry eyes into mine, and then in surprise—for I do not think he had ever seen me showing such resolve—he looked away. He could not know for what I had just prepared.

"Are you," I asked, "working on Sunday?"

"You haven't been down to the West End today, have you?"

I shook my head.

"You don't know what's going on?"

"No."

"Every cop in town was at The Widow's Walk. Every cop in town." He looked past me. "Do you mind if I sit down?"

I did. I didn't. I made some gesture to indicate as much.

He sat down.

"Look, Madden," he said, "I know you lead a very busy life, but maybe you can recollect receiving a phone call this morning from Merwyn Finney."

"The proprietor of The Widow's Walk?"

"You eat there all the time but you don't know his name?"

"Hey," I said, "don't break my chops."

"All right," he said. "Why don't you sit down, too?"

"Because I'm ready to go out."

"Finney called about a car, correct?"

"Is it still there?"

"You told Merwyn Finney," Alvin Luther now said, "that you couldn't remember the name of the woman who was with Pangborn."

"I still can't. Is it important?"

"Probably not. Unless she's his wife."

"I don't think she was."

"Well, good. You're a shrewd judge of people."

"I'm not smart enough to guess what's going on now."

"Oh, I could tell you," he said, "but I don't want to slant your opinion." He looked into my eyes again. "What's your make on Pangborn?"

"Corporate lawyer. Sharp. On tour with a blonde lady."

"Anything wrong with him?"

"Just not likable."

"Why?"

"Cause I wanted to get somewhere with Jessica and he was in the way." I stopped. There was much to be said for Regency as a cop. Pressure came off him and it was constant. Soon, you made a mistake. "Oh," I said, "that's her name. It just came to me. Jessica."

He wrote it down. "Her last name?"

"Still blank. She may never have told me."

"What was she like?"

"Society lady. Southern California society, I'd say. No real class. Just money."

"But you liked her?"

"I had the feeling she'd carry on in the closet like a porny star." I said this to shock him. It succeeded more than I had expected.

"I don't approve of pornies," he said. "I don't go to them. I wouldn't mind slaughtering five or ten of those porny stars, though."

"That's what I like about law enforcement," I answered. "Put a killer in uniform and he can't kill anymore."

He cocked his head. "Cheap hippie philosophy," he said.

"You could never stand up to a discussion," I told him. "Your brain is full of minefields."

"Maybe so," he said slyly, and winked. "Let's move back to Pangborn. Would you say he was unstable?"

"Not particularly. I'm tempted to say not at all."

"Don't."

"Don't?"

"Did he impress you in any way as a swish?"

"He might wash his hands after making love, but, no, I would not call him a swish."

"Was he in love with Jessica?"

"I'd say he liked her for what she could offer, and was getting a little fatigued. She may have been too much of a woman for him."

"You don't think he was in love with her uncontrollably?"

I was about to say, "Not my impression," when I decided to ask, "What do you mean by 'uncontrollably'?"

"I'd say it's loving somebody to the point where you're not in command of your actions."

Somewhere in my mind a mean calculation came forth. I said, "Alvin, what are you leading to? Did Pangborn kill her?"

"I don't know," said Regency. "Nobody has seen her."

"Well, where is he?"

"Merwyn Finney called this afternoon and asked if the car could be removed from his lot. But it was legally parked in the first place. So I told him we'd have to put a warning on the windshield. This afternoon I was making a turn around town and thought I'd take a look. It didn't add up right to me. Sometimes you see an empty buggy that's all wrong. So I tried the trunk. It was unlocked. Pangborn was inside."

"Murdered?"

"Interesting you say that," said Regency. "No, my friend, he was a suicide."

"How?"

"He put himself in the trunk and closed it. Then he laid himself under a blanket, stuck a pistol in his mouth, and pulled the trigger."

"Let's have a drink," I said.

"Yeah."

His eyes were fixed with fury. "Very strange business," he said.

I could not help myself. A. L. Regency had his powers. "Are you sure it's suicide?" I asked, although I could see no advantage to myself in the question.

Worse. Our eyes met clearly with that lack of concealment which is palpable: both people are remembering the same sight. I was seeing blood on the passenger seat of my car.

He kept the silence before he said, "There's no doubt it's suicide. The powder marks are all over his mouth and palate. Unless someone drugged him first"—Regency took out his notebook and set down a few words—"only I don't see how you can ram a gun into someone's mouth, shoot him, and then rearrange his body without betraying yourself on the blood spill. The dispersal of blood on the floor and side of the trunk is wholly consistent with suicide." He nodded. "But I don't," he said, "have a high opinion of your acumen. You read Pangborn all wrong."

"I certainly didn't see him as a suicide."

"Forget that. He's a degenerate faggot. Madden, you don't even have a clue who's really in the closet."

Now he looked about the living room as if to count the doors and classify the furniture. Nor was it comfortable to see the place through his eyes. Most of the furniture had been chosen by Patty and her taste was flouncy and full of Tampa Beach money—that is, white furniture and splashy hues in the cushions and the draperies and the throw rugs, loads of flowers on the fabrics, many barstools in puffy leatherette—pink, lemon-lime, orange and ivory for her boudoir and her drawing room—quite a candystripe for Provincetown in winter. Will it give some idea of my state if I admit that most days my mood did not rise to the differences between the hues in Nissen's house and mine?

Regency studied our furniture. "Degenerate faggot" was still smoking on his lips.

I could not leave it there. "What makes you so certain Pangborn was homosexual?"

"I wouldn't term it that. I'd call him *gay*." How the word offended him. "They ought to spell it 'Kaposi's syndrome.' " He drew a letter from his pocket. "Call themselves *gay* and go around infecting one another *systematically*. They're laying in a plague."

"Well, all right," I said. "Count your plagues. I'll count mine." He was that opinionated it would have given me combative pleasure to argue—nuclear pollution for your side, herpes for mine—but not now.

"Look what's in this envelope," he said. "Was Pangborn gay or was he gay? Just read it!"

"Are you certain he wrote it?"

"I checked the handwriting against his address book. He wrote the letter, all right. About a month ago. It's dated. But he never sent it. I guess he made the mistake of rereading it. That's enough to put the barrel right in your throat and blow it out."

"Who was he writing to?"

"Oh, you know faggots. They're so intimate with each other, they don't bother with names. Just chat away soul to soul. Maybe at the end they'll deign to use your name once. That's so the flower who receives the epistle will know the dirt is in the right pot." He went off on his whinny.

I read the letter. It was in strong purple-blue ink, a firm round hand:

I've just dipped into your volume of verse. I know so little about the fullest appreciation of poetry and classical music, but I know what I like. I like symphonies to rise up from the private parts. I like Sibelius and Schubert and Saint-Saëns and all the esses, yes, yes, yes. I know I like your poems because I'm tempted to write you back and make you twitch, bitch. I know you hate my vulgar side, but let us never forget, Lonnie's a guttersnipe and had to stretch a little to marry his chain-store heiress. Who's bringing the chains?

I liked your poem "Spent" because it made me feel for you. There you were, tight as a tick, nervous about yourself, as always, locked up so terribly, well, you were serving time, after all, and I was out in Nam patrolling the China seas. Do you know the sunsets there? You speak so beautifully of the rainbow that comes before your eyes after you are "Spent" but I lived those rainbows. How vividly your lines bring to mind the lush sex-ridden months I spent in Saigon, yes, sweetheart, *spent!* You write about those heavies surrounding you and tell this reader: "I feel they have fires inside, well-stoked fires glowing through their hide, heating the summer air." Well, kiddo, that's not true only for your heavy criminal types. I have had the same thoughts about many a sailor I knew. Many a fire I've warmed my hands and face by. You almost cracked up denying yourself what you want, but then, you're a gentleman. Of sorts. But I sought and I *found*. I seduced indiscriminately, playing the male slut. I fed like a clown's pig from the oversize bottle with the long rubber nipple. No crack-ups for Lonnie, thank you. He's wise enough to get the most out of his queer blood.

How much you missed in those China seas. I remember black-eyed Carmine coming to the quonset hut door near Danang and calling softly, 'Lonnie, baby, come on out!' I remember the tall thin blond lad from Beaumont, Texas, who brought me his letters to his wife. She was leaving him and I had to read the letter, I was his *censor*, and how he lingered at the edge of Officer's Country as it grew dark, and I love the way he kept talking about the chicken ranch until I just reached over and fondled him and he spread out and relaxed, and, lovey, he wasn't about to ask for anything more for his chicken ranch until the next night when he'd prowl about Officer's Country until it was dark again and I who was hungry could satisfy his hunger. And I remember the lovely lad from Ypsilanti named Thorne and the taste of love-impregnated sherry within his lips, those lovely eyes, the quietness of him and the tender, halting poor sixth-grade grammar of the sweet letter he wrote me the day I was leaving the ship, and he came up on the bridge to give it to me.

Or the signalman from Marion, Illinois, who sent me his first amorous advance in semaphore, not knowing I could keep up with the great speed at which he sent it: "Hey, honey, how about you and me in my boat tonight?" And my answer, "What time, honey?" I can still see the look of surprise on his face. And the glorious scent of him—sweat and Aqua Velva.

How much your poem brings back. Those were the glory days. No legal briefs. No scions of society—don't take it personally—to suck up to. Just Admirals and grunts. What a pity you've never known a Marine. Or a Green Beret. They're green, sweetie, but don't fire until you see the pink of their privates! I haven't had the leisure to think of these things in ages, but now I will. Your poems bring it back. I think of the Chief Hospital Corpsman I met in the Blue Elephant on Saigon Boulevard and later I remember the room I took him to in some half-gutted hotel and the glorious gushing forth of him until he caught me to drink a little himself because he had to slake the great thirst his pouring out had given him. And he looked for my name in my hat so he could see me again though I didn't want that and told him so. Burying my nose in his sack and the frenzied smell of it knocking all sense out of my head all over again.

Yes, they had fires in them that warmed the sensuous air. Legions of great, begging, dripping pricks, angry red as the wattles of a turkey gobbler, lovely, lovely glorious days, while you languished in Reading Gaol, poor Wardley, fighting a nervous collapse because you wouldn't do what your heart cried out for you to do.

Maybe I better read no more of your fine poems. You see how mean they make me. Never reject a friend as dear as me, or watch out, you'll lose me forever. But then, you have!!! This time it's not a boy from the Air Force just in for the weekend, nor am I being oh so discreet with a gay churchman who's awfully hot to be indiscreet, no, I have the surprise of all time, Wardley. I'm with a blonde creature. Do you think me awfully drunk? I am.

Never fear. This woman looks as feminine as Lana Turner, but maybe she ain't, not altogether. Maybe she's had a sex change. Do you believe it? One of our mutual friends saw her with me, and had the crust to say she was so gorgeous she had to be a lie. Has *she* once been a *he*, they asked. Well, bad news for all of you, I said, she hasn't. It's an honest-to-god real woman, fuck-face! That's what I said to our mutual friend. In fact, it's the *first* woman I've had since I got to marry my heiress with her dime-store chains. So I know chains. I've been in them for years. Let me tell you, Wardley, it's heaven to be out of them. It's as carnal with this new woman as it used to be on Saigon Boulevard, pure carnal rut-copulating-fucking-sucking heaven for a faggot—should I say ex-faggot?—like me. What intoxication to cross the great divide. Wardley, I'm a man to this woman. She says there has never been a better. Baby, it has kicked off personal energies you wouldn't believe. High is high, but I am maniacally high. If someone tried to take my blonde lady away, I would kill.

See what I mean? High! But why get you upset? You've been down this road, haven't you, Wardley? Lived with your blonde beauty too. Well, no hard feelings. Ex-roommates of the heart we may be, but let us remain dear old friends. This is God's gift to women, your own Lonnie.

P.S. Have you ever seen the commercial for the electric razor named ——. I leave the name blank because I daren't tell you which one. I represent them, after all. But you know which one. Look for it on TV. There's a 21-year-old boy—Mr. Body!—shaving himself and looking as pleased as concupiscence-in-cream all the while he's doing it. Know the secret? He told me. He thinks of this electric razor as looking just like a nice fat cock. He thinks of his boyfriend rubbing that fat pretty penis all over his face. The ad men are slain by how wonderful this commercial turns out. Oh, well, I'm high on hetero, and have to say goodbye to all that.

P.P.S. I know the 21-year-old well. Believe it or not, he's the son of my blonde lady. In fact, I'm the boyfriend he's thinking of. Don't you think he's a little jealous now of Mom and me?

P.P.P.S. All this is top-secret ultra-confidential.

I handed the letter back. I think we both made an effort not to look into each other's eyes, but they met nonetheless. Truth, they caromed off each other like magnets bearing the same pole. Homosexuality was sitting between Regency and me as palpably as the sweat you breathe when violence is next to two people.

" 'Vengeance is mine, saith the Lord,' " said Regency. He put the letter back in his breast pocket and breathed heavily. "I'd like to kill those faggots," he said. "Every last one of them."

"Have another drink."

"There is corruption in this letter," he said, patting his breast, "that leaves a taste no drink is going to wash."

"I'm not the one to give the speech," I said, "but have you ever asked yourself whether you should be Chief of Police?"

"Why say that?" he asked. At once, all of him was on guard.

"You ought to know. You've been here. In summer, this town has a huge homosexual contingent. As long as the Portuguese desire their money, you will have to accept their habits."

"It may interest you to know I'm not the Acting Police Chief anymore."

"As of when?"

"As of this afternoon. When I read that letter. Look, I'm just a country boy. Know what I know of Saigon Boulevard? Two whores a night for ten nights, that's all."

"Come on."

"I saw a lot of fine men get killed. I don't know any Green Berets with pink privates. It's good Pangborn is dead. I'd have done it myself."

You could believe him. The air was this side of the gap from lightning.

"Did you resign formally?" I asked.

He put out his hands as if to hold off all questions. "I don't want to get into it. I was never supposed to become Chief of Police. The Portugee under me is actually running the job."

"What are you saying? Your title is a cover?"

He took out his handkerchief and blew his nose. As he did so, he wagged his head up and down. That was his way of telling me yes. What a hick. He had to be from the Drug Enforcement Administration.

"Do you believe in God?" he asked.

"Yes."

"Good. I knew we could have a conversation. Let's have one soon. Get drunk and talk."

"All right."

"I want to serve God," he said. "What people don't comprehend is that if you want to serve, you have to grow balls big enough to take on His attributes. That includes the heavy responsibility of exercising vengeance."

"We'll talk," I said.

"Good." He stood up to leave. "Do you have a clue who this guy Wardley could be?"

"I assume it's an old lover. Some rich, uptight country squire."

"I like your acumen. Ha, ha. Ha, ha. Say I heard that name somewhere. It's too unusual to forget. Somebody said the name Wardley just in passing. Could it have been your wife?"

"Ask her."

"When I see her, I will ask her." He took out his notebook and wrote down an item. "Where," he said, "do you think this Jessica lady is?"

"Maybe she went back to California."

"We're checking that now."

He put his arm around my shoulder as if to console me for I knew not what, and we walked together through the living room to the door.

Given my height, I never have to think of myself as a small man, but he was certainly larger.

Now at the door he turned and said, "I have a regards for you. It's from my wife."

"Do I know your wife's name?"

"It's Madeleine."

"Oh," I said. "Madeleine Falco?"

"The same."

What is the first maxim of the streets? If you want to die with a slug in your back, fool around with a cop's wife. What did Regency know of her past?

"Yes," I said, "once in a while she used to take a drink in a place where I did some bartending. Many years ago. But I do remember her. What a lovely girl she was, what a fine lady."

"Thank you," he said. "We have two lovely children."

"That's a surprise," I said. "I didn't know . . . you have children." It was a near-miss. I had been about to say, "I didn't know Madeleine could have children."

"Oh, yes," he said, fishing out his wallet, "here's a picture of us."

I looked at Regency and at Madeleine—it was certainly my Madeleine ten years older than the last time I saw her—and with two tow-headed boys who looked a little like him and not at all like her.

"Very nice," I said. "Tell Madeleine hello."

"Sayonara," said Regency, and took off.

Now I could not begin to go to the Truro woods. I could not bring myself up to such concentration all over again. At this hour, I could not. My mind was yawing like a wind in the hills. I did not know whether to think about Lonnie Pangborn, Wardley, Jessica or Madeleine. Then sorrow came down on me. I had all the sorrow of thinking of a woman I had loved, and the love was gone, and it should never have been lost.

I brooded upon Madeleine. Perhaps an hour later I went to the top floor, and in my study unlocked a file drawer. There, out of a pile of old manuscript, I found the pages I was looking for and read them again. They were written almost twelve years ago—was I twenty-seven when I did them?—and done very much in the style of the cocky young man I tried to be then, but that was all right. If you are no longer one man, only a collection of fragments, each with its own manner, the act of looking back on writing done when one was full of identity (even phony identity) can put you together for a little while, and did while I was rereading these pages. As soon, however, as I concluded, I was bathed in an old woe. For I had made the mistake of showing the manuscript to Madeleine years ago, and it helped to break us up:

The best description of a pussy I ever came across was in a short piece by John Updike called "One's Neighbor's Wife":

Each hair is precious and individual, serving a distinct rôle in the array: blonde to invisibility where the thigh and abdomen join, dark to opacity where the tender labia ask protection, hearty and ruddy as a forester's beard beneath the swell of belly, dark and sparse as the whiskers of a Machiavel where the perineum sneaks backward to the anus. My pussy alters by the time of day and according to the mesh of underpants. It has its satellites: the whimsical line of hairs that ascend to my navel and into my tan, the kisses of fur on the inside of my thighs, the lambent fuzz that ornaments the cleavage of my fundament. Amber, ebony, auburn, bay, chestnut, cinnamon, hazel, fawn, snuff, henna, bronze, platinum, peach, ash, flame, and field mouse: these are but a few of the colors my pussy is.

It is a beautiful description of a forest, and makes you ponder the mysteries of scale. Somebody once wrote that Cézanne shifted our perception of magnitude until a white towel on a table was like the blue-shadowed snows in the ravines of a mountain, and the treatment of a patch of skin became a desert valley. An interesting idea. I always saw more in Cézanne after that, just as I realized I had never looked at a pussy properly until I read Updike. For that alone, John would be one of my favorite writers.

They say Updike used to be a painter, and you can see it in his style. Nobody studies surfaces so closely as he does, and he uses adjectives with more discrimination than anybody who's writing in the English language today. Hemingway said not to use them, and Hemingway was right. The adjective is the author's opinion of what's going on, no more. If I write, "A strong man came into the room," that only means he is strong in relation to me. Unless I've established myself for the reader, I might be the only fellow in the bar who is impressed by the guy who just came in. It is better to say: "A man entered. He was holding a walking stick, and for some reason, he now broke it in two like a twig." Of course, this takes more time to narrate. So adjectives bring on quick tell-you-how-to-live writing. Advertising thrives on it. "A superefficient, silent, sensuous five-speed shift." Put twenty adjectives before the noun and no one will know you are describing a turd. The adjectives are the cruise.

Therefore, let me underline it. Updike is one of the few writers who can enhance his work with adjectives rather than abuse it. He has a rare talent. Yet he irks me. Even his description of a pussy. It could as easily be a tree.

(The velveteen of moss in the ingathered crotch of my limbs, the investiture of algae on the terraces of my bark, etc.) Just once I would like to have him guide me through the inside of a cunt.

Right now, for instance, my mind is pondering the difference between Updike's description of a pussy and a real cunt, that is, the one I am thinking of at this instant. It belongs to Madeleine Falco, and since she is sitting next to me, I need only reach over with my right hand to feel the objective correlative on my fingertips. Still, I would rather remain in the simpler state of a writer in reverie. Being nothing if not competitive—as which unheralded writer is not?—I am trying to put the manifest of her cunt into well-chosen words, and so implant a small standard of prose on the great beachhead of literature. Therefore, I will not dwell on her pussy hair. It is black, so black against the cemetery-white of her skin that my bowels and balls resound against one another like cymbals whenever her bush is displayed. But then, she loves to display it. She has a little pink mouth within the larger one (like Governor Nelson Rockefeller) and it is a true flower that pants in the dew of her heats. When aroused, however, Madeleine's cunt seems to grow right out of her buttocks, and this little mouth always remains pink no matter how wide she spreads her thighs, whereas the outer meat of her vagina—the larger mouth—reveals a sullen grease-works, and the perineum (which we boys out on Long Island used to call the Taint—'tain't vagina, 'tain't anus, ho, ho) is a gleaming plantation. You don't know whether to eat her, devour her, revere her or root about. I used to whisper, "Don't move, don't move, I'll kill you, I'm about to come." How her cooze would pullulate in reply.

Whenever I was inside of Madeleine, the other girl she usually was, the dear brunette on my arm that I walked with down the street, ceased to exist. Her belly and her womb became all of her—all that fatty, saponaceous, sebaceous, unctional, unguinous quiver of lubricious worldly delights. Let me not claim I can do without adjectives when it comes to meditating on cunt. Fucking her, I would be afloat with all the belly dancers and dark-haired harlots of the world—their lust, their greed, their purchase on the swarthier ambitions of the cosmos, all now in me. God knows through which designs of karma was my come pulled by her belly. Her cunt was more real to me than her face.

After she read this much, Madeleine said, "How could you write such things about me?" and wept in a way I could not bear.

"It's only writing," I said. "It's not what I feel about you. I'm not a good enough writer to say what I really feel." I hated her, however, for making me disavow my writing. But then, we were in trouble in any event. She read those pages just a week before we decided to get into a wife-swapping sort of half-orgy (I know no quicker way to describe it) that I talked Madeleine into attending with me, and the use of the word "attend" must come from my Exeter French, since we had to drive all the way from New York to North Carolina to get there, and didn't know the people. All we had was an ad in *Screw* magazine with a post office box for an address:

> Young but mature white couple, male a gynecologist, are seeking fun weekend. No water sports, golden showers, S&M or B&D. Send photograph and SASE. You must be married.

I answered the letter without telling Madeleine, and sent a photo of us nicely dressed and standing on the street. Their Polaroid came back. They were in bathing suits. The man was tall and half bald with a long sad nose, knobby knees, a small potbelly and a sallow look.

Madeleine said, on looking at the picture, "He must have the longest prick in Christendom."

"Why do you say that?"

"There's no other explanation for him."

The wife was young and wearing a flouncy bathing suit. She looked saucy. Something about her spoke to me right out of the photograph. On an impulse I said, "Let's visit."

Madeleine nodded. She had large dark eyes that were luminous and full of tragic knowledge—her family were not without rank in the Mafia and had put a few curses on her head when she left home (which was Queens) for Manhattan. She wore those wounds of departure like a velvet cloak. She had gravity, and to counterbalance it, I would go through great pains to make her laugh, even trying to walk on my hands around our furnished room. A moment of merriment from her gave a bouquet to my mood that could last for hours. That was why I had fallen in love. She had a tender marrow within her depths that I found with no other woman.

But we were too close. She began to pall on me. How harsh and Irish I must have come to seem. After we'd been together for two years, we were in the season when one marries or one parts. We talked about dating other people. I cheated on her from time to time and she had all the night for choosing to do the same to me since I worked the bar four times a week from five to five, and much love can be made in twelve hours.

Therefore, when she nodded her agreement to the trip down South,

I needed no more confirmation to proceed. One of her gifts was to be able to convey it all by one wry humorous dip of the head. "Now tell me the bad news," she said.

So we went to North Carolina. We assured each other that we would probably not like the other couple, and get out fast. Then we could enjoy an extra night or two on the drive back. "We'll stop in Chincoteague," I said to her, "we'll try to sneak up on a Chincoteague pony," and explained how they were the last wild horses, just about, east of the ·Mississippi.

"Chincoteague," she said. "I would like that." She had a rich husky voice, whose timbre would resonate in my chest, and she let me rock on every syllable in Chincoteague. Thereby, we laid salve on each other against the incision we had just made on the nature of our future flesh. And went.

That was where I first encountered Patty Lareine. (It was long before she met Wardley.) She turned out to be the wife of Big Stoop (as she called him) and Big Stoop turned out to be (1) possessor of a truly long dick and (2) a liar, for he was not the most successful gynecologist in the county, but a chiropractor. He was also a prodigious lover of pussy. Could you conceive of how deep he dived into Madeleine's treasure chest?

In the adjoining bedroom (for he was hygienic about these wife-swapping sports—no threesies or foursies!) Patty Erleen—who had not yet renamed herself Patty Lareine—and I began our own weekend. I may yet bring myself to describe it, but for now, suffice it to say that I thought of her on the ride back to New York, and Madeleine and I never stopped off in Chincoteague. Nor was I smoking in those days. It was my first attempt to kick the addiction. So I had gone through some quick rises and free falls of the ego, passing through two days and a night of mate-switching (Big Stoop never knew that Madeleine and I were not married, although, truth to tell, for the damage it did, we were) and never a cigarette for the moments I felt *impaled*—that is the word for listening to my woman give voice to pleasure (and how Madeleine could moan) while another man was in her. No male ego is the same after hearing the same ongoing female cry of pleasure given to a strange new (very long) dick. "It is better to be a masochist than a faggot," I said to myself more than once during those two days, but then I spent hours that had their own glory for me, since the chiropractor's wife, formerly his nurse, this Patty Erleen, had a body as pneumatic as a nineteen-year-old model in *Playboy* standing unbelievably before you in life, and we had one hot high school push-on romance, that is, I kept pushing her to put her mouth into places she swore she had never put it before, which kept us in each other's pits, we had such hooks for each other, so mean and intimate and nasty and superpleasureful (as Californians say) for being nasty. God, Patty Erleen was nice, you could fuck her till you died. Even now, twelve years later, I was close to that first night again, and did not want to be, as if to think well of Patty would betray Madeleine once more.

Instead, I suffered the memory of the long return of Madeleine Falco and myself to New York. It was a very long return. We quarreled, and Madeleine shrieked at me (which was most out of character for her) when I went too fast around a few turns, and finally—I blame it on trying to go cold turkey without cigarettes—I lost the car on an unexpectedly sharp turn. It was a big boat of a Dodge, or a Buick or a Mercury—who can remember? They all acted like sponge rubber on a hard curve, and we squeaked and squeegeed over a hundred yards of hardtop before we slammed into a tree.

My body felt equal to the car. Part was crunched, part was stretched, and a fearful racket like a trailing muffler knocked inside my ears. Without, a silence. One of those country silences when the unrest of insects vibrates through the fields.

Madeleine was in worse shape. She never told me, but I learned that her womb was injured. And, indeed, there was a frightful scar on her belly when she came out of the hospital.

We lasted for another year, cutting ourselves away from each other over the months that followed. We got into cocaine. It filled the rift. Then the habit froze, and the rock of our relation was cracked by the habit, and the rift was larger. It was after we broke up that I got busted for selling cocaine.

Now I sat in my study in my home in Provincetown sipping my bourbon neat. Could it be that these pains of the past in conjunction with a little bourbon were proving a sedative for three days of shocks and starts and turns and absolute dislocations of all I understood? Sitting in that armchair, I began to feel sleep coming on like a blessing. The murmur of what was gone rose over me, an infusion, and the colors of the past grew deeper than the present. Was sleep the entrance to a cave?

In the next instant I was plucked back from sleep. What could I do when even my simplest metaphor saw an entrance to a cave? That was not calculated to keep one's mind away from the burrow in the Truro woods.

All the same, I kept sipping at the bourbon, and a few resources returned. Was I beginning to digest the impact of Mr. Pangborn's suicide? For now it seemed not improbable that Pangborn could be the maniac who did it. Certainly the letter might be seen as the anticipation of a crime. "If someone tried to take my blonde lady away, I would kill." But whom? The new lover or the lady?

This, which offered a working premise, became, when added to the bourbon, the sedative I needed, and I fell at last into a deep sleep, as bruised about as if I were still playing wide receiver for that Exeter team which could not throw a pass, and went down to such a depth in sleep that the voices of Hell-Town were not even with me when I awakened. Instead, I came back to a clear recollection that three nights ago—yes, for certain!—Jessica and Lonnie and I had stepped out of The Widow's Walk about the same time, they from the Dining Room, I from the Lounge, and there, in the parking lot, had resumed—much against Pangborn's will and much to her taste—our conversation, and Jessica and I laughed so much and so quickly that it was soon decided we must go to my house for a nightcap.

Then began a discussion about the car. Did we go in two or one? Jessica was for two cars, Lonnie in his rented sedan, and she and I in my Porsche, but he could read ahead and had no desire to be sent packing, so he solved it all by getting in the passenger seat of my Porsche, whereupon she was obliged to fit herself in and all around him, and managed to do this only by laying her legs across my lap so that I could shift gears only by maneuvering my hand in and around her knees and under her thighs, but then, it was only two miles and a little to my house, and once there, we talked for a long time about property values in Provincetown and why Patty's and my old ramble was worth so much when it consisted only of two salt-boxes and two sheds and a tower we had built ourselves for my third-floor study, but frontage, I told them, was the factor. We had one hundred feet of bay frontage, and the length of our house ran parallel to the shore, rare in our town. "Yes," said Jessica, "that's wonderful," and I swear her knees parted a little further.

Now, I cannot say whether this was a recollection or a dream, for if it had all the clarity of the real event, the logic seemed to belong to that theater of sleep where only those impossible actions take place which are too incisive for the day. What I now recalled is that as we sat in my living room and drank, I began to sense the sachet in each of Lonnie's moves. The deeper he got into drink, the less the Bar Association seemed able to shore up his masculine frontage, and I woke up in my chair on this, the third morning after they first disappeared, ready to swear on the stand that the other night, looking at her and at him in my living room, I developed a prodigious erection—one of those few we remember with excessive pride—and so peremptory was my understanding of this kind of bonus that I made a point of undoing my fly right into the warp and woof of a long, rich—I must say it—pregnant silence. Yes, I took it out and held it up for them, like a six-year-old or a happy lunatic, and said, "Which of you gets first licks?"—a cataclysmic remark, since the evening rather than my phallus could certainly have been blown, but if this memory is true, she got up from where she was sitting, knelt by me, put her blonde head in my lap and her red mouth on my cock and Lonnie gave vent to a sound that was half joy and half agony pure.

Then, it seems, we were all in my Porsche again, and on a crazy trip to Wellfleet. Once I stopped the car in the woods just before we got to Harpo's house, and made love to her on the front fender, yes, because on this morning, awakening in the third-floor-study chair, recalling it all, I could still feel the grasp of the walls of her vagina on my monster of an erection. How I had to fuck her! Down with Patty Lareine! It was as if Jessica and I had been designed in some heavenly shop, part for part, our privates were inseparable, and where was Lonnie but watching! He was crying, if I remember, and I never felt more of a brute. His misery was as good as blood to my erectile tissue. That was the state of my affections near to four weeks after being deserted by my wife.

Then all three of us were talking again in the car. He said he had to be alone with the woman, he had to talk to her—would I let them talk? In the name of decency, would I let them talk?

"Yes," I said, "but we must have a séance afterward." Why, I did not know. "I'll bet you," I said, "she's still with me after you talk." And I remember going up the stairs to Harpo, and the tattoo, yes, Harpo was humming as he put in the needles, and his good battered face had the expression of a seamstress, and then—no, I could not remember stopping in the Truro woods to show them my marijuana patch, but we must have—yes, now I could not see how I would have failed to do that.

What had happened after? Had I left her alone with him? How little my balance on awakening this morning was for love, and how much for self-interest! I was now hoping I had left her with him, and that it was her head—so much for my fealty to great pussy on marijuana—yes, it was her head I wished to find in the burrow. For if she was there—and now I was convinced it had to be Jessica—why, then I could find other clues. If he had killed her in some motel room and brought her body (or was it only her head?) back to my patch, there ought to be tire marks still on the side of the sandy road. I could drive by his car, wherever it was now impounded, and check the tires, yes, I was thinking like a sleuth at last; and all of this, as I soon came to realize, was an exercise to drive my psyche up the high vertical wall of my fear until I felt strong enough, yes, psyched up enough once more to make the trip a second time in my mind in order to make it a first time in reality. So, waking up in the chair at eight in the morning, refreshed with all the carnal stimulations of Jessica, I converted the high hard adrenaline of each lustful thought into the will to lift myself out of my morass. And it took all of that day, all of the morning and afternoon. Even though I did not wish to return in the dark, I was obliged to. For long hours that day my will was silent, and I sat in my chair or I walked on the beach at low tide, and suffered as much as if I had to climb our Monument again. By evening, however, I had gotten myself back once more to the place I was when Regency knocked on my door almost twenty-four hours ago, and so I got into my Porsche, yes, once again, even thinking that Pangborn might, after disposing of Jessica, have come by my car and painted the front seat with the last of her blood—how would I ever prove that?—and drove out to the woods, parked, went up the trail, and with my heart pounding like a battering ram on a cathedral door, and the perspiration coming off my face like founts of eternal water, I drew in the mist of the night air in Truro, removed the rock, reached in with my arm and came out with nothing at all. I cannot tell you how I searched that burrow. I could have burned a hole in the earth with my flashlight, but when the footlocker was removed, all else was out. There was nothing there. The head was gone. Just the footlocker with its jars of marijuana remained. I fled those woods before the spirits now gathering could surround me.

Five

By the time I reached the highway, however, my panic was gone. If many a night of drinking had on many a bad morning brought me close to committing myself (so little could I remember of what I had done) it now seemed to me that since the evening at The Widow's Walk I had not—despite my agitation—been cut off again from my memory. If this was true, then I did not remove that blonde head from the burrow. Someone else was involved with the deed. It was even likely that the murder had not been my act.

Of course, how could I swear that I had stayed in bed each night? On the other hand, no one had ever accused me of walking in my sleep. Like the rustle along the beach that comes with the turning of the tide (if you have ears to hear it) so did a kind of confidence begin to return to me, a belief, if you could so call it, that I had not lost the last of my luck (just the sort of recovered faith that gets a man back to the crap tables).

In my case it was the bravado to believe I could return home, stay reasonably sober and fall asleep. Indeed, I did, which impressed me in the morning as a species of small wonder. Be it said, I had gone to bed with a purpose. It was to debate (in the deepest regions of sleep) whether I should try to see Madeleine or not. The readiness with which I took to my bed, and the force with which I slept, were testimony to that purpose.

By morning, there was no question. On this, the Twenty-eighth Day of Patty's departure, I would go to see Madeleine. All else could wait. I had breakfast and cleaned the dog's dish, noting that his fear of me had now been replaced by a huge reserve. He had kept his distance this week. Yet before I would allow myself to ponder the withdrawal of his friendship and thereby risk my mood, I picked up the Cape Cod book and found Alvin Luther Regency's number in the Town of Barnstable.

It was nine o'clock, a good time to call. Regency had probably driven the fifty miles to Provincetown already, or failing that, was on the road.

Nor was I wrong. It was Madeleine on the line. I knew she was alone.

"Hello," she said. Yes, she was alone. Her voice was clear. When another person was in the room with her, she always betrayed distraction.

I waited, as if to prepare the occasion. Then I said, "I hear you send regards."

"Tim."

"Yes, it's Tim."

"The man of my life," she said. It was with an edge of mockery I had not heard for a long time. She could just as easily have said, "Aren't you the fellow in the short chapter?" Yes, her voice had echoes.

"How are you?" I asked.

"I'm fine," she said, "but I don't remember sending you regards."

"I have it on good authority you did."

"Yes, it's Tim," she said, "oh, my God!" as if now, the second time around, it was reaching her. Yes, Tim—on the phone—after all these years. "No, baby," she said, "I didn't send you regards."

"You're married, I hear."

"Yes."

We had a silence. There was a moment when I could feel the impulse mount in her to hang up, and perspiration started on my neck. All hope for the day would be smashed if she put the receiver down, yet my instinct was not to speak.

"Where are you living?" she asked at last.

"You mean you don't know?"

"Hey, friend," she said, "is this Twenty Questions? I don't know."

"Please, lady, don't be harsh."

"Fuck off. I'm sitting here putting my head together"—that meant I had interrupted her first toke of the morning—"and you ring up like you're the fellow from yesterday."

"Wait a minute," I said, "you don't know that I'm living in Province-town?"

"I don't know anybody there. And from what I hear, I'm not sure that I want to."

"That's right," I said. "Every time the clock chimes, your husband busts another one of your old dealer friends."

"How about that?" she said. "Isn't it awful?"

"How could you marry fuzz?"

"Do you have another dime? Try calling collect." She hung up.

I got into my car.

I had to see her. It was one thing to blow on the embers of an old romance, it was another to feel the promise of an answer. I had at that moment an insight into the root of obsession itself. No wonder we cannot bear questions whose answers are not available. They sit in the brain like the great holes that were dug for the foundations of buildings that never went up. Everything wet, rotten, and dead collects in them. Count the cavities in your teeth by the obsessions that send you back to drink. No question, therefore. I had to see her.

How quickly I took myself through the landscape. It was the day for me. Just outside Provincetown, a wan November sun gave a pale light to the dunes and they looked like the hills of heaven. The wind blew sand until the ridges were obscured by an angelic haze of light, and on the other side of the highway, toward the bay, all the little white cabins for summer tourists were lined up as neatly as kennels on a pedigree-dog compound. Now, with their windows boarded, they had a mute, somewhat injured look, but then, the trees were bare as well and bore a hue as weathered as the hide of animals going through a long winter in a land without forage.

I took my chances and drove at a rate that would have put me in jail if a State Trooper had caught my vehicle on radar. Yet I did not make such fine time, after all, since it occurred to me in the middle of this high speed that Barnstable was a small enough town to notice a man in a Porsche asking directions to Regency's house, and I did not want a neighbor inquiring of Alvin Luther this evening who the friend might be who parked his sports car three hundred yards away from the door. In this part of the Cape, the winter people, mean and quick-sighted as birds, orderly as clerks, write down license numbers when they don't recognize your car. They anticipate interlopers. So I parked in Hyannis and rented an anonymous dun-colored blubber-boat, a Galaxy, or was it a Cutlass?—I think a Cutlass, it didn't matter, I was hyper enough to joke about the ubiquity of our American auto with the young airhead behind the Hertz counter. She must have thought I was on LSD. She certainly took a time checking my credit card and made me wait through one of those ten-minute ready-to-slay delay warps before she put down the phone and gave the card back. That gave me opportunity to brood a bit over my financial condition. Patty Lareine had emptied our checking account when she left, and had cut off my Visa, my MasterCard and my American Express cards, all of which I discovered in the first week. But husbands of my ilk have resources even wives like Patty Lareine cannot eradicate entirely, and so my old Diners Club, which I would renew but never use, had been overlooked by her. Now its viability was keeping me in food, drink, gas, this rented car, and—well, it was near to a month—sooner or later Patty Lareine was going to get a few bills from the outpost. Then, after she cut me off, lack of money might become my preoccupation. I didn't care. I would sell off the furniture. Money was the game other people played that I tried to avoid by having just enough not to play it. No one ever trusts a man who makes such a claim, but do you know?—I believe myself.

All this is making an excursion from the point, except that the nearer I came to Barnstable, the more my mind was afraid to contemplate what I would do if Madeleine did not let me in. Such uneasiness was, however, soon replaced by the need to concentrate on getting there. That was no automatic deed in these parts. The environs of Barnstable had in the last decade become little more than freshly paved roads and newly erected developments slashed through the flat scrub pine that covered most of the land here. Even old-timers had often not heard of new streets two miles from where they lived. So I took the precaution of stopping at a real estate office in Hyannis where they had a large up-to-date map of the county, and finally located Alvin Luther's little lane. As I had suspected, it looked, by the map, to be not more than a hundred yards long, one of six similar and parallel mini-streets all depending from a trunk road like six teats on a sow, or, would it be kinder to say, like one of six cylinders on an in-line engine designed for the kind of car I was now driving? Dependably, the short road to his house ended in a nipple the size of an asphalt turnaround. Around that dead-end circle were set out five identical highly modified Cape Cod–type wooden houses, each with a planted pine tree on the lawn, a set of plastic rain gutters, asbestos shingles, differently painted mailboxes, trash-can bins, tricycles on the grass—I parked just short of the circle.

It would certainly attract attention to be seen walking fifty needless steps to her door. I could hardly go up, ring her bell and later make it back to my car without being observed. Yet it would be worse to leave the car in front of another house and in consequence agitate the owner. What a loneliness hung over this enclave in the sorry scrub-pine woods! I thought of old Indian graves that once must have sat on these low brush-filled lands. Of course, Madeleine would accept a situation whose gloom matched her own worst moods—from that she could rise. But to live in a house like Patty's, where one could plummet below the cheerfulness of the colors—well, not much, for Madeleine, could be worse.

I pressed the doorbell.

It wasn't until I heard her step that I dared to be certain she was in. She began to tremble as soon as she saw me. The intensity of her disturbance went through me as clearly as if she had spoken. She was delighted, she was furious, but she was not startled. She had put her make-up on, and thereby I knew (for usually she did not do anything to her face until evening) that she was expecting a visitor. Doubtless, it was me.

I received no great greeting, however. "You're a clod," she said. "I'd expect you to do something like this."

"Madeleine, if you didn't want me to come, you should not have hung up."

"I called you back. There was no answer."

"You discovered my name in the book?"

"I discovered *her* name." She looked me over. "Being kept doesn't agree with you," she told me at the end of this examination.

Madeleine had worked as a hostess for years in a good New York bar and restaurant and she did not like to have her poise nicked. Her trembling had most certainly stopped, but her voice was not where she would have placed it.

"Let me lay the facts of life on you," she said. "You can stay in my house about five minutes before the neighbors will start phoning each other to find out who you are." She glanced out the window. "Did you walk here?"

"My car is down the road."

"Brilliant. I think you better go right away. You're just asking directions, right?"

"Who are your neighbors that they inspire such respect?"

"There's a State Trooper's family to the left, and a retired couple to the right, Mr. and Mrs. Snoop."

"I thought maybe they were old friends from the Mafia."

"Well, Madden," she said, "ten years have gone by, but you still show no class."

"I want to talk to you."

"Let's find a hotel room in Boston," she said. It was her good way of telling me to go peddle a few papers.

"I'm still in love with you," I said.

She began to cry. "You're such a bad guy," she said. "You really are rotten."

I wanted to embrace her. I wanted, if the truth be told, to go right back to bed with her, but it was not the hour. That much I had learned in ten years.

Her hand made a little gesture. "Come on in," she said.

The living room went with the house. It had a cathedral ceiling, factory-prepared paneling, a rug of some synthetic material, and a lot of furniture that must have come from the shopping mall in Hyannis. There was nothing of herself. No surprise. She paid great attention to her body, her clothing, her make-up, her voice and the expressions on her heart-shaped face. She could register with the subtlest turn of her fine mouth every shade of the sardonic, the contemptuous, the mysterious, the tender and the cognizant that she might need to express. She was her own work of brunette art. She presented herself as such. But her surroundings were another matter. When I first met Madeleine she was living in an apartment totally drab. I need only describe Nissen's place again. That was cool. I had a queen who was independent of her habitat. I can tell you that was one good reason I tired of her over a couple of years. An Italian queen was no easier to live with than a Jewish princess.

Now I said, "Alvin bought all this?"

"Is that your name for him? Alvin?"

"What do you call him?"

"Maybe I call him the winner," she said.

"It was the winner who told me that you send regards."

She was hardly quick enough to conceal the news. "I never spoke your name to him," she said.

I was thinking that could be true. When I knew her she never talked about anyone before me.

"Well," I said, "how did your husband find out I knew you?"

"Keep trying. You'll come up with the answer."

"You think Patty Lareine told him?"

Madeleine shrugged.

"How do you know," I asked, "that Patty Lareine knows him?"

"Oh, he told me how he met the two of you. Sometimes he tells me a lot. We're lonesome here."

"Then you knew I was in Provincetown."

"I managed to forget it."

"Why are you lonesome?" I asked.

She shook her head.

"You have two sons to take care of. That must keep you hopping."

"What are you talking about?"

My instinct was sound. I did not think children lived in this house. "Your husband," I said, "showed me a photograph of you with two little boys."

"They're his brother's children. I don't have any. You know I can't."

"Why would he lie to me?"

"He's a liar," Madeleine said. "What's the big news? Most cops are."

"You sound as if you don't like him."

"He's a cruel, overbearing son of a bitch."

"I see."

"But I like him."

"Oh."

She began to laugh. Then she began to cry. "Excuse me," she said and stepped into the bathroom that was off the entrance hall. I studied the living room some more. There were no prints or paintings, but on one wall hung about thirty framed photographs of Regency in various uniforms. Green Beret, State Trooper, others I did not recognize. He was shaking hands in some of them with political officials and men who looked like bureaucrats, and there were two fellows that I would have cast for high FBI men. Sometimes Regency was receiving athletic or memorial cups, and sometimes he was giving them away. In the center was one large framed glossy of Madeleine in a velvet gown with deep cleavage. She looked beautiful.

On the facing wall was a gun rack. I do not know enough to say how fine a collection it might be, but there were three shotguns and ten rifles. To one side was a glass case with a steel-mesh front, and within was a pistol rack with two six-shot revolvers and three fat handguns that looked like Magnums to me.

When she still did not come out, I took a quick trip upstairs and passed through the master bedroom and the guest bedroom. There was more shopping-mall furniture. It was all neat. The beds were made. That was not quintessentially characteristic of Madeleine.

In the corner of the mirror was tucked a piece of paper. On it was written:

> *Revenge is a dish which people*
> *of taste eat cold.*
>
> *—old Italian saying*

It was in her handwriting.

I moved downstairs just before she came out again.

"Are you feeling all right?" I asked.

She nodded. She sat in one of the armchairs. I put myself in the other.

"Hello, Tim," she said.

I didn't know whether to trust her. How much I needed to talk I was just beginning to realize, but if Madeleine did not prove to be the best person to whom to unburden myself, she would almost certainly be the worst.

I said, "Madeleine, I'm still in love with you."

"Next case," she said.

"Why did you marry Regency?"

It was wrong to use his last name. She stiffened as if I had touched her on the marriage itself, but I was already weary of speaking of him as the winner.

"It's your fault," she said. "After all, you didn't have to introduce me to Big Stoop."

Nor did she have to finish the thought. I knew the words she was inclined to say, and held back. However, she could not hold herself. Her voice came forth in a poor imitation of Patty Lareine. She was too angry. The mimicry was strained. "Yessir," said Madeleine, "ever since Big Stoop, I've had a taste for good old boys with mammoth dicks."

"You serving any drinks?" I asked.

"It's time for you to go. I can still pass you off as an insurance salesman."

"Say, you *are* afraid of Regency."

She was not hard to manipulate when all was said. Her pride had to remain intact. She now said, "It's you he'll be irritated at."

I said nothing. I was trying to calculate the size of his anger. "Do you think he'd be bad?"

"Buster, he's in another league."

"What does that mean?"

"He can be bad."

"I'd hate to watch him cut my head off."

Now she looked startled. "Did he tell you about that?"

"Yes," I lied.

"Vietnam?"

I nodded.

"Well," she said, "any man who can behead a Viet Cong with one stroke of a machete is doubtless to be reckoned with." She was not horrified altogether by such an act. Not altogether. I was remembering the depth of the sense of vengeance in Madeleine. Once or twice a friend had insulted her over what I deemed a small matter. She never forgave it. Yes, an execution in Vietnam could stir up much in her.

"I gather that you're miserable with Patty Lareine," Madeleine now said.

"Yes."

"She left you a month ago?"

"Yes."

"Do you want her back?"

"I'm afraid of what I'd do."

"Well, you chose her." There was a decanter of bourbon on the sideboard, and she now picked it up and came back with two glasses, pouring each of us a half-inch of liquor without water, and no ice. That was a ritual from the past. "Our morning medicine," we used to call it. As before, so again—she shuddered as she sipped it.

"How the hell could you pick her over me?" was what Madeleine wanted to say. I could hear the words more clearly than if she had uttered them.

That was one question she would never ask aloud, and I was grateful. What could I have replied? Would I have said, "Call it a question of Comparative Fellatio, dear heart. You, Madeleine, used to take a cock into your mouth with a sob, or a sweet groan, as if hell were impending over this. It was as beautiful as the Middle Ages. And Patty Lareine was a cheerleader and ready to gobble you up. Albeit with innate skill. It came down to whether you wished your lady to be demure or insatiable. I chose Patty Lareine. She was as insatiable as good old America, and I wanted my country on my cock."

Of course, my long-lost medieval lady had now developed a taste for men who could behead you with a blow.

The greatest virtue of living with Madeleine had been the way we could sit in a room together hearing each other's thoughts so clearly that we seemed to be drawing them from the same well. So she as much as heard my last unsaid speech. I knew that by the mean twist of her mouth. When she looked at me again, Madeleine was full of hatred.

"I didn't tell Al about you," she said.

"Is that what you call him?" I said to hold her off. "Al?"

"Shut up," she said. "I didn't tell him about you, because there was no need for it. He burned you right out of me. Regency is a *stud*."

No woman had ever flayed me with that word so well before. Patty Lareine could not have come close. "Yes," said Madeleine, "you and me loved each other, but when Mr. Regency and I began our little court-ship, he would fuck five times a night, and the fifth was as good as the first. On the best day you'll ever have, you'll never come near Mr. Five. That's what I call him, you dolt."

Against every intent of my will, there were tears in my eyes from the pain this speech gave me. It was equal to suffering while sand is cleaned out of a wound. Yet, at that moment, I fell in love with her all over again. Her words would show me where I put my feet for the rest of my life. It also stirred a pride I thought was dead. For I took a vow that one night before I was done, I would obliterate her admiration for Mr. Five.

Before I left, however, our conversation took another turn. We sat in silence for a time, and then it was longer than that. Maybe it was half an hour later that the tears began to come out of her eyes and wash away the mascara. After a while she had to wipe her face.

"Tim, I want you to go," she said.

"All right. I'll be back."

"Call first."

"Okay."

She walked me to the door. Then she stopped and said, "There's one thing more I ought to tell you." She nodded to herself. "But if I do," she went on, "you'll want to stay and talk."

"I promise not to."

"No, you'll break your word." She said, "Wait. Wait here," and she went to a shopping-mall replica of a Colonial kneehole desk in the living room, where she wrote a few words on a note, sealed it and came back.

"This promise you can keep," she said. "I want you to hold this note until you're better than halfway home. Then, open it. Think about it. Don't ring me to talk about it. I'm telling you what I know. Don't ask how I know."

"That's six promises," I said.

"Mr. Six," she said, and came close, and gave her mouth to me. It was one of the most remarkable kisses I have ever had, and yet there was little passion in it. All the tenderness of her heart, however, and all her pall of rage both passed into me, and I confess that I was stunned by the combination, as if a good boxer had just caught me with a startling left hook and a stultifying right, which is not the way to describe a kiss and gives none of the balm it also offered my heart, but I say this to emphasize how rubbery were my legs on the walk past the neighbors down the road to my car.

I kept the six promises and didn't open her note until long after I turned in the blubber-wagon at Hyannis and got back into my Porsche and drove all the way to Eastham. There I stopped on the highway to peruse her message, and it took three seconds. I didn't phone her, I just read the note again. It said: "My husband is having an affair with your wife. Let's not talk about it unless you're prepared to kill them."

Well, I started up my Porsche again, but it will come as small surprise that I was not able to concentrate on the road, and coming to a sign for the Marconi Beach Site of the National Park Service, I turned off Route 6 and drove out to the bluffs overlooking the Atlantic Ocean. I left my wheels in the space allotted by the Park Service and walked off to sit on the top of a low dune, passing sand through my hands while I meditated on the Pilgrims and wondered if it might be out in the seas right here that they turned north to sail up the tip of the Cape and around to Provincetown. What better place than this promontory for Marconi to send his early wireless messages across the ocean's space? My mind, however, on pondering such large concepts, grew empty, and I sighed, and thought of other wireless messages that had gone between Joan of Arc and Gilles de Rais, Elizabeth and Essex, the Czarina and Rasputin, and in our own most reduced and modest way, Madeleine and myself. I sat at the top of this low bluff and passed sand back and forth in my hands and tried to estimate my situation now that I had seen Madeleine. Did it all come down to Alvin Luther Regency?

It occurred to me that I could just about use a rifle and had hardly any competence with my pistol. For that matter, I had not had a fist fight in five years. With drinking, and, of late, my smoking, I must have a liver large enough for two. Yet at the thought of facing Regency, I also felt some of the old blood come back. I did not start as a fighter, and I did not seem to have ended as one, but the years in the middle when I tended bar taught me a few tactics, which knowledge I had doubled in the slammer—I was a compendium of dirty tricks—and then finally, it didn't matter. I had gotten so evil in my last few street fights that they always had to pull me off. Something of my father's blood had passed on to me, and I seemed to have bought his code. Tough guys don't dance.

Tough guys don't dance. On that curious proposition my memory, like a boat coming around a buoy into harbor, returned to my adolescence and I could feel myself dwelling again in the year I turned sixteen and went into the Golden Gloves. That was far away from where I now found myself with Madeleine's note. Or was it not so far? After all, it was in the Golden Gloves that I tried for the first time to hurt someone seriously, and sitting here, on the beach at South Wellfleet, I started to smile. For I was able to see myself in the way I used to, and at sixteen, I always pictured myself as tough. I had, after all, the toughest father on the block. While I knew, even then, that I would never be his equal, still I told myself that I was enough like him to make my high school football varsity by my sophomore year. That was a feat! And I remember how that winter, once football was over, I used to feel a mean and proud hostility toward the world which I could hardly control. (It was the year of my parents' divorce.) I started to go to a boxing gym near my father's bar. It was inevitable. Being Dougy Madden's son, I had to sign up for the Golden Gloves.

A Jewish boy I knew at Exeter told me that the year before he turned thirteen was the worst in his life. He spent it getting ready for his Bar Mitzvah, and never knew if on a given night he could fall asleep or would be wide awake reciting the speech he had to give next winter in the synagogue to two hundred friends of his family.

That wasn't as bad, I suggested to him, as your first night in the Gloves. "For one thing," I said, "you walk in half naked, and nobody has prepared you for that. Five hundred people are there. Some of them don't like you. They're for the other guy. They're very critical when they stare at you. Then you see your opponent. He looks like dynamite."

"What made you do it?" my friend asked.

I told him the truth. "I wanted to make my father happy."

For a boy with such a good purpose, I had, all the same, a nervous stomach in the dressing room. (I was sharing it with fifteen other fighters.) They, like me, were to be in the blue corner. On the other side of a partition was a dressing room with fifteen contenders from the red corner. Every ten minutes or so, one of us on each side would go out to the auditorium and another would come back. There is nothing like the danger of humiliation to build fast alliances. We didn't know each other, but we kept wishing each guy luck. Devoutly. Every ten minutes, as I say, one kid would go out, and soon after, the previous kid would return. He would be ecstatic if he won, and in misery if he lost, but at least it was over. One kid was carried in, and they sent for an ambulance. He had been knocked out by a black puncher with a big rep. In that minute I considered forfeiting my match. Only the thought of my father sitting in the first row kept me from speaking up. "Okay, Dad," I said to myself, "my death is for you."

Once the fight started, I discovered that boxing, like other cultures, takes years to acquire, and, immediately, I lost the little culture I had. I was so scared I never stopped throwing punches. My opponent, who was fat and black, was just as frightened and never stopped either. At the bell, neither of us could move. My heart felt ready to explode. By the second round, we could not do a thing. We stood still, we glowered, we used our heads to block punches because we were too tired to duck—it cost less to get hit than to move. We must have looked like longshoremen too drunk to fight. Both of us were bleeding from the nose and I could smell his blood. I learned on this night that blood has a scent as intimate as body odor. It was an horrendous round. When I got to my corner, I felt equal to an overraced engine whose parts were ready to seize.

"You got to do better, or we don't win," said the trainer. He was a friend of my father's.

When I could catch my voice, I said as formally as I could—you would have thought I was already in prep school—"If you want to terminate the fight, I will abide by that."

The look in his eye, however, told me he would repeat my remark for the rest of his life.

"Kid, just go beat the shit out of him," my trainer said.

The bell rang. He gave me my mouthpiece and a shove toward the center of the ring.

Now I fought with desperation. I had to eat the entrails of my remark. My father was shouting so loudly, I even thought I was going to win. Boom! I ran into a bomb. The side of my head could just as well have stopped the full swing of a baseball bat. I suppose that I careened around the ring because I only saw the other boxer in jump cuts. I was in one place, then I was in the next place.

New adrenaline must have been shaken loose by the punch. My legs were shocked full of life. I began to circle and to jab. I ran and I ducked and I jabbed (which is what I should have done from the beginning). At last I could recognize the given: my opponent knew less about boxing than me! Just as I was measuring him for a hook (since I had now discovered that he lowered his right each time I feinted with my left to the belly) why, the bell rang. Fight was over. They lifted his hand.

Afterward, when the well-wishers were gone and I was sitting alone with my father in a coffee shop, a second wave of pain just commencing, Big Mac muttered, "You should have won."

"I thought I did. Everybody says I did."

"That's friends." He shook his head. "You lost it in the last round."

No, now that it was over and I had lost, I thought I had won. "Everybody said it was beautiful the way I took that punch and kept moving."

"Friends." He said it in so lugubrious a voice that you would have thought it was friends, not drink, that was the bane of the Irish.

I never felt more argumentative with my father. There is no surliness like sitting around, half dislodged in every vale of your mind, torso and limbs, your organs hot and full of lead, your heart loaded with consternation that maybe you did lose the fight your friends say was stolen from you. So I said out of my own puffed mouth, and I probably never sounded cockier to him, "My mistake was that I didn't dance. I should have come out fast at the bell and stuck him. I should have gone: Stick! Stick! Slide," I said, moving my hands, "and circled away. Then back with the jab, dance out of range, circle and dance, stick him! Stick him!" I nodded at this fine war plan. "When he was ready, I could have dropped the bum."

My father's face was without expression. "Do you remember Frank Costello?" he asked.

"Top of the mob," I said with admiration.

"One night Frank Costello was sitting in a night club with his blonde, a nice broad, and at the table he's also got Rocky Marciano, Tony Canzoneri and Two-ton Tony Galento. It's a guinea party," my father said. "The orchestra is playing. So Frank says to Galento, 'Hey, Two-ton, I want you to dance with Gloria.' That makes Galento nervous. Who wants to dance with the big man's girl? What if she likes him? 'Hey, Mr. Costello,' says Two-ton Tony, 'you know I'm no dancer.' 'Put down your beer,' says Frank, 'and get out there and move. You'll be very good.' So Two-ton Tony gets up and trots Gloria around the floor at arm's length, and when he comes back, Costello tells the same thing to Canzoneri, and he has to take Gloria out. Then it's Rocky's turn. Marciano believes he's big enough in his own right to call Costello by his first name, so he says, 'Mr. Frank, we heavyweights are not much on a ballroom floor.' 'Go do some footwork,' says Costello. While Rocky is out there, Gloria takes the occasion to whisper in his ear, 'Champ, do me a favor. See if you can get Uncle Frank to do a step with me.'

"Well, when the number is over, Rocky leads her back. He's feeling better and the others got their nerve up too. They start to rib the big man, very careful, you understand, just a little tasteful chaffing. 'Hey, Mr. Costello,' they say, 'Mr. C., come on, why don't you give your lady a dance?'

" 'Will you,' Gloria asks, 'please!'

" 'It's your turn, Mr. Frank,' they say.

"Costello," my father told me, "shakes his head. 'Tough guys,' he says, 'don't dance.' "

Now, my father had about five such remarks and he never dropped them on you until he did. "*Inter faeces et urinam nascimur*" became the last and the unhappiest, even as "Don't talk—you'll spill the wind out of the sails" was always the happiest, but through my adolescence, it used to be: "Tough guys don't dance."

At sixteen, a half-Mick from Long Island, I did not know about Zen masters and their koans, but if I had, I would have said the remark was a koan, since I didn't understand it, yet it stayed with me, and the older I became, the more meaning it offered, until now, sitting on a beach at South Wellfleet, looking out at the surf that came to me at the end of the three-thousand-mile ride of the waves, I thought again of the wonders of erosion that Patty Lareine had worked on my character. The wells of self-pity rose predictably, and I thought it was time to stop thinking of my koan unless I could bring a new thought to the circle.

Surely my father had meant something finer than that you held your ground when there was trouble, something finer that doubtless he could not or would not express, but it was there, his code. It could be no less than a vow. Did I miss some elusive principle on which his philosophy must crystallize?

It was then that I saw a man approaching on the beach. The closer he came, the nearer I came to recognizing him, and with that, many of my preoccupations with myself began to fade.

He was a tall man but not menacing in appearance. In truth, he was plump, and soon in danger of looking like a pear, for at any weight he would have had a potbelly and not much in the way of shoulders. Moreover, his gait as he walked on the sand was comic. He was well-dressed, in a three-piece pin-stripe charcoal-gray flannel suit with a white collar on a striped shirt, a club tie, a small red handkerchief in his breast pocket, and a camel's-hair coat folded on his arm. To avoid scuffing his brown loafers, he was carrying them in his hand, and so marching in argyle socks over the cold November sand. That gave him the prancing, skittery foot of a show horse stepping over wet cobblestones.

"How are you, Tim?" the man now said to me.

"Wardley!" I was twice stupefied. Once, because he had put on so much weight—he was slim when I saw him last in divorce court—and again, that we should meet on this beach at South Wellfleet I had not visited in five years.

Wardley leaned over and stuck out his hand in the general direction of where I was sitting.

"Tim," he said, "you were a perfect son of a bitch in the way you acted, but I want you to know, I don't sit on bad feelings. Life, as one's friends constantly admonish, is too short for that."

I shook his hand. If he was willing, I did not see how I could refuse. After all, his wife had run across me dead broke in a bar in Tampa—it was the first time she had seen me in close to five years—had given me a job as their chauffeur, had taken me to her bed under his nose, thereby resuming the romantic possibilities we had begun on our night in North Carolina, and had then motivated me to the point where I certainly tried to think up a fail-safe method to kill him. That failing to spark, I certainly did testify against him in the divorce trial, taking the stand to swear—and some of it happened to be true—that he had solicited me to testify against her for a very good sum. I had added that he proposed I take Patty Lareine to a house in Key West that he was prepared to raid with a detective and a photographer. That was not wholly true. He had merely mused aloud over such a possibility. I also said that he had asked me to seduce her with the aim of becoming a witness for him, and that was successful perjury. It is possible my testimony did as much for Patty Lareine as her lawyer with his video coaching. Wardley's legal guns certainly treated me like a star witness and did their best to paint me as an ex-con and a beach bum. They were as nasty as you would expect, but how could I keep any kind of good conscience about my role? Through all of that gig as a chauffeur in his home, Wardley had treated me as an Exeter classmate down on his luck. It had been no way to treat him back.

"Yes," he said, "I was hurt for a little while, but Meeks always said to me, 'Wardley, extirpate self-pity. It's one emotion this family can't afford.' I hope they're dipping Meeks now in the worst pits, but that's neither here nor there. One must take one's advice where one can find it."

He had the damnedest voice. I will come to describe it in a moment, but for now, his face was over me. Like many ungainly people, he had a habit, when speaking to someone who was seated, of leaning forward from the waist and putting his mug into the air space around your own, so that you were always uneasy you'd receive the dew of his patrician spit. With the sun on his face he looked, particularly at this short distance, like a dollop of oatmeal. He would have been oafish in appearance if he weren't so neat, for his thin dark hair was straight, and his features, left to themselves, were lumpy, lacking in strength and sullen, but the eyes were startling. They were luminous, and had the curious gift of goggling into a blaze at a passing remark as if the devil had just rammed a thumb up Wardley's track.

So his eyes did their best to own you, staring into your face as if you were the first soul he had ever found remotely like his own.

Then there was his voice. My father would have hated it. God certainly used Wardley's voice to display His decency. Whatever Wardley lacked in any other way was made up for by his diphthongs. A snob would turn to cream before those diphthongs.

If I have taken a while to describe my old classmate, it is because I was still in shock. I had long been a believer in the far reach of coincidence; indeed, I went so far as to think one must always expect it when extraordinary or evil events occur—a bizarre but forceful notion I hope to explain. That Wardley, however, should choose to appear on this beach now—well, I would have been happier at first with a rational explanation.

"It's incredible that you're here," I said despite myself.

He nodded. "I have absolute faith in chance meetings. If I had a saint, her name would be Serendipity."

"You seem glad to see me."

He considered this, his eyes intent on mine. "Do you know," he said, "everything considered, I think I am."

"Wardley, you have a good nature. Please sit down."

He complied, which was a relief. Now, I did not have to look constantly into his eyes. His thigh, however, which had ballooned up as much as the rest of him, rested against mine, a large soft amiable physical object. The truth is that if one had a vocation in that direction, one could have grabbed him, etc. His flesh had the kind of nubile passivity that begged to be abused. In prison, I remembered now, they used to call him "the Duke of Windsor." I used to hear cons say of Wardley, "Oh, the Duke of Windsor. He's got an asshole as big as a bucket."

"You don't look well," Wardley now murmured.

I let this pass, and took my turn to ask, "How long have you been in these parts?" I could have meant this Marconi Beach, South Wellfleet, the Cape, New England, or for that matter, all of New York and Philadelphia too, but he just waved his hand. "Let's talk," he said, "about vital matters."

"That's easier."

"Easier, Mac, you're right. I've always said—in fact, I used to say it to Patty Lareine, 'Tim has an instinctive gift for good manners. Just like you, he tells it as it is. But he puts the best face on the matter.' I was trying to smuggle a clue, of course, into her obdurate head. How I tried to give her a notion of how to behave." He laughed. It was with the great pleasure exhibited by people who have spent their lives laughing aloud when they are by themselves, and so, if there was much loneliness in it, there was also extraordinary individuality, as if he didn't care how much was revealed of the most godawful sinks and traps in his plumbing. The liberty of being absolutely himself was worth the rest.

When he had finished this laugh, and I had begun to wonder what was amusing him so, he said, "Since you, me and Patty have been down this road before, let me make it brief. What would you think of doing her in?"

He said it with a gleam, as if proposing the theft of the Koh-i-noor diamond.

"Total?"

"Of course."

"You don't take long to get to the point."

"That's the other piece of advice I received from my father. He told me, 'The more important the matter, the quicker you must broach it. Otherwise, the importance itself will weigh on you. Then you'll never get it proposed.'"

"Maybe your father was right."

"Of course."

He was obviously leaving the option to pursue this suggestion entirely to me.

"I'm inclined to ask," I said. "How much?"

"How much do you want?"

"Patty Lareine used to promise me the moon," I said. " 'Just get rid of that awful faggot,' she'd say, 'and you'll have half of all I'll be worth.' " I said this to be as rude to him as I could. His compliment about my good manners had irritated me. It was so blatant in its stroking. So I said this to see if his wounds had dried. I'm not so certain they had. He blinked rapidly, as though to keep a few emotional paces in front of any loose tears, and said, "Well, I wonder if she now has equally agreeable things to say about you."

I began to laugh. I had to. I had always assumed that when we were done, Patty Lareine would be kinder to me than she had been to Wardley, but that might be a large supposition.

"Are you in her will?" he asked.

"I have no idea."

"Do you hate her enough to do the job?"

"Five times over."

I said it without pause. Talking on the beach gave a great freedom to say anything. But then the number came back. Had I uttered a true sentiment, or was it merely a repetition of the noxious idea that Madeleine Falco Regency's husband ejaculated five times a night inside that temple I had once adored. Like a boxer, I only seemed to ache hours after the ugly exchanges had taken place.

"I've heard," Wardley said, "that Patty treated you badly."

"Well," I said, "you could use the word."

"You look whipped. I don't believe you could perform the deed."

"I'm sure you're right."

"I don't want to be."

"Why don't *you* commit it?" I asked.

"Tim, you'll never believe me."

"Tell me anyway. Maybe I can find the truth by comparing the lies."

"That's a good remark."

"It's not mine. It's Leon Trotsky's."

"Oh. It's worthy of Ronald Firbank."

"Where is Patty Lareine now?" I asked.

"She's around. You can count on that."

"How do you know?"

"She and I are vying for the same piece of property."

"Are you trying to slay her or defeat her in a business deal?"

"Whichever comes first," he said with a droll flash of the whites of his eyes. Could he be trying to emulate William F. Buckley, Jr.?

"But you would rather see her dead?" I persisted.

"Not by my own hand."

"Why not?"

"You simply won't believe me. I want her to look into the eyes of her killer and have it all wrong. I don't want her to see me as the last thing in her life and say, 'Oh, well, it's Wardley going in for pay-back.' That's too easy. It'll give her peace. She'll know who to haunt as soon as she gets her stuff together in the next place. And I'm not hard to find. Believe me, I prefer her to die in a state of profound confusion. 'How could Tim have done it?' she'll ask herself. 'Did I underestimate him?' "

"You're marvelous."

"Well," he said, "I knew you wouldn't comprehend me. But you hardly can, considering the gap in our backgrounds."

He had turned around sufficiently so that his eyes were looking into mine again. On top of it all, his breath was not too fragrant.

"But if you scotch her in the real estate deal," I said, "she'll know it's you paying her back."

"Yes, she will. I want that. I want my living enemies to see my expression. I desire them to know on every breath they take that, yes, yes, it's Wardley who did this to them. Death is different. Send them out in confusion, I say."

I would have been less inclined to take him seriously if, in prison, he had not had a man killed who was threatening him. I was present when he bought the killer's services, and he had not sounded all that different from now. Convicts would laugh at him, but not to his face.

"Tell me about the real estate deal," I said.

"Since your wife and I have an eye on the same place, I'm not certain I should tell you. One never knows when Patty Lareine will come back and wrap her arms around you."

"Yes," I said, "I could be vulnerable," and wondered how Patty would reek of Acting Police Chief Regency.

"I shouldn't tell you." He paused, then he said, "On impulse, however, I will."

I had to look now into those abominably large, searching eyes. "I don't want to roil your feelings, Tim, but I'm not certain you truly understood Patty Lareine. She pretends that she couldn't care less what the world thinks of her, but I will tell you that she's really the stuff from which the world's flagships are made. It's just that she's too proud to work her way up the daily rungs. So she pretends no interest."

I was thinking of the first gathering to which I had taken Patty Lareine when we came to Provincetown five years ago. Some friends of mine brought their wineskins out to the dunes for a party, and the women contributed tea-cakes and Acapulco Gold, Jamaica Prime, and even a few Thai sticks. We had a moon blast. Patty had actually been nervous before it began—I was to learn that she was always nervous before a party—which might have been hard to comprehend considering how good she was at giving them, but then, Dylan Thomas, they say, used to throw up just before going out to give an unforgettable poetry reading. So had Patty taken them for a great ride on this first party, and before the end, even bent over to play a bugle between her legs. Yes, she had been the life of that party and many another.

All the same, I knew what he meant. She gave so much for so little. Often I felt the wistful note of a good artist painting ashtrays to make Christmas gifts. So I did not ignore what he said; indeed, I considered whether he could be right. Her unrest at living in Provincetown had become considerable of late.

"The secret to Patty Lareine," Wardley said, "is that she sees herself as a sinner. Hopelessly lost. No return. What can a girl do next?"

"Drink herself to death."

"Only if she's a fool. I would say the practical answer for Patty Lareine is to build great works to the devil."

His wait was portentous, as if to allow endless space for this to sink in. "I've kept my eye on her," he said. "There is little she has done in the last five years I haven't heard about."

"You have friends in town?"

He made a gesture with his hands.

Of course he did. With half the winter population on welfare, he would not have to pay a great deal for information.

"I've kept in touch," he said, "with real estate agents. Haunted the tip of the Cape in my own way. Provincetown impresses me. It's the most attractive fishing village on the Eastern seaboard, and if not for the Portuguese, bless them, it would have been ruined long ago."

"Are you saying Patty Lareine wants to get into real estate?"

"Not at all. She wants to pull off a coup. She has her eye on a fabulous house on a hill in the West End."

"I think I know the place you mean."

"Of course you do. Don't I know that! Those people you had drinks with at The Widow's Walk were my surrogates. They were planning to step into the agent's office next day to get that house you were already kind enough to put me in." He whistled. "Provincetown is haunted. I'm convinced of it. How else could you come up with my name while speaking to them."

"It is remarkable."

"It is directly spooky."

I nodded. My scalp felt alert. Did Patty Lareine tune the orchestra in Hell-Town? While blowing her bugle at the moon?

"Do you realize," said Wardley, "that poor Lonnie Pangborn got up the same night in the middle of dinner with his blonde lalapalooza, and phoned me? He was half convinced I was double-dealing. How, he asked, could he keep a low profile as the purchaser when my name was being bruited about?"

"Well, chalk one up," I said.

"That always happens with master plans," said Wardley. "The better the plan, the more you may count on something unforeseen getting in to bend the works. Someday I'll tell you the real story of how Jack Kennedy got killed. It was supposed to be a miss! What a set of accidents! The CIA didn't know anus from appetite that day."

"You want to buy the estate in order to keep Patty Lareine from getting it?"

"Exactly."

"What would you do with it?"

"I would take great pleasure in hiring a caretaker to watch over its empty glories. Calculated to put dry rot into every one of Patty Lareine's apertures."

"But what better can she do, if she gets it?"

He held up a white plump hand. "This is just my speculation."

"Yes."

"Newport is Newport, and you can leave it where it is. Martha's Vineyard and Nantucket have become no better than real estate. The Hamptons are a disaster! Le Frak City is more attractive on Sunday."

"Provincetown is jammed worse than any of them."

"Yes, in summer it's hopeless, but then, so are all the other spots on the Eastern seaboard. The point is, Provincetown has natural beauty. The others are nature's culls. And for fall, winter and spring, nothing is superior to little old P-town. I suspect that Patty Lareine wants to start a chic hotel right there on that estate. Done properly, it could, in a few years, have more cachet than anything around. In the off-season, once in, it could sweep all before it. That's how Patty is thinking, I reckon. And, with proper assistants, she would make a fabulous hotelier. Tim, whether I'm right or wrong, I know this. She's got her heart set on the place." He sighed. "Now that Lonnie's packed it in and the blonde has disappeared, I've got to find a representative in a hurry or go speak for myself. That will kick the price way up."

I began to laugh. "You've convinced me," I said. "You'd rather screw Patty on a piece of real estate than kill her."

"You bet." He made his point of laughing with me. I didn't know what to believe. His story sounded wrong.

We watched the waves for a while.

"I adored Patty Lareine," he said. "I don't want to bring out the crying towel, but for a little while, she made me feel like a man. I always say that if you're AC-DC, it's nice to have power in both lines."

I smiled.

"Well, it was no laughing matter. All my life, I would remind you, I've been trying to regain property rights to my rectum."

"Given up?"

"I'm the only one who would care what the answer is by now."

"Back in my chauffeuring days, Patty Lareine used to harangue me on how we had to off you, Wardley. She would say that there would be no peace until you were dead. That if we didn't kill you, you would certainly kill us. She said she'd known some evil types in her day, but you were the most vindictive. You had, she said, so much time to plot and scheme."

"Did you believe her?"

"No, not really. I kept thinking of the day we got kicked out of school together."

"Is that why you didn't try to terminate me? I always wondered. Because, you know, I didn't suspect a thing. I always trusted you."

"Wardley, you have to see my situation. I was broke. I had a police record and couldn't work any good places as a bartender, and the wealthiest woman I ever knew acted as if she was mad about me, and promised me all the drugs and booze and toys that money could buy. I did get pretty serious about how I was going to total you. Psyched myself up. But I couldn't get that heavy shit to flush. Know why?"

"Of course not. I'm asking."

"Because, Wardley, I kept thinking of the time you got your moxie together and inched out along a third-floor ledge to get into your father's room. That story moved me. You were one wimp who got his nerve up. Finally, I had to call it off. You can choose not to believe me."

He laughed, and then he laughed again. The sound of his humor as it cawed through his bends brought a flight of sea gulls near, much as if he were the lead bird crying out, "Here's food, here's food!"

"That's marvelous," he said. "Patty Lareine's plans gone kerflooie because you didn't have the heart to kill the little boy on the ledge. Well, I've enjoyed this talk and am delighted that as old classmates we are finally getting to know one another. Let me fill you in on what a liar I used to be. I never *inched* out along that ledge. I made up the tale. Everybody has to have a war story in prison, so that became mine. I wanted people to recognize that I was too desperate to fool around with. But the truth is that I gained entry to my father's private library by way of the butler—who was also the photographer, remember? He just took out his key and let me in. And all for no more than the promise that I would unbutton his fly—old-fashioned buttons for the butler, not zippers!—and go gooey-gooey down there. Which I did. I always pay my debts. Paris is well worth a Mass!"

With that he stood up, lifted his shoes on high as if he were the Statue of Liberty, and started off. When he was ten feet away, he turned around and said, "Who knows when Patty Lareine may pop in on you? If you get the impulse, off her. Her head, since we have to put a figure on it, is worth two million and change." Then he lowered the arm that was carrying the shoes and pranced off on stiff cold feet.

He was not out of earshot before I told myself that if I could find the blonde head that had now disappeared, that very blonde head which probably belonged to Jessica Pond, it might, by now, be sufficiently decomposed to be successfully presented as the remains of Patty Lareine. I might be the lucky inheritor of a high-powered scam. Tricky as hell, but worth two million.

Then I told myself: Anyone who is capable of thinking this way is capable of homicide.

Then I told myself: Thought is cheap. The best guide to my innocence is that the idea of such a scam hardly stirs me.

I waited until Meeks Wardley Hilby III was a distance down the beach before I went back to my Porsche, and left Marconi Beach for the drive to Provincetown.

On the way home I learned a little more about the tarnished nature, on occasion, of coincidence.

It seemed to me that I was being followed. I could not swear to this because I could not locate a car behind me. When I would speed, no vehicle came rushing up to keep me in sight. Even as I might sometimes sense, however, who was on the telephone before I picked it up, so now I could not relinquish the conviction that somebody was on my tail. They might be keeping a good distance, but they were following. Had a beeper been put on my Porsche?

I turned right down a side road for a hundred yards and parked. No other car came along. I got out and looked in the front trunk, and at the motor in the rear. Under the back bumper I found a small black box, half the size of a pack of cigarettes, held in place by a magnet.

The black box made no noise and offered no ticking. It felt inert in my hand. I could not be certain what it was. I replaced it, therefore, on the bumper, went back to Route 6, and drove for another mile. Then I parked at the summit of a long straightaway. I kept a pair of field glasses in the side pocket for watching gulls and I scanned the highway with them. There, behind me, just within the useful range of these binoculars, was a brown van also parked on the shoulder. Had they stopped when I did? Were they waiting for me to start up again? I kept driving until I came to Pamet Road in Truro, which went east from the highway for a mile, then north for a mile, then back west to join the four-lane. Three quarters of the way around I stopped at a turn where I could see much of the southern arm of Pamet Road on the other side of the Pamet River Valley, and again the brown vehicle had halted. I had seen this closed brown van before, I knew it!

I parked my car by a house and stepped back into the woods. Whoever was in the van waited another ten minutes but then must have concluded that I was visiting someone, so they drove by to look at the house before which my Porsche was parked, then turned around to go back from where they had come. I listened to the motor, which was not hard to follow. Our roads are empty in winter. It was the only sound in the valley.

Now they stopped again, perhaps three hundred yards away. They would wait for me to start up. The beeper would tell them when I began to move.

I was inclined, what with all natural sense of outrage, to throw their gadget right into the woods—or, better, leave it on some parked car and oblige my followers to wait on Pamet Road for the rest of the night. But I was too furious for that. It offended me that the exceptional meeting of Wardley and myself on Marconi Beach came down to no more than using a beeper to follow my Porsche. Apparently the first precept to recollect was that not all coincidence was diabolical or divine. I was back with the common people!

After all, it was not Wardley I had seen behind the wheel of the van, but Spider Nissen, and Stoodie was in the bucket seat beside him. Wardley was doubtless reading Ronald Firbank in some country inn with a CB radio at his side waiting for Spider and Stoodie to send the word.

Yes, I would keep the beeper, I told myself. Maybe I could use it to good purpose when the opportunity arose. That, however, was only a small satisfaction, considering how much unrest this little machine aroused in my blood, but I could now recognize that the more events began to impinge on me, the closer I could come to the first cause.

Six

After all these maneuvers on the highway, I was angry, I was curious, I was thirsty, and it occurred to me I had not been in a bar since the night at The Widow's Walk. Ergo, so soon as I came back to my house, I parked and walked down to the town wharf. We have good bars in the center of town: The Bay State (which we call The Brig), The Poop Deck and The Fish and Bait (unofficially renamed The Bucket of Blood to honor the number of fights that take place in there), good bars, but you would not call them great, for they have none of the working-class panache that bartenders like my father bring to a place. Still, they are dark, and just dirty enough to make you comfortable. One can hunker down to drinking as comfortably as an unborn babe in a good dependable womb. Few fluorescent tubes will be overhead and the old jukebox is too feeble to blast your ears. In summer, of course, a bar like The Brig would be more crowded than a New York subway at rush hour, and the story is told—I believe it—that one summer some PR men at Budweiser or Schaefer or one of those warm-urine brews decided to run a contest for the bar-and-restaurant that sold the most beer in the state of Massachusetts. Well, a place in Provincetown called The Bay State showed the greatest volume of beer sales for July. So, on a weekday morning in August, some high executives in lightweight summer suits flew over, accompanied by a television crew, to film the presentation of the award, expecting no doubt to drop in on one of those lobster cum fish-and-chips places, large as an armory, that you can find around Hyannis, and instead encountered our dark, funky Brig with no customers rich enough to buy anything better than ale, but two hundred beer drinkers packed in standing up. Maybe The Brig was the length of a boxcar from the front door to the stinking garbage cans in the rear, and for food, you could get a submarine with ham and cheese or linguiça sausage. The TV cameras rolled and the freaks stood up and said, "Yeah, that's the beer. Stinks. What you got that red light on your TV camera for? I'm talking too much, right? Stop! Right?"

Well, in winter it was still crowded, but you could sit down and take a taste of the marrow of the mood of what was coming down in the town that day. A lot of commercial fishing boats would return by afternoon and the crews would be drinking. The carpenters and the dope dealers and the narcs and some of the handymen for summer cottages, and unwed young mothers on Fridays with their welfare checks, and others generally scuffling for bread or looking for a friend to buy them a glass were also downing our good urine. I knew most of these people in varying degree and would speak of them if they figured in what was happening to me now, since they were all most individual no matter how much they looked alike, but in winter, as I say, we looked alike. We were sallow, and everybody dressed in Army surplus clothes.

Let one story suffice. I live in a Portuguese town, after all, and have no natives in my story but Stoodie, who is a disgrace to the Portuguese. One afternoon in winter when The Brig was unnaturally empty, a Portuguese fisherman about eighty years old was sitting at the bar. He was as bent over and twisted from a life of work as a cypress growing out of a boulder on a rocky coast. Into the bar walked another fisherman as arthritic as himself. They had grown up together, played football together, graduated from high school together, worked on fishing boats together, got drunk together, probably seduced each other's wives, and now at eighty didn't like each other any more than when they used to have fist fights in recess. The first, nonetheless, got off his stool, stood up, and bellowed across the bar in a voice as hoarse as the March wind, "I thought you was *dead!*" The other stopped, glared back, and out of a larynx shrill as a gull, replied, "*Dead?* I'll go to *your* funeral." They had a beer together. It was merely another exercise in dispelling the spirits. The Portuguese know how to bark when they speak.

We imitate them. In other places, they measure the acid rain, or the index of air pollution, or the amount of dioxin in the soil. Here, where we have no industries but fishing, and room renting, and no farming, the air and sand are clean, but it is a rare day when you cannot feel the weight of spirits in a bar, and when I walked in full of my sleepless nights with the wraiths of Hell-Town, I could feel everybody's awareness of me. I might just as well have been a spill of ink in a pool. I was about as welcome as a sullen log on a slow smoldering fire.

All the same, each bar, like each hearth, had, as I had observed through working a few, something like the same hitches to their habits. The log that smokes up one fireplace gets another ablaze, and the mixture of my depression, my good store of adrenaline at being followed, plus the company of manic, anxious haunts I doubtless carried in my hair soon put The Brig in a roaring mood. People who had been expiring at their own tables got up and moved to others. Dudes and their old ladies who had hardly been speaking began to feel the rosy itch. And I, who in this hour may have been closeted with horror more than anyone there—winters in Provincetown can be named by whose year it is for that—took the credit to myself for such kindling, although I did no more than nod to a face in my path and take up an insular position by the bar.

Pete the Polack was the first to approach, and we had a short conversation that came near to twisting my neck on its bearings. "Hey," he began, "I been talking to your wife."

"Today?"

He took a while replying. My dry throat had a little difficulty managing to ask the question, and by then he was in the middle of slugging down his beer. Besides, his mind had already disconnected as well. That happened often in The Brig. People would start conversations, and their brains, particularly on beer and speed, would veer off like waterbugs.

"Today," said Pete, "no. Couple of days ago."

"When?"

He waved his hand. "Couple of days." He could as well have said, "A couple of weeks ago." I had noticed that winter people kept constant intervals for time. Something could have happened two weeks ago, or two nights ago, but if it was your habit to say, "Five days ago," then that was how you would remember it. So I pushed him no further. Instead I returned to the topic.

"What did Patty want to talk to you about?"

"Oh, yeah. Hey. She wants me to look after the big house on the hill in the West End."

"The one she's thinking of buying?"

"That's what she said."

"Wants *you* to look after it?"

"Well, me and my brother."

It made sense. The brother was a good carpenter. In effect, Pete was saying that his brother would take care of the place. Patty might have asked Pete to contact him.

I knew it was stupid, but I had to ask. "Can you remember if you talked to her before or after the Patriots game?"

"Oh, yeah, that game." He nodded profoundly. The speed was taking him somewhere deep. He pondered—whatever it was—the game, the date, the money in his back pocket, then he shook his head. "About two days ago."

"Yeah," I said, "figures."

Beth Nissen slipped up to us. She was drunk, which was rare for her, and she was animated, which was even more unusual.

"What did you do to Spider?" she asked me.

"Hey, honey," Pete said, "old hassles is old hassles. I got to move on." He bent over, kissed her sweater where her nipple ought to have been and took his beer down the road to a table.

"Is Spider truly hassled?" I asked.

"Who knows?" Her eyes turned starry. "Spider is crazy."

"Well, we all are," I said.

"Don't you believe that you and I are crazy in a special way?" she said.

"How?"

"We've never fucked each other."

That was par for winter. I made a point of laughing and put my arm around her waist, and her pale eyes stared out from behind her eyeglasses with a far-gone electric glow.

"Spider lost his knife," said Beth, "and claims you stole it." She giggled as if Spider without his knife was like another man without his pants. "He lost his motorcycle, too," she said. "Did you tell him the Patriots were going to win?"

"At half time."

"Well, they did win," said Beth. "But at half time, he decided to reverse his bet. Said he was going against you. Now he says it's your fault he lost his motorcycle."

"Tell Spider to stick it up his giggie."

She giggled. "In the Midwest," she said, "we used to say 'giggie.' I think I'll send a letter to my parents and tell them their daughter can no longer distinguish her pussy from her giggie." She hiccuped. "I'm not going to tell Spider anything," she said. "He's in a terrible mood. After all, why not?" she asked. " 'The worst are filled with a passionate intensity,' right?" She gave me an outsize lewd look.

"How's Stoodie?" I asked.

"Oh," she said, "watch out for Stoodie."

"Why?" I asked.

"Oh," she said, "I tell everybody to watch out for Stoodie."

I could not decide whether it was due to the constant flashes I kept having of a blonde head in a dark plastic bag, but every word I heard seemed connected to my own situation. Was there a real fever in the air? No one but myself and—I must pray—someone else knew what had been buried in my marijuana patch, yet this thought was all but shrieking out of every cry for beer from every table. I suppose the spirits were tugging at the beer-drenched sponge of whatever collective mind was here.

Beth saw my look wander away from her. "Is Patty Lareine still split?" she asked.

I shrugged. "I hear she's been around."

"I think she is. Bolo is back in town."

"You saw him?" Bolo was Mr. Black, although indeed his name was Green. Joseph "Bolo" Green. He got the name Bolo on the first day he walked into a bar here. "There are bad niggers," he announced to a table of ten of us, "but I am *baaaaad*," and everybody was silent for a moment as if paying respect to the dead he had left behind—we are the Wild West of the East!—but Patty Lareine began to laugh and said, "Stop waving your bolo. Nobody is going to steal your *black*." By the look of pure happiness in her eyes, I could see that the next Mr. Black had just been anointed.

"Yes," said Beth, bringing me back to her—I, too, had a mind that could veer like a waterbug—"Bolo is certainly back in town. He was in and out of The Brig ten minutes ago."

"Did you talk to him?"

"He propositioned me."

I would have been certain she was lying if she had not looked so happy.

Now the bartender was signaling as well. He pointed to the phone behind his service sink.

My extrasensory attainments failed me on this occasion. I thought I was going to hear Patty's voice, but it was Harpo.

"Mac," he said, "I've been trying to get you. I had to force myself to call you."

"Why?"

"Because I betrayed you."

"How could you do that?"

"I lost my nerve. I want to warn you."

Harpo's speech had a metallic anxiety. He sounded as if he were speaking out of a mechanical diaphragm. I tried to decide what he might be on, but there must have been many chemicals in his brain.

"It's Laurel," he now said.

"The tattoo?"

"The woman. *Laurel.* I called up Police Chief Regency and told him about her *and* the tattoo."

That could have no significance for Regency, I decided. Not unless Patty Lareine, when in his company, spoke of Madeleine as Laurel.

"Great," I said, "Alvin now knows I have a tattoo. Where's the treachery?"

"I told him that Laurel was waiting for you in the car downstairs."

"But why do you think the name is Laurel?"

"You spoke to her. Through my window."

"I did?"

"That's what you shouted. 'I'm going to win this bet, Laurel.' That's what you said."

"I may have said Lonnie. I think I was yelling to a man."

"No, it was Laurel. I heard the name. I believe that Laurel is dead."

"Who told you?"

"I was up on the roof. I heard it. That's why I called the Chief. I knew I shouldn't have given you the tattoo. People do terrible things after a tattoo."

"What else did you tell Regency?"

"I said I thought you killed Laurel." He began to cry.

"How can you believe that?" I asked.

"I saw Laurel dead. When I stood on the roof last night, I saw her on the horizon. She said you did it." I heard him blowing his nose at the other end of the phone. "I wrestled with my conscience. Then I called Regency. It was the wrong thing to do. I should have spoken to you first."

"What did Regency say?"

"He's an asshole! He's a bureaucrat. He said he wanted to take it under consideration. Mac, I don't trust him."

"Yeah," I said, "it's me you trust."

"Well, I realized you didn't do anything. I could tell by the sound of Regency's voice. It wasn't right."

"I'm happy to hear that."

His breathing got heavy. Over the wire, I could feel his senses rattling. "I may not have the right to say who killed her," he added, "but now I know."

"It's Nissen," I said.

"I hate Spider's knife," said Harpo. "A vicious instrument." With that, he hung up.

A hand was tapping me on the shoulder. I turned around to stare into Bolo's golden-brown eyes blazing into mine with all the light of a lion. He was deep-black in color, purple-black like an African, so his eyes were disconcertingly golden. I had known from the moment I first saw him that he was going to be no good news for my marriage. I was right. There had been three earlier models, but Mr. Green proved to be the definitive Mr. Black. After all, Patty Lareine had never left me before.

The worst was that now I could not feel any hatred for him, not even some rage at my drear and cuckolded state. The proof was that he could come up to me while I was on the phone, even lay his hand on me, and I, in reply, merely gave a nod.

Of course, I might as well have been lifted by a helicopter from the summit of one peak to the next. I had none of the bother of descending through the scree to the canyon floor and up the other ridge, no, I had gone directly from a number of remarks by Harpo (each capable of blasting me off my mind) to the lights in Bolo's eyes, and by now I might as well have been stuffed with Novocaine, just so far did I feel removed from this overabundance of stimulations—yes, it had all caught up, and I was one candidate who could call himself Mr. Marble Eyes, totally zonked and zombied by the quick turns of the race course this evening, except that at this moment Mr. Green put his hand on my shoulder again and dug his fingers in—viciously, I tell you—and said, "Where the fuck is Patty Lareine?," all of his fury passing into me. With that, I woke up and shook off his hand with an equally violent move, and replied, "Get your filthy lunch hooks off of me," words that came right out of an old high school fracas. But for the first time, I was not afraid of him. I didn't care if we went out to the street and had a fight. The thought of being knocked cold was an anodyne dear as nepenthe.

Let me say there was little doubt in my mind what he could do to me. If you have ever been in an interesting penitentiary, you come to know that there are blacks and blacks, and a few you never mess with. Mr. Green was not on that high shelf, or I would have been dead. But he could fit on the second level: mess with him under few circumstances. Now his eyes glared into mine and I looked back, and the light in the room turned red between us—I mean it literally—I do not know if his rage on meeting mine was so intense that the nerves which reflect color to the brain were strained by the voltage passed through or if all the firebrands of Hell-Town raced toward us, but I had to stand in the considerable wrath of all that had happened to him over his last twenty-five years (from the first cuff in the cradle) and he stood in the maniacal disproportion of all that had been happening to me. I think it was dazzling to both of us to endure for even a little while in such a hellish red light. Indeed, we both stood there looking at each other for so long that I had time to remember the sad tale of his life as he told it to Patty Lareine and me on the night we met: it was how he lost his boxing career.

If it strains belief that I could think of such a story while the steam of his madness was scalding my eyes—well, I can hardly believe it myself. Maybe I was not as brave as I pretended and clung to his tale in the hope that it would mollify his rage. You cannot strike a man who is filled with compassion for you.

This was the story: He was illegitimate, and his mother claimed he wasn't hers. Said they messed up the name tags in the hospital. She used to beat him every day. When he got older, he beat everybody he faced in the Golden Gloves. He was in line to make the U.S. team for the Pan-American games, but he went down to Georgia to look for his father. Never found him. Went into a white bar dead drunk. They wouldn't serve him. They called the State Troopers. Two came in, and asked him to leave.

"You got no alternative," he informed them. "Serve me, or piss on you."

One of the troopers hit him so hard with a billy club that he began to lose the Pan-American games right there. But he didn't know it yet. Just felt a great happiness. Because he was bleeding as if he had been butchered, but he wasn't shook. In fact, he was wide awake. He proceeded to injure both cops and it took the entire bar to subdue him. They brought him in restraints to the jail house. Among other things, his skull was fractured. He could box no more.

That was the sad tale he told. He related it as an example of his stupidity, not his valor (although it had the opposite effect on Patty) and when we came to know him better, he proved to be a funny man. He used to do imitations of black whores to make us laugh. We saw a lot of Mr. Green, and I would lend him money.

Will it give you an idea of how close I felt to annihilation, and how comfortable this idea had become (after all the rat-scurry of keeping myself alive) that I could now recognize that Bolo had not treated me so badly as I had treated Wardley. The remains of my rage began to fade and a peace came in to replace it. I do not know what Mr. Green was thinking of, but even as my anger departed, so did his. "Well," I said, making my offering to the silence, "what do you say, motherfucker?"

"I never had a mother to fuck," he replied. Sadly, he held out his hand for five. Sadly, I tapped it.

"I don't know where Patty Lareine is," I said.

"You aren't looking for her?"

"No."

"I'm looking for her, and I can't find her."

"When did she leave you?"

He frowned. "We had it on together for three weeks. Then she got restless. Took off."

"Where were you?"

"In Tampa."

"Did you see her ex-husband?"

"Wardley, is that the guy?"

I nodded.

"We saw him. He took us out to dinner one night. Then she went to see him alone. That was cool. He was no threat. I figured she was hitting on him for something good. But the next day she took off." He looked like he was about to cry. "She treated me decent. She was the only bitch ever treated me that decent." He looked very sad. "I just ran out of things to talk to her about. Used them up." His eyes studied mine. "You know where she is? I got to find her."

"She may be around."

"She is."

"How do you know?"

"A guy called me. The guy said Patty Lareine told him to call. She wanted me to know. She was back here in P-town with Wardley. She missed me, the fellow said."

"Who was the fellow?"

"Didn't give his name. He gave it, but there's nobody by that name. I knew it was no good when he gave it. He was talking with a handkerchief over the phone."

"What was the name?"

"Healey. Austin Healey."

A mote of town lore came back. A couple of years ago a few of us, tired of the sound of Stoodie, began to speak of him as Austin Healey. That went on for a little while. But Stoodie was not told our name for him. It had to be Spider who called.

"This Healey said Patty L. was at the Provincetown Inn," Bolo said. "I called there. Shit, she wasn't nowhere near a place like that."

"When did you get back?"

"Three days ago."

"When did she leave you?"

"One week ago, about."

"Seven days for sure?"

"Eight. I counted them."

Yes, he was counting his days. I was counting mine.

"I could kill her," he said, "for leaving me."

"There's no man she won't leave," I said. "She comes from a narrow background. It's sin to her."

"I'm just as narrow as she is," he said, "and I'm going to take a big hit on something when I see her." He looked at me from an angle as if to say, "You can hustle others, but, baby, get trustworthy with me."

Then he put his doubts away. He would tell. "Austin Healey said Patty Lareine was seeing you again. When I heard that, I figured I would have to treat you to a welcome." He paused to let me feel the weight of the thought. "But I knew I couldn't do it to you."

"Why?"

"Because you treated me like a gentleman."

He measured the truth of this and seemed to agree with himself. "Moreover," he said, "Patty Lareine don't like you anymore."

"Probably not."

"She said you trapped her into marriage."

I began to laugh.

"What are you laughing about, honkie?"

"Mr. Green, there's an old Jewish saying: 'A life, a wife!' "

He, too, began to laugh.

We went on long enough to draw attention to ourselves. History was being made in The Brig tonight. The cuckold and the black lover were having a big time together.

"Joseph, I'll see you around," I said to Bolo Green.

"Keep the peace."

I had to take a long walk. More had come into my head than I could put in order.

It was drizzling, and I was walking down Commercial Street with my hands in my pockets and my head so withdrawn into my parka hood that I did not become aware that a car was following me until the headlights on my back could no longer be ignored. I turned. Behind me was a police cruiser with one man in it. He opened the door. "Get in," he said. Regency, at my service.

We had not driven fifty feet before he began to talk. "Got a make on your woman, Jessica," he said. He pointed to a piece of paper on the front seat. "Take a look," he told me and handed over a pencil flashlight that he drew from his breast pocket.

I studied a photostat of a photograph sent by wire. It was Jessica clearly enough. "I'd say that's her."

"Well, we don't need you to inform us, pal. There's no doubt. The waitress and the proprietor at The Widow's Walk have both confirmed."

"Good work," I said. "How did you track her down?"

"No big deal. We contacted Pangborn's office in Santa Barbara and there were a couple of blondes he associated with socially or business-

wise. We were looking into that when her son called. He knew she was
in Provincetown with Pangborn—as you might guess from Don Lon's
little billet-doux."

"You're speaking of the son who was Lonnie's lover?"

"Correct," said Regency. "The kid with the cordless razor." He
opened his window and hawked a throaty yield. "I think I'll never watch
a commercial again."

"You may not."

"Now, here, Madden, is where the soup starts to stick to the spoon.
It seems her name isn't Jessica."

"What is the real name?"

"Laurel Oakwode. It's a fancy spelling: w-o-d-e for 'wood.' "

Recollection came back to me of what I had said to Harpo before the
séance that ended with Nissen's scream. "Harpo," I had said, "tell everybody we're trying to reach Mary Hardwood, who is my mother's cousin.
But the woman I really want to talk to is named Laurel."

Such a coincidence could not have been produced by a beeper. Despite myself, I began to shiver. Sitting beside Regency in the police car,
cruising fifteen miles an hour down Commerical Street, I began to
shiver visibly.

"You need a drink," said Alvin Luther.

"It's all right," I said.

"Maybe you'd be in better shape," he suggested, "if the tattoo on
your arm didn't say 'Laurel.' "

"Do you want to stop the car?"

"No objection at all."

We were at the end of Commercial Street. We had come to the place
where the Pilgrims once landed, but in the drizzle, I could see nothing.

"Okay," he said, "get out."

My panic had subsided. The thought of walking two and a half miles
home with no more than this amputated encounter for company encouraged me to take a chance.

"I don't know what point you're trying to make," I said, "but it's no
big deal to me. I got shit-face and drove out to see Harpo, and had him
put on a tattoo. Maybe Jessica told me that her real name was Laurel,
but I don't remember."

"Was she with you?"

I had to make a decision. "Harpo says she was."

"You're saying you can't remember?"

"Not clearly."

"So you could have knocked her off, and forgotten it?"

"Are you accusing me?"

"Let us say that I am working on the outline of the first scenario. In my way, I'm a writer too." He could not restrain himself. The wild stallion gave his great neigh and whinny.

"I don't like the way you're talking."

"Hey, pal," said Regency, "kidding is kidding, but get your ass off my pillow. I could take you in right now."

"On what? There's no crime. The lady might be on her way back to Santa Barbara. You're not about to hurt your record with a false arrest."

"Let me rephrase myself," he said. "I could take you in right now as a suspect in the possible murder of Leonard Pangborn."

"You said it was a suicide."

"So I thought. But the forensics have taken a look. They came in on a special from Boston at our request. The supercoroners, they like to be called, but my private tag for them is: the supercoronaries." Once again he laughed at his own joke. "They mess up your heartbeat considerably with what they find."

"What did they find?"

"I'll tell you. It's going to be no secret very soon. Pangborn may have killed himself, but if he did, who drove the car?"

"You told me that he got into the trunk and closed the lid on himself before he fired the shot."

"The congealed blood on the floor of the trunk has a shirred movement as if, soon after it began to coagulate, the car was driven, from wherever the event occurred, to The Widow's Walk."

"Wouldn't the staff at the restaurant have heard the car come back?"

"Not if it was three in the morning. They wouldn't be around. Look, let's not argue. The car was moved. The patterns of the blood show that it was." He shrugged. "What it comes down to, Madden, is that somebody drove this vehicle back to The Widow's Walk after Lonnie committed suicide."

"Could Jessica have done that?"

"Yes, Laurel Oakwode certainly could. Let me ask: Did you bang her?"

"I believe I did."

He whistled. "God, is your head a mess. You can't even remember that?"

"What bothers me is I believe I did it in front of Lonnie Pangborn."

"I hate to quote a nigger, but Cassius Clay said it: 'You ain't as dumb as you look.' "

"What do you mean?"

"Don't let my praise linger in your mouth." He lit a cigar and puffed on it like it was a Bangalore Torpedo. "Madden, you have just given me *your* scenario. One: You bang Jessica in front of Lonnie. Two: You wipe your cock and walk off. Three: Jessica comforts Lonnie. Four: He starts to complain: 'Us faggots are not built for such competition.' He hides in the trunk. Bang! He's left her a gift—his body. These gay people can be spiteful. Well, she's a respectable cunt and doesn't want publicity. So she drives back to The Widow's Walk, leaves the car and starts home to Santa Barbara." He nodded his head. "It holds up beautifully if—One: You can find where she slept that night, although I'll tell you in advance to save part of your lawyers' fees that you can always claim she walked back to your house and slept in tears on your sofa. Unless you gave her your bed." He opened his window and threw the cigar away. "Two: She must, when she shows up, be alive, and corroborate your story. You have to pray she doesn't come back to us as a corpse in these dunes and woods."

"You've done some thinking on this."

I had hoped to stroke him. He merely nodded. "Let me give you another scenario. You and she and Pangborn go out to Wellfleet in your car. On the way back Lonnie can't stand losing her, so he waves his pistol at you. You stop the car and wrestle his shooter away. In the fracas, she gets shot. Mortally. You leave her in the woods and drive him to his car, make him get into the trunk—he's limp as a worm by now. Then you drive away to a quiet place, open the trunk, lay the barrel in his throat, say sweetly, 'I'll never hurt you, Lonnie, this is only fun and games. This is how I get my kinks out. Kiss the barrel for me, Lonnie.' Then you pull the trigger, do a little wiping and leave his finger on it. Next, you drive the car back to The Widow's Walk, get back in your car, go to the woods again and dispose of her body. Son, you do it all except you forget to wipe your front seat. As my wife says, 'Nobody's perfect.' Neither am I. I let you get away with blood on the front seat. I'm a hick and trust my friends. Yes," he said, "you better hope and pray her body doesn't show up. I'll be the first one after you because I bought the story about the nose bleed."

"Well," I said, "why don't you take me in now?"

"Figure it out."

"You have no case. If she was shot at close quarters in my car, her blood would have been all over his clothing."

"Maybe you're right. Let's have a drink."

Nothing could have been more unsatisfactory. The last thing I wanted was to drink with him. But he started up the car, began to whistle "Stardust" and took off in a spray of road sand and rubber.

I thought we'd go to the VFW bar, for it was his favorite place to have a few, but instead he turned in at Town Hall and walked me down the basement corridor to his office where he pointed to a chair and took out a bottle of bourbon. I assumed we had come here to serve some of the recording equipment he kept in his desk.

"I figured I'd show you the amenities of this place," Regency said, "before you have to use the jail."

"Can we talk about something else?"

He grinned. "Name your topic."

"Where's my wife?"

"I was hoping *you* could tell me."

"I talked to the fellow she ran off with. She left him eight days ago. I believe his story."

Regency said, "That checks."

"With what?"

"According to Laurel Oakwode's son—his name, by the way, is also Leonard, but they call him Sonny, Sonny Oakwode—Patty Lareine was in Santa Barbara seven nights ago."

"I didn't know that."

"Yes, she was there with this fellow Wardley."

I had never known exactly what was meant by the remark: *I could not part my lips.* Now I knew.

"Good bourbon?"

I gave one mute nod.

"Yes, she was in Santa Barbara with Wardley and they had dinner with Laurel Oakwode and Leonard Pangborn at Lonnie's beach club. All four of them at one table. Sonny joined them later for coffee."

I still couldn't speak.

"Want to know what they talked about?"

I nodded.

"I need some input from you a little later."

I nodded.

"Good. According to what I get from Sonny . . ." Here he stopped to remark, "By the way, on the phone Sonny doesn't sound like a cocksucker. Do you think Pangborn was lying in that letter?"

I drew a question mark with my finger.

"But Pangborn didn't seem gay to you?"

I shook my head.

"I can't believe how much of life," he said, "is in the closet. God, you or I could be queer."

"Whatever you say, dear," I lisped.

He took that as a big laugh. I was glad to get my voice out under any auspices. Being speechless is a shock one does much to get out of.

We each took a sip of bourbon.

"Want some pot?" asked Regency.

"No."

"Mind if I smoke?"

"Aren't you afraid of being caught in your office?"

"By whom? I'm trying to put a suspect at his ease, that's all." Now, he did take out a stick of pot, and he did light it.

"Beautiful," I said.

"Yeah." He exhaled. "There's a joke in every toke."

"Yessir."

"Madden, what I hear from Sonny is that Pangborn and Laurel were to fly to Boston, drive to P-town and pretend to be tourists in love with the Paramessides estate."

"Is that the name of it?"

"Yeah. Some Greek fronting for Arabs bought it a few years ago. Now Wardley wanted to buy it for Patty. That's what they talked about at dinner."

He took another toke.

"They were talking of getting married again," he said.

"Immense." I think I was contact-high from the smoke.

"Do you know why Patty wanted the place?" asked Regency.

"She never told me."

"According to Sonny, she's had her eye on the estate for a year. Ward-

ley wanted to buy it for her the way Richard Burton used to buy Elizabeth Taylor a diamond."

"Isn't such news upsetting to you?" I asked.

"What do you mean?"

"Haven't you and Patty Lareine been getting your fingers in the jam
together?"

If we had been boxers, I would have said to myself, This is the first
punch he has to acknowledge. He blinked, and an aura of spacy rage
came off him. That's the only way I can describe it—as if the cosmos
had been poked and now was cranking up an electric storm.

"Hey, hey," he said. "Tell you what, buster. Ask me no questions
about your wife, and I won't ask about mine."

The stick of marijuana was burning close to his knuckles. "I think I
will have a toke," I said.

"Nothing to hide, eh?"

"No more than you, maybe."

He handed over the roach and I took a pull from the ember.

"Okay," he said, "tell me what you and Wardley talked about this
afternoon."

"How do you know we met?"

"Can you begin to conceive how many informants I have in town?
This phone," he bragged, tapping it, "is a marketplace."

"What do you sell?" I asked.

"I sell the deletion of names from rap sheets," he said. "I sell the
quashing of petty indictments. Madden, go fuck yourself, and when you
come all over your jockey shorts, get right down here with the real folks
and tell your friend Alvin what Wardley said on the beach today."

"Suppose I don't?"

"It will be worse than a society divorce in Tampa."

"You figure you can beat me in a pissing contest?"

"I work harder."

I found that I wanted to tell him. Not because I was afraid (you are
too far gone, the marijuana was telling me, to fear any man) but because
I was curious. I wanted to know what he would make of it. "Wardley,"
I said, "told me that he and Patty Lareine were in competition to buy
the house."

Regency whistled. "Wardley is planning to double-cross Patty Lareine or you." He weighed options at a great rate in his mind like a computer going zippity-click-dick-pick, and said, "Maybe he wants both of you."

"He has cause."

"Would you mind telling me why?"

"When we were all back in Tampa years ago, Patty Lareine wanted me to off him."

"You don't say."

"What are you coy about?" I asked. "Didn't she ever tell you?"

He had his weak spot. No question. He wasn't certain how to deal with remarks about Patty. "It's not clear what you're referring to," he said at last.

"Pass," I said.

That was a mistake. He picked up momentum immediately. "What else did you and Wardley talk about?"

I didn't know whether to tell him or not. It had occurred to me that Wardley might have tape-recorded our conversation on the beach. Cleverly edited, it could leave me looking as if I were up-for-sale on a murder job. "Wardley was concerned," I said, "that Pangborn was dead, and he was curious why Jessica had disappeared. He kept saying that now he would have to bid on the house directly and that was going to drive up the price."

"Did he indicate where Patty Lareine might be?"

"He wanted me to try to find her."

"What did he offer?"

"Money."

"How much?"

Why protect Wardley? I was wondering. Was it my vestigial family prejudice against talking to cops? Then I thought of the beeper. "Two million," I said.

"Did you believe him?"

"No."

"Was it an offer to kill her?"

"Yes."

"Will you testify to that?"

"No."

"Why not?"

"I'm not sure he was serious. In any event, I didn't agree. As I found out in Tampa, when it comes to contracting for a hit, I'm a wet fire-cracker."

"Where can I find Wardley?"

I smiled. "Why don't you ask a couple of your informants?"

"Which ones?"

"The ones in the brown van."

He nodded as if I had made a good move in a chess game. "I'll tell you what," he said, "they don't know. He just meets them here and there."

"What is he driving?"

"He talks to them by CB radio. Then he meets them. He just walks up to them. Then he walks away."

"You believe that?"

"Well, I haven't shaken them so hard that their teeth rattle."

"Why not?"

"You get a bad reputation bruising informants. Besides, I believe them. Wardley *would* behave that way. He wants people to think he's a class act."

"Maybe you're not very concerned to find out where Patty is."

He made an elaborate to-do about showing his cool. He took the roach and pinched it out with his thumb, rolled it into a small ball of paper and popped it into his throat. No evidence, said his smile. "I'm not hungry," he said. "Your wife will show up intact."

"Are you positive? I'm not."

"We have to wait," he said mildly.

I wondered how much he was lying about, and how deep were the lies. Nothing came off him but a hint of the void. I took another sip of the bourbon. It did not go with the marijuana.

He seemed to like the combination, however. He took out another stick and lit it. "Murders are damnable," he said. "Once in a while you get a case that leaves its roots in you."

I had no idea what he was up to. I took the marijuana he offered and pulled in some smoke, handed it back.

"There was one case," he said, "of a good-looking bachelor who would pick up a girl and get her to go to a motel with him. He would make love to her, and convince her to spread her legs while he took Polaroids. Then he would kill her. Next, he'd take another photograph. Before and after. After which he would decamp, leaving the girl in the bed. You know how he got caught? He used to put his photographs into an album. A page for each lady. His mother was a jealous watchdog, so she broke the lock on the album. When she saw the contents, she fainted. When she came to, she called the authorities."

"Why do you tell this story?"

"Because it turns me on. I'm a law enforcement officer and it turns me on. Every good psychiatrist has a touch of the psycho in him, and you can't be a good cop without sitting on a kettle of potential monstrosities in yourself. Does my story turn you on?"

"You didn't tell it well enough."

"Ho, ho, wouldn't a good DA love to get you on the witness stand."

"I want to go now," I said.

"Can I drive you?"

"Thank you. I'll walk."

"I didn't mean to upset you."

"You didn't."

"I have to tell you. That guy with the Polaroids interests me. There's something in the nitty-gritty that he is close to."

"I'm sure," I said.

"Sayonara," said Regency.

On the street, I began to shiver all over again. Most of it was simple relief. For the last hour I might as well have been touching every word I uttered. They had all had to be put into position. It was natural to feel relief at getting out of his office. But I hated his intelligence. The story he told *had* turned me on. One tickle down at the core.

What had he been trying to communicate? I recollected nude Polaroids I had taken of Madeleine years ago and of Patty Lareine not so long ago. They were hidden somewhere in my study like fish nibbling on the reef. I felt a mean sense of possession at the very thought of their existence. It was as if I held the key to some dungeons. I began to ask myself again: Was I the bloody dispatcher?

I cannot describe how much revulsion came to me then. I was physically ill. The marijuana magnified the spasms of my throat until they were near to orgasmic in the power of their heaves. Up from the esophagus came bile and bourbon and whatever little food had been in me, and I bent over a fence and left this misery on a neighbor's lawn. One could hope the rain would absolve me.

Yes, I had been like a man half crushed beneath a rock who by the most extraordinary exertion against the pain has just managed to extricate his body. Then the weight topples over on him again.

I knew why I had thrown up. I had to go back to the burrow. "Oh, no," I whispered to myself, "it's empty!" But I did not know. Some instinct in myself, powerful as Hell-Town, told me to go back. If the killer, as we would have it, always returns to the scene of the crime, then some switch may have been thrown, for I was convinced that the only way I could demonstrate to myself for another night that I was not guilty of slaughter was to go back. If I did not return, I was guilty. Such was the logic, and it grew so powerful that by the time I reached my home it was for no more pressing purpose than to get the keys to my Porsche. I began to prepare, as I had before, all the mental concomitants of this trip: the highway, the country road, the humpbacked sand road—and I saw in advance the puddles that would be forming in the hollows with this rain, then the trail, the moss-covered stone by the burrow. I even saw, by way of my imagination, a plastic bag revealed by my flashlight. It was as far as I could go in my thoughts. Prepared, now, as well as I could make myself, I was about to depart, when the dog began to lick my fingers. It was his first sign of affection in four days. So I took him along. Practical reasons came to me with the flat thrust of his big tongue on my palm: he could certainly be of use. For if there was nothing in the burrow, who was to say that nothing was buried nearby? His nose could bring us to it.

Yet I confess that the old smelly reek of the dog so assailed my tender stomach that I had a second impulse not to take him. He was, however, already in the car, as solemn as a soldier going to the front, one big black Labrador. (His name, by the way, was Stunts, bestowed on him because he was too dumb to learn any.)

We set out. He sat beside me in the bucket seat, his nose pointed to the window, and with equal solemnity we drove. It was only when I was more than halfway to the turnoff in Truro that I remembered the beeper. The thought that I was still being followed stirred a rage in me. I pulled the car over to the highway shoulder, parked, removed the little box and laid it in a shallow trench at the foot of the mileage marker. Then we went on.

I see no need to describe the rest of the drive. It became as hesitant as the ones before, and the closer I came over the last sandy road, the less of my foot I gave to the pedal, until I began to stall, first once, then twice. The last was in a puddle, and I had a fear, intimate as the passing of a ghost, that I could not start the car again. During Colonial times, there had been a gallows at a clearing in these woods, and through the drizzle, every overhanging branch looked to have a man dangling from it. I do not know who was more deranged by the effort, the dog or myself. He whimpered steadily in a dying plaint as if his paw were caught in a trap.

I blundered down the trail holding a flashlight, and the mist was so heavy, my face felt washed in froth. The dog kept his shoulder against my thigh until the last few yards before the twisted dwarf pine, where-upon he began to run ahead, his voice now raised in a mixture of elation and fright as if, like us, he could call upon two deep and divided halves of himself. Indeed, he never sounded more human than with his throat coming forth in these cries of pleasure and wheezes of panic. I had to hold him back, or he would have scraped the moss from the stone at the burrow.

Yet when I drew the rock away, he gave a little moan. It was equal to the sound I might have made, for I did not wish to look. Then I could bear it no longer. The flashlight revealed a black and slimy plastic bag over which bugs crawled, and in a lathering of my own sweat, with fingers that shook as if they were being touched by spirits, I invaded the domain of the burrow—so it felt!—reached in, pulled out the bag. It was heavier than expected. I will spare you how long it took me to untie the knot, but I did not dare to rip my way inside, as if the rivulets of Hell-Town might well forth from such a tear.

At last the knot came apart. I lifted the flashlight and looked at the face of my wife. A pistol might as well have fired through the fabric of a thousand nights of sleep. My wife bore a look of consternation on her face, and showed a red jungle at the base of her neck. I took one look, could not take another, closed the bag. I knew in that instant that I had a soul. I felt it turn in my heart even as my fingers retied the knot at the top of the bag.

I stood up to leave then, swaying on one foot, then the other. I did not know if I could move. Nor could I decide whether to take her with me or whether I was obliged to let her rest in this foul place. As the swoon of my will continued, the dog ceased whimpering, stirred about, and began to push his head and shoulders into the burrow, pushed farther, and, on an instant, all of his movements reversed and he came out backward, dragging the end of a green plastic bag in his mouth. Now I saw the face of Jessica Pond. I could not call her Laurel Oak-wode.

Will it sound strange to you that I picked up both heads and carried them back to the car? One bag was in each hand, and I laid them in the trunk with some care not to confound whatever veils of death still adhered—how poor a shroud is a plastic bag! The dog walked with me like a mourner, and the trees on either side of the trail offered silence. The sound of the Porsche motor starting up was as loud as an explosion in that pall.

We drove out. Since I did not know what I was doing, will it make any more sense to you that I stopped to get the beeper, and when I did, Stoodie and Nissen came up to attack?

Later, when I could puzzle it through, I decided that they must have been following my car until the moment when I detached their instrument. Then they must have waited for a while. Then they must have driven to where they thought I was parked but found no car, no house, only the sound of the beeper tantalizing them. It was off the road, but where they could not quite determine. So they parked, and waited.

I only saw them coming after I stood up in the trench by the mile-stone marker with the beeper in my hand. By then they were moving toward me on a run. I remember thinking that they wanted to recover what I had stolen from the burrow—that is the indication of where my mind had gone. There is this to be said for madness: your blood can pass from one transcendental moment to another without fear. I think, now that I consider it, they were befouled with rage after all the frustration of waiting for their beeper through thirty rain-filled fucked-up minutes. So they were ready to waste me for so misusing their fine technique.

They came down on the dog and me, and Nissen had a knife in his hand and Stoodie a tire iron. The animal and I had never been bound in that compact of dog and man that vows you will die together, but he was with me then.

I could not name the strength that came to us. I had the heads of two blonde ladies to guard in the trunk of my car. Those heads, if I were found with them, had to be worth two hundred years of incarceration, and that gave the strength to fight. My lunacy gave more. For by the exaltation of its logic, I was transporting my ladies from a foul grave to a finer one.

So my rage was near to maniacal. It had packed itself like gunpowder these last five days into my head and limbs. The sight of Spider and Stoodie approaching with menace was as good as cocking a trigger. I remember how the dog stood at attention beside me, his fur stiff like steel nails. Then it all happened and was over for him. I do not know if it took even ten seconds, but the dog sprang at Nissen and caught Spider's face and throat in his jaws. He also caught the point of Spider's knife in his heart and died on top of Spider, who shrieked and ran away, holding his face. Stoodie and I took longer.

He circled, looking to swing his iron, and I kept away, ready to hurl my beeper—it was my beeper now—at his head, but the instrument weighed no more than a small rock.

Rage or no, I wasn't in shape to fight. My heart was burning already, and I could never match the tire iron. I had to catch him one perfect right shot to the jaw—my left would never be good enough—and for that I had to wait until he swung the iron. There is no other course when fighting a tire iron but to get the opponent to commit himself. You can only strike after the weapon goes by. Stoodie knew this. He lashed the iron back and forth and committed himself to no full swings. He would wait. Let me come undone from the tension. Stoodie waited, and we circled, and I could hear my breathing louder than his. Then I hurled the beeper and it struck him on the head. I threw my right after it, but only caught his nose, not his chin, and he brought the iron down on my left arm. He was off-balance, and so it was not with whole force, but my arm was dead and I was in such pain I barely dodged his next swing. Now he lashed the air again as the blood from his nose went into his mouth, and bones in his face, it came to him, were broken.

He swung again. I ducked, grabbed two handfuls of roadside pebbles and threw them in his face. Blinded, he brought one huge swing down on me, and I skipped to the side and threw my right as hard as I ever hit anything, a thunderbolt went down my arm, and he and his iron fell together. Then I made the mistake of kicking him in the head. That broke my big toe. Be it said for the new pain that it kept me from beating on his skull with the tire iron. Picking that up, I hobbled down the road to the van. Spider was leaning against it, his head in his hands, moaning, and I knew the joys of going berserk. With the tire iron I smashed in his windows, his headlights, his taillights, and then, not content, tried to pry one of the doors off, but failing that, sprung the hinge at least.

Spider watched, and said at the finish, "Hey, man, have a heart. I need medical attention."

"Why did you say I stole your knife?" I answered him.

"Somebody did. I got a new one that's no fucking good."

"It's in my dog."

"I'm sorry, man. I got nothing against your dog."

It was as fractured as that. I left him by the van, walked carefully around Stoodie so that I would not turn the iron on him, knelt by Stunts, who had died near the Porsche, his favorite chariot, and managed with my good arm to get him into the front seat.

Then I drove home.

Shall I tell you the virtues of such a war? I held myself together long enough to take both plastic bags down to the basement, where I laid them in a carton. (I have not yet spoken of this, but their odor in another twenty-four hours would be a disaster.) Then I dug a grave in the yard for my dog and buried him, doing it all with one good arm and one good foot—the ground in this mist was soft—and then I took a shower and went to bed. If not for the war by the side of the road, I could never have slept and would have been ready for a mental home by morning. As it was, I slumbered as well as any of those who were dead and awoke in the morning to find my father in the house.

Seven

I cannot say that either of us was cheered a good deal by how the other looked. My father was making instant coffee, but at his first sight of me, he put down the jar and whistled softly.

I nodded. I had come downstairs with a swollen foot, a left arm I could not raise above my head, and a bucket of ice water inside my chest. Who knows what circles were beneath my eyes.

Dougy was the greater shock, however. There was almost no hair left on his head and he had lost a lot of weight. High on his cheeks was a fierce pink flush that reminded me of a fire in a windswept place.

The recognition came like a touch of the crud itself. He must be on chemotherapy.

I guess he had become accustomed to the quick wipe from people's eyes of the initial aversion, for he said, "Yeah, I got it."

"Where's it situated?"

He made a gesture to indicate that was neither here nor there.

"Thanks for sending a telegram," I said.

"Kid, when there's nothing anybody can do about your story, keep it to yourself."

He looked weak, which is to say, he did not look all-powerful. I couldn't tell, however, if he was in discomfort.

"Are you on chemotherapy?" I asked.

"I quit it a couple of days ago. The nausea is a disgrace." He walked forward and gave me a little hug, not too close, as if he felt infectious.

"I heard a joke," he said. "This Jewish family is waiting in the hospital lobby. The doctor comes up to them. He's a prosperous son of a bitch with a peppy voice. He choips like a boid." My father liked on occasion to remind me, as he used to remind my mother, that the roots were back in Hell's Kitchen and be damned to you. His snobbery remained unflaggingly inverse, so he would go out of his way to say "boid" for "bird."

Now he could proceed with his joke. " 'I have,' says the doctor, 'good news *and* bad news for you. The bad news is that your father's disease is incurable. The good news is that it is not cancer.' The family says, 'Thank God.' "

We laughed together. When we were done, he handed me his untouched cup of instant coffee and started to spoon himself out another. "Here we have bad news," he said.

"It's incurable?"

"Tim, who the fuck can say? Sometimes I think I know the moment I got it. If I'm that close to the source, maybe I can find my cure. I tell you, I hate those pills the doctors push. I hate myself for taking them."

"How do you sleep?"

"I never been a famous sleeper," he said. Then he nodded. "Kid, I can handle anything but the middle of the night." That was quite a speech for him. He cut it off. "What happened to you?" he asked.

I found myself telling him about the fight.

"Where'd you leave the dog?" he asked.

"Buried him in the yard."

"Before you went to sleep?"

"Yes."

"Somebody raised you right."

We stayed in the kitchen all morning. After I made some eggs, we tried the living room, but Patty's furniture was not for an old longshoreman. Soon we were back in the kitchen. Outside it was another gray day, and looking through the window, he shivered.

"What do you like about this godforsaken place?" he said. "It's like the back coast of Ireland in winter."

"No, I love it," I told him.

"Yeah?"

"The first time I came here was after being kicked out of Exeter. Remember we got drunk?"

"I sure do." It was a pleasure to see him smile.

"Well, in the morning you went back to New York, and I decided to come here for the summer. I'd heard of this town. I liked it right off, and then when I was here a week, I went to a dance joint out near the highway one night. There was a good-looking girl I kept watching, but I didn't go near her. She was with her crowd and dancing. I just kept observing. At closing, I took a shot at it. I went up to her on the dance floor, looked in her eyes, she looked in mine, and we went out the door together. Screw the dudes she was with. They didn't do a thing. So the girl and I crossed the road, went into the woods, lay down, and, Dougy, I was in her. I figure it took six minutes from the time I walked up to her till I was in. That impressed me more about myself than anything I'd done till that day."

He enjoyed my story a good deal. His hand reached out in an old reflex for his tumbler of bourbon and then he realized it wasn't there. "So this place is your luck," he said.

"To a degree."

"Are you all right?" he asked. "For a guy who's just beaten up a hood with a tire iron, you don't look too happy. Are you afraid he'll return?" What a look of happiness came into my father's eyes at the thought that Stoodie might decide to come back.

"There's a lot to talk about," I said, "but I don't know if I'm ready to tell you."

"Have to do with your wife?"

"Some."

"Say, if I was going to be around for another ten years, I wouldn't say a word, but since I won't, I'll tell you. I believe you married the wrong broad. It should have been Madeleine. She may be a vindictive guinea, but I liked her. She had class. She was subtle."

"Is this your blessing?"

"I kept my mouth shut on too many things for too many years. Maybe it started to rot inside. One of the causes of cancer, says the choipy boids, is a harsh environment."

"What do you want to tell me?"

"A guy who marries a rich woman deserves every last thing he gets."

"I thought you liked Patty." They had loved to drink together.

"I liked her guts. If all the other rednecks was as macho as her, they'd be running the world. But I didn't like what she was doing to you.

Certain dames ought to wear a T-shirt that says: 'Hang around. I'll make a cocksucker out of you.' "

"Thanks."

"Hey, Tim—it's a figure of speech. Nothing personal."

"You were always worried about me, weren't you?"

"Well, your mother was delicate. She spoiled you a lot. Yeah," he said, looking at me out of his ice-blue eyes, "I worried about you."

"Maybe you didn't have to. I took my three years in the slammer without a fall. They called me Iron Jaw. I wouldn't take cock."

"Good for you. I always wondered."

"Hey, Dougy," I said, "what's the virtue? You think I feel like a man most of the time? I don't. What was I protecting? You're an old-line fanatic. You'd put all the faggots in concentration camps including your own son if he ever slipped. Just cause you were lucky enough to be born with tiger's balls."

"Let's have a drink. You're off your feed."

"Should you have a drink?"

He made a move with his hands again. "It's an occasion."

I got two glasses and put bourbon in them. He added a considerable amount of water to his. If nothing else, that was enough to tell me he was ill.

"You have me wrong," he said. "Do you think I've been living alone for twenty-five years in a furnished room, and I do no thinking? I try to keep up. In my day, if you were queer, you were damned. Don't even ask. You were an agent of hell. Now, they got Gay Liberation. I watch them. There's faggots everywhere."

"Yeah, I know," I said.

"Ha, ha," he said and pointed a finger at me. The early liquor was obviously doing angel's work on his spirits. "My son wins the round."

"Good at dancing," I said.

"I remember," he said. "Costello, right?"

"Right."

"I'm not sure I know what that means anymore," he said. "Six months ago they told me to stop drinking or I was dead. So I stopped. Now, when I go to sleep, the spirits come out of the woodwork and make a circle around my bed. Then they make me dance all night." He gave a cough filled with all the hollows of his lungs. It had been an attempt to laugh. " 'Tough guys don't dance,' I tell them. 'Hey, you bigot,' the spirits answer, 'keep dancing.' " He looked into the lights of the bourbon as if their kin could be found there, and sighed. "My illness makes me less of a bigot," he said. "I think about faggots and you know what I believe? For half of them, it's brave. For the wimps, it takes more guts to be queer than not. For the wimps. Otherwise they marry some little mouse who's too timid to be a dyke and they both become psychologists and raise whiz kids to play electronic games. Turn queer, I say, if you're a wimp. Have a coming-out party. It's the others I condemn. The ones who ought to be men but couldn't show the moxie. You were supposed to be a man, Tim. You came from me. You had advantages."

"I never heard you talk so much before. Not once in my life."

"That's cause you and I are strangers."

"Well, you look like a stranger today," I said. It was true. His large head was no longer crowned by his rich white hair, white with the corrupt splendors of ivory and cream. Now he just had an enormous bald head. He looked more like a Prussian general than the model of an Irish bartender.

"I want to talk to you now," he said. "I may be acting thick, but it came over me at Frankie Freeload's funeral: Tim is all I got."

I was moved. Sometimes a couple of months would go by, sometimes a half-year, before one of us called. Still, it seemed all right. I had always hoped so. Now he confirmed it.

"Yes," he said, "I got up early this morning, borrowed the widow's car and told myself all the way here that this time we speak it out face to face. I don't want to die without you knowing of my regard for you."

I was embarrassed. Therefore, I leaped on the way he said "the widow's car." "Did you have any hanky-panky with Freeload's wife?" I asked.

Not often did I see my father look sheepish. "Not lately," he said.

"How could you? With a friend's wife!"

"For the last ten years, Frankie was pickled in booze. He couldn't find his tool or the pot."

"A friend's wife?" I gave him the family laugh. High tenor.

"It was only once or twice. She needed it. An act of mercy."

I laughed until the tears came. " 'I wonder who's kissing her now,' " I sang. It was wonderful to have your father at his own wake. Suddenly I felt like crying.

"You're right, kid," he said. "I hope and pray Frankie never knew." He looked at the wall for an instant. "You get older and you begin to feel as if something is wrong. You're in a box, and the sides keep coming closer. So you do things you didn't do before."

"How long have you known you were sick?"

"Ever since I went into St. Vincent's forty-five years ago."

"That's quite a while to have cancer and never show it."

"None of the doctors have a feel for the subject," he said. "The way I see the matter, it's a circuit of illness with two switches."

"What are you saying?"

"Two terrible things have to happen before the crud can get its start. The first cocks the trigger. The other fires it. I've been walking around with the trigger cocked for forty-five years."

"Because you couldn't recover from all those hits you took?"

"No. Cause I lost my balls."

"You? What are you talking about?"

"Tim, I stopped, and I felt the blood in my shoes, and there was St. Vincent's in front of me. I should have kept chasing the bastard who did the shooting. But I lost my nerve when I saw the hospital."

"Hell, you had already gone after him for six blocks."

"Not enough. I was built to be that good anyway. The test came when I stopped. I didn't have the nerve to go on and catch him. Cause I could have. Something in the scheme of things might have made him trip. I didn't push my luck. Instead, I stopped. Then I heard a voice clearly in my head. It's the only time I would say that God or someone *highly superior* was speaking to me. This voice said, 'You're out of gas, kid. It's your true test. Do it.' But I went into St. Vincent's and grabbed the orderly by the collar, and just at the moment when I got tough with that punk in the white jacket was when I felt the first switch get thrown in the cancer."

"What threw the second switch?"

"It never got thrown. It corroded. Cumulative effects. Forty-five years of living with no respect for myself."

"You're crazy."

He took a big belt of his watered bourbon. "I wish I was. Then I wouldn't have cancer. I've studied this, I tell you. There's buried statistics if you look for them. Schizophrenics in looney bins only get cancer half as often as the average population. I figure it this way: either your body goes crazy, or your mind. Cancer is the cure for schizophrenia. Schizophrenia is the cure for cancer. Most people don't know how tough it is out there. I was brought up to know. I got no excuse."

I was silent. I stopped arguing with him. It is not easy to sort out what effect his words were having. Was I coming to understand for the first time why the warmth he had for me always seemed to cross a glacial field? I may once have been a seed in Douglas Madden's body but only after that body was no longer held by him in high esteem. I was, to a degree, defective. Agitation had to be stirring in all my old wounds, well-buried and long-resigned. No wonder my father had taken no great joy in me. Intimations came how in years ahead—if I lived—the memory of this conversation might make me shake with rage.

Yet, I also felt compassion for my father. Damnable compassion. He had cast a long shadow across my understanding of him.

Next, I knew a considerable amount of fear. For now it seemed real to me again that I had murdered two women. How many times over these last few years had I come to the edge of battering Patty Lareine with my bare hands? And each time I resisted the impulse, had not a sense of oncoming illness settled more firmly into me? Yes, like my father I had been living in a harsh environment. I thought once more of the impulse that led me to climb the tower. Had that been the night when I hoped to keep the first switch from being thrown?

I knew then that I would confide in Big Mac. I had to talk about the two murders and the plastic bags in the damp cellar of this house. I could hold it no longer. Yet I could not bring myself to speak about it directly. Instead, I more or less sidled up to the topic.

"How much do you believe," I asked, "in predestination?"

"Oh, yeah," he answered, "what kind of predestination?" The shift in subject made him happy. Long years behind a bar had left my father adept at living with questions as wide as the heavenly gates.

"The football spreads," I said. "Can God pick the team that will cover?"

It was obviously a question Dougy had lived with. He revealed that glint in his eye which showed that he was debating whether to disclose useful knowledge. Then he nodded. "I figure if God bet the spread, He'd win eighty percent of the time."

"How do you come up with that number?"

"Well, let's say the night before the game He passes over the places where the players are sleeping and takes a reading. 'Pittsburgh is up for this game,' He says to Himself. 'The Jets are jangled.' Pittsburgh, He decides, is worth a lot more than three points. So He bets them. I'd say He's right four times out of five."

"But why four out of five?"

"Because footballs," said my father ominously, "take funny bounces. It is not practical to get better than four out of five. That's good enough. If He wanted to take account of the physics of every bounce, He'd have to do a million times more work in His calculations in order to get up from eighty to ninety-nine percent. That's not economical. He's got too many other things to work at."

"But why did *you* settle on four out of five?"

My father took this as a most serious question. "Sometimes," he told me, "a football handicapper can get a great streak going and hits up around seventy-five percent against the spread for a month or more. I figure that's because he's got a pipeline for a little while into higher places."

I thought of Harpo. "Can some keep it going longer?"

My father shrugged. "Dubious. These pipelines are hard to maintain." He showed no concern at mixing his metaphor: "It's a high-wire act."

"What about a terrible losing streak?"

"Those guys are on the pipeline too. Only the flow is in reverse. Their hunches are one hundred and eighty degrees wrong."

"Maybe it's just the law of averages."

"The law of averages," he said with disgust, "has done more to mess up people's minds than any idea I know. It's horse manure. The pipeline is either feeding you or it's tricking you. Greedy people get fucked by the pipeline."

"What if your bets turn out fifty-fifty?"

"Then you're nowhere near the pipeline. You're a computer. Look in the papers. The computer predictions end up at .500."

"All right," I said, "that's prediction. What I really want to talk about is coincidence."

He looked troubled. I got up and freshened our drinks. "Put a lot of water in mine," he said.

"Coincidence," I said. "What do you make of it?"

"I've been doing the talking," he said. "You tell me."

"Well," I said, "I think it's not unlike the pipeline. Only it's a network. I believe we receive traces of everyone's thoughts. We're not aware of it usually, but we do."

"Wait a minute. You're saying people are able to send and receive wireless messages? Telepathy? Without knowing it?"

"Whatever you want to call it."

"Well," he said, "for the sake of argument, why not?"

"Once," I said, "I was up in Fairbanks, Alaska, and you could feel it. There was a network."

"Yes," he said, "near magnetic north. What were you doing in Fairbanks?"

"A scam. Nothing significant." Actually, I had gone up on a cocaine run after Madeleine and I had split. It was in the month before I got busted on a quick trip to Florida for the same deed. Selling two kilos of cocaine. Only the services of a lawyer well paid for his powers of plea bargaining got it down to three years (with parole).

"I had a ruckus one night with a guy in Fairbanks," I told him. "He was bad news. In the morning when I woke up, I saw his face in my thoughts. His expression was ugly. Then the phone rang. It was the same fellow. His voice sounded as ugly as his face. He wanted a meet with me late that afternoon. All day I kept running into people I had seen the night before, and not once was I surprised by their expression. They looked angry or happy in just the way I expected them to look. It was as precise as a dream. At the end of the day I met with the heavy. But now I was no longer uptight about it. Because, as the afternoon went on, I could see him clearly in my thoughts and he was looking wasted. Sure enough, when I met up with him, that's how he was, a bigger coward than me."

My father chuckled.

"I tell you, Dougy," I said, "I think everybody in Alaska drinks so they can shut themselves out from living in everybody else's head."

He nodded. "Northern climes. Ireland. Scandinavia. Russia. Drunk like skunks." He shrugged. "I still don't see what this has to do with your argument."

"I'm saying people don't want to live in each other's heads. It's too scary. It's too animal. Coincidence is the sign that they're approaching such a state."

"What kicks it off?" Dougy asked.

"I'm not sure," I said. I took a breath. Everything considered, there were worse matters to contend with than my father's scorn. "I think that when something big and unexpected is about to happen, people come out of their daily static. Their thoughts start pulling toward one another. It's as if an impending event creates a vacuum, and we start to go toward it. Startling coincidences pile up at a crazy rate. It's like a natural phenomenon."

I could almost feel him brooding over his own past. Had he lived through experiences to compare with this on the morning he was shot? "What kind of impending events do you mean?" he asked.

"Evil events."

He was being cautious. "What kind of evil events?"

"Murder, for one."

He pondered what I said. Then he shook his head as if to say, "I do not like your input." He looked at me. "Tim," he said, "do you remember the bartender's guide?"

In my turn, I nodded. When I started my first job as a bartender, he had given me a schedule. "Son," he had said, "keep this in mind. In New York, on the streets, it's Peeping Toms from twelve A.M. to one A.M., fires from one to two, stickups two to three, bar fights three to four, suicides four to five, and auto accidents from five A.M. to six A.M." I had kept it in my head like a typed schedule. It had proved useful.

"Nothing special about murders," he now said.

"I'm not talking about New York," I said, "but here."

"You're saying a murder in this place is an extraordinary event?" I could see him all but measuring the cold damp of Cape Cod air against the blood and steam of the act. "Yeah," he said, "all right, I'll grant the point." He looked not altogether happy. "What's the purpose of this discussion?"

"I'm tangled up in coincidences," I said.

"Well, by your line of reasoning, you must be close to something bad," he said.

"I'm closer than that."

He took the pause.

"There was a suicide last week," I said, "although the man may have been killed. I believe I stole his woman the night it happened." The most curious thought came to me next: because my father had cancer, whatever I told him would never touch the air for others. That might be one of the virtues of his cancer. He could receive messages like a tomb and never send them out again. Was my father now on the other side of the spirits from all of us?

"There's more to tell than that," I said. "It's not public knowledge as yet, but two women have been killed in this town in the last week."

"My Lord," he said. That was a lot of news, even for him. "Who did it?"

"I don't know. I have a few ideas, but I'm not certain."

"Have you seen the victims? Are you sure of your facts?"

I hated to reply. As long as I said no more, we might still cling to the premise that we were drinking in the kitchen: we could surround his visit with lulling recollections of other boozy meanderings through the uncharted spaces of philosophy. But by my next remark, we would both be brought up dripping, sober, and on another beach.

I suppose I took so long to reply that my father repeated the question. "Have you seen the victims?"

"Yes," I said. "They're in the cellar."

"Oh, criminey!" His tumbler was empty. I saw his hand go for the bourbon bottle and then withdraw. Instead, he turned his glass upside down. "Tim, you do it?" he asked.

"No." I couldn't refuse my own liquor. I swallowed what was left in my glass. "I don't think I did," I said, "but I can't be certain."

So we got into it. Bit by bit, detail by detail, I told him more and more of what I could remember of each of these days after the night I went to The Widow's Walk, and when I soon confessed (for confession is indeed how it felt) that Patty Lareine was one of the two women dead, my father gave one groan of the sort you might utter if you fell from a window to be impaled on a spike.

Yet I cannot say he looked terrible. The fierce pink flush, which had been restricted to his cheekbones and left the rest of his face pale compared to his once red color, now spread a flush to Dougy's forehead and chin. That provided the illusion he was less ill than before. Indeed, I think he was. No matter his antipathy to cops, he looked so much like one himself—Captain of the Precinct or Lieutenant of Detectives would have been seized on instantly by any casting director—that willy-nilly he found himself playing the role for a good part of his life. I have to say on the strength of his questions, he was no mean interrogator.

Finally I came to a halt in my account (although in the telling we passed from morning to afternoon, made a few sandwiches and drank a little beer). He said at last, "There are two questions that keep me from seeing straight on this. One is whether you are innocent or guilty. I find it hard to believe the first, but then, you're my son." He stopped and scowled, and said, "I mean, I find it hard to believe the second—that you're guilty."

"What you're saying," I told him, "is that I could have done it. You said it! The reason is: *You* are capable of murder. In fact, maybe you did pull off one or two in the union days."

Dougy gave no reply to that. Instead he said, "Good people kill for duty, or for honor. Not for money. A sleazo kills for money. A coked-up greed bag slays for money. But not you. Do you stand to benefit from her will?"

"I have no idea."

"If her will leaves you real money, you're in a load of trouble."

"She may have had no money left. She was always secretive about how much was there. I suspect Patty Lareine made some terrible investments in the last couple of years. We could be broke."

"I sure hope so," he said. Then he laid his frozen blue eyes on me. "The problem is in the manner of those killings. That's my second question. Why? Why would someone decapitate those two women? If you did it, then you and me, Tim, have to pack it in, I figure. Our seed has got to be too hideous to continue."

"You speak calmly about such matters."

"That's because I don't believe you're capable of such an atrocity. I mention it only as an option. Set the record straight."

His monumental sense of always knowing the right thing to do irritated me in the most peculiar fashion. It was as if we were not speaking of ultimate matters so much as having a family spat. Ideological divergences. Kill the son of a bitch, says Dougy Madden. No, says the son, put him in a home for the mentally ill. I wanted to shake my father.

"I am capable of such atrocities," I said to him. "I can tell you. I know that. I'm prey to the spirits. If I did do it, I was in some kind of coma. I would have been carried to it by the spirits."

Big Mac gave me a look full of distaste. "Half the killers in this world make that claim. Fuck 'em all, I say. What does it matter if they're telling the truth? They're just a lightning rod for all the shit that other people are putting on the air. So they're too dangerous to have around." He shook his head. "You want to know my real feelings? I'm hoping and praying you didn't do it because, in fact, I couldn't off you. I couldn't even turn you in."

"You're playing with me. First it's one option, then the other."

"You damn fool," he said, "I'm trying to find my own head."

"Have a drink," I said and spilled a little more bourbon down my throat.

"Yes," he said, ignoring me, "the second big question takes care of the first. Why would anyone perform a decapitation? All you do is avoid a maximum prison in order to get a maximum mental hospital. You can even bring capital punishment on yourself by the hideousness of the crime—at least if they hang you in this state. So you'd have to be nuts. I don't believe you are."

"Thank you," I said, "but I don't believe the killer is nuts either."

"Why would anybody sane cut off the head?" he repeated. "There's only one good reason. To entrap you." Now he beamed like a physicist who has found his hypothesis. "Is the burrow in your marijuana patch large enough to hold an entire body?"

"Not unless the footlocker is removed."

"Could it hold two bodies?"

"Never."

"The decapitation may have been reasoned-out. There are people capable of anything once they decide it gives them a practical advantage."

"You're saying . . ."

But he was not about to relinquish the fruits of his thinking process to me. "Yeah, I'm saying those heads were cut off so they'd fit your burrow. Somebody wants you to take the fall."

"It's got to be one of two people," I said.

"Probably," he said, "but I can think of a few others." Now he tapped the table with his middle fingers. "Were the women shot in the head?" he asked. "Can you see from the heads how they were killed?"

"No," I said. "I didn't study them."

"What about their necks?"

"I couldn't look at that."

"So you don't know if the beheading was done by a hacksaw, a knife, or whatever."

"No."

"Don't you think you ought to find out?"

"I can't disturb them any more."

"Tim, it's got to be established. For our own sakes."

I felt ten years old and ready to blubber. "Dad," I said, "I can't look at them. It's my wife, for God's sakes."

He took that in. The heat of the chase had made him oblivious to much.

"Okay," he said at last, "I'll go down and take a look."

While he was gone I went to the bathroom and threw up. I wish I could have wept instead. Now that I was alone and no longer had the fear of breaking down in front of my father, there were no tears. Instead, I took a shower, put my clothes back on, splashed my face with after-shave lotion and went back to the kitchen. He was there and looking pale. All of the flush was gone. His cuffs were damp and I realized he must have washed up at the cellar sink.

"The one who's not your wife . . ." he began.

"Jessica," I said. "Oakwode. Laurel Oakwode."

"Yeah," he said, "that one. She was decapitated with a sword. Or maybe it was a machete. One big stroke. Patty is a different business. Somebody who didn't know how to do it sawed her head off with a knife."

"Are you certain?"

"Want to look for yourself?"

"No."

I saw it anyway. I do not know whether it was in my imagination or a true glimpse of his retina, but I saw Jessica's throat. There was a straight slash across, and the nearest flesh was bruised by the weight of the blow.

Patty's neck I did not have to visualize. I would not forget a red jungle.

My father opened his hand. The fragment of a spent bullet was in it. "That's from Oakwode," he said. "I can't get the rest without making a mess in your cellar but I've seen stuff like this before. It comes from a .22 with a hollow tip. That's what I'd say. It spreads on contact. In the brain, one .22 can do all the work. Probably with a silencer."

"Fired into her mouth?"

"Yes," he said. "Her lips look bruised, like somebody forced her to open her mouth. Maybe with the gun muzzle. You can still see the powder burns on her upper palate where the entrance hole is. Small enough. Just right for a .22. No exit wound. I was able to fish this much out." He pointed to the bullet fragment.

Tough guys don't dance. You had better believe it. *Fish this much out.* My knees were quivering and I had to put both hands on the glass to get the bourbon to my lips. I found that I was not ready to ask about Patty.

He told me all the same. "There are no marks, entrance wounds or bruises on her face and scalp. I would assume she was shot in the heart and died quick."

"What makes you think that?"

"Just a guess. I don't know. It could have been a knife. Her head tells me nothing but who she is." He frowned as if forgetting a most important detail. "No—it tells me one more thing. You would need a coroner to be sure, but I would guess that your wife,"—now he could not say Patty Lareine either—"was killed twenty-four to forty-eight hours later than the other woman."

"Well, we'll find out," I said.

"No," he said, "we will never know."

"Why?" I asked.

"Tim," he said, "we have to dispose of these heads." He held up his hand to forestall me. "I know the price," he said.

"We'll never be able to find out who did it," I blurted.

"We'll determine that, I think. We just won't be able to prove it." The flush was coming back to his face. "If you want satisfaction, we'll have to look for other means."

I let that pass for now.

"Follow my reasoning," he said. "I figure there's more than one executioner. People who use machetes don't fuck with knives."

"People who use machetes don't usually have .22s with special bullets and silencers."

"I have to think about that," he said.

We were silent. I was doing very little thinking myself. A numbness was settling through my limbs as if I had been walking for many hours through the November woods and had just stopped to rest.

"Here's what I am clear on," he said. "Somebody chose to use your marijuana stash to hide Jessica's head. That implicates you so deeply you still can't say you didn't do it. Then the head is removed. Why?" He

held up both fists as if he were steering a car. "Because somebody has
decided to kill Patty. This person wants to be certain both heads will be
found there later. He doesn't want you or the first killer going back to
destroy the evidence. Or suppose you panic. You might reveal it to the
authorities. Therefore, this second person, he takes the head."

"Or she," I said, "takes the head."

"Or she," said my father, "although I don't know what you mean by
that." When I said nothing further—I had spoken out of impulse—he
said, "Yes, I figure two principals. The one who killed Jessica, and the
one about to kill Patty. The first puts the head there to implicate you.
The second removes it so that both can be put back later. At which time,
or soon after, you will have to take the onus for both crimes."

"You're assuming an awful lot," I said.

"When people do these things," my father said, "they believe they are
viewing the scene clearly even if all they're doing is dropping one more
ingredient into the soup."

"Who's the cook?" I asked.

"Wardley, for one. He could have known Patty was dead all the while
he was talking to you. He could have done it, and been setting you up."

"I don't see how."

"He has a low opinion of you. I don't blame him. Maybe he heard
Jessica's head was now floating around, and he supposed you knew
where it was. So he decided to ask, instead, for Patty's head. He figured
you'd try to pass Jessica off as Patty. Then he'd have what he wanted—
both heads."

"Can you stop repeating that word?"

"Heads?"

"It's getting to me."

"There's no substitute for it."

"Just use their names."

"Until we find their bodies, it's misleading."

"Just use their names," I repeated.

"Hey," he said. "You're as fancy as your mother."

"I don't care if my great-grandparents cut peat in Irish bogs every
stinking day of their lives, I'm, yes, I'm as fancy as my mother."

"Ho, ho," he said, "score one for her side. May she rest in peace."
He belched. The bourbon, the beer and his illness were working on
him together. "Pass the bottle," he said.

"You're assuming too much," I said. "Why wouldn't Wardley know where Jessica was? If Regency did, Wardley would. Spider is their go-between."

"Let's say they're crossing each other up a little. It's amazing what people know and don't know in such situations." He tapped the table with his knuckles. "I say Wardley didn't know where Jessica was, and wanted you to bring her to him."

"I think Wardley had put them both in the burrow already. Keep to the given. Spider and Stoodie were following me. Wasn't that so they could be there when I went back to the burrow? To grab me just as I'm coming out with the heads? They would have been the foulest scumbags ever to make a citizen's arrest."

That impressed him. My father's brow gave his assent. "It rings true," he said. "They think you're going to the burrow, but the beeper tells them you've stopped. No wonder they go apeshit when you come back."

"I think we have a case against Wardley," I said.

"Concerning Patty, you have the beginnings of a real possibility. But who killed Jessica?"

"Maybe Wardley did that also."

"He would enjoy using a .22 with a silencer. But do you see Mr. Hilby with a machete?"

"How about Stoodie?"

"Maybe."

"Who are you thinking of?" I asked.

In how many conversations across his bar had my father served as surrogate private detective, acting criminal lawyer or honorary appeals court judge? He brought his hand to the corner of his mouth as if debating whether to peel the truth from his lips like an adhesive plaster.

Now he removed his hand. "I don't like this Regency," he said. "Not the way you describe him. He could be the fellow."

"Do you think he killed Jessica?"

"He could use a high-powered .22 handgun *and* a machete. He's the only one who could. You told me about his house. He's a weapons freak. He probably has flamethrowers in the basement. He would study how to kill you by putting a bamboo spear with poison on its tip in your path. I have met the type. 'When it comes to weapons,' they say, 'I know them all. I'm a Renaissance man.' "

"Yeah, but you hate cops."

"You bet I do. Only, some are less unreliable than others. This guy's a prairie wolf. A professional soldier who becomes a cop! I read him for a narc all the way. He's no Acting Chief of Police. That's a cover. He's a troubleshooter for the Drug Enforcement Administration, and I'll bet, back at the agency, they're scared of him. They pee in their pants when he's around."

"I find that hard to believe."

"I know cops better than you do. For how many years did I have to pay off the Mafia on Wednesday night and the police on Thursday? I know cops. I know their psychology. Why do you think a high-powered gung ho like Regency has been buried on Cape Cod?"

"It's a big narcotics center."

"Nothing next to Florida. They could really use him there. They're fobbing him off. You have to understand police psychology. No cop likes to work with a fellow professional who makes him uneasy. You can't give orders that are resented, or you make an enemy. A guy with a legal weapon has too many opportunities to shoot you in the back. So when cops have to put up with a crazy, they don't try to fire him. They fob him off. Make him Head-of-the-Universe in Twin Acres, Montana. Pee-town, Mass. No," he concluded, "I don't like Regency one bit. That's why we're going to dispose of the heads."

I started to argue with him, but he kept cutting me off. "If those plastic bags are found in your cellar," he said, 'there is no way out of it for you. You're a sitting duck. And if you try to remove them, it's worse. The moment they see you getting into your car, they'll follow you."

"I've got to bury my wife."

"No, you don't. I'll do it. I'll take your boat and your fishing gear and two tackle boxes. Do you have an extra anchor on board?"

"No."

"Then I'll use the one that's there. For Patty and Jessica both."

Now it was my turn to say "Oh, criminey!"

"Hey," said Dougy, "you look at me and see a crude man. I look at you and see a sitting duck."

"I have to go with you. It's the least I can do."

"If I set out alone, it's just an old gink fishing. They won't look twice. But you! They'll see you there. They'll alert the Coast Guard. What's your story when they find the two ladies on board complete but for their bodies? 'Oh,' you'll say, 'I found them. Voices told me where to look.' 'Yeah,' they'll say, 'you're Joan of Arc. Next case.' " He shook his head. "This, Tim-Boy, is where you firm up. I'll be gone a few hours. Why don't you, in the interim, make a few phone calls."

"To whom?"

"Try the airport. Maybe you can find out when Jessica arrived."

"She and Lonnie came by car."

"How do you know that was her first night in town? Or his?"

I shrugged. I didn't.

"Find out," he said, "who the real estate agent is."

When he went down to the cellar, however, I stayed immobile in my chair. I would not have moved if he had not called up the cellar stairs, "Tim, I'm ready to row the dinghy out to your boat. Go for a walk. I want to get *them* away from the house."

I saw spirits and he saw real people. All right. He was taking the chances, and the least I could do was walk.

I put on a parka, and went out the front door and down Commercial Street in the deserted afternoon sunlight, but I could not keep on the street for too long. It was a silent day, quiet as the sunlight that came down in fluted pillars through the gray banks overhead, and I knew there would be a play of brights and shadows on the beach. Just when I was certain I heard the motor starting on our twenty-foot Whaler (Patty's boat) I turned into an empty beach lot and onto the sand and, yes, there on the water, the dinghy left behind at the mooring, and all but alone in the harbor, no Coast Guard in sight and only a couple of fishing boats coming into Town Wharf, was my father heading the Whaler out to the bay, and I took a breath and returned with my aching foot over the sand.

Back in the house, surprisingly refreshed by this walk, I decided, by way of Dougy's suggestion, to make those phone calls. I tried the airport first and had a piece of good fortune. The girl at the ticket desk was a drinking friend, and she was on duty. So I could ask if Jessica Pond or Laurel Oakwode and/or Lonnie Pangborn had been in or out of Provincetown in the last few weeks. A few minutes later she called me back: Jessica Pond came in on an afternoon flight fifteen days ago. She left nine days ago on the first morning plane. The airline booked her return ticket from Provincetown to Boston to San Francisco to Santa Barbara. Nobody named Pangborn had come in or out. However, the girl recalled she was at the desk on the morning the Pond passenger left, and Chief Regency brought her to the airport. " 'Take good care of this lady,' he told me," said the girl.

"Did he and she look friendly?" I asked.

"Tim, I was too hung-over to take a look." She deliberated. "I guess there was some oovie-groovie going on."

Well, that opened the possibilities. If Jessica Pond had been here for a week alone, then flew to Santa Barbara and came back, the question became: Was she working with Pangborn for Wardley or was she working for herself?

I called the real estate agent in town whom I knew best. She could, however, give me no more than the name of the Boston lawyer who represented the Paramessides estate. As far as she knew, the property was not for sale. When I rang the lawyer's office, I gave my name as Lonnie Oakwode. When the lawyer came on, I said, "Mr. Thwaite, my mother, Mrs. Oakwode, had to go over to Europe to take care of an urgent matter but asked me to contact you."

"Well, I'm glad you called. We've all been standing on tiptoe the last few days. Your mother was supposed to be here with a certified check."

"Yes, I know," I said.

"Good. Give her a message for me. I'm a bit concerned that the price is going to be given an adjustment upward. Or will be if we don't hear from her. I can't hold the fort on short rations, you see. A promise is a promise, but we've got to have her check. Another party put in a bid last week."

"I'll get to her quickly."

"You must. It's always like that. Years go by and an estate gets back nothing from the property but penalties and taxes. Then everybody wants it all at once, and in the same business week." He coughed.

"Mr. Thwaite, she'll get back to you."

"Hope so. Lovely woman, your mother."

"I'll tell her."

I hung up quickly. I was playing her son with much too little knowledge to stay on the line for long.

Still, my guess had been given some confirmation. Laurel Oakwode must have been planning to acquire the property for herself. Was it to hold up Wardley and, thereby, Patty Lareine?

I posed the question: What would Patty Lareine do to a woman who tried such a maneuver?

"She would kill" was the unmistakable reply that came back to me.

In that case, if Patty Lareine had done it, and with a .22 silencer, why did Regency behead the victim? Was it to leave the most recognizable part of her on my plot of marijuana? Did Patty Lareine hate me to that extent, or did Regency?

He did, I decided. It was Regency who had suggested I should go to the patch.

I got up from the phone with more clarity, more anger and more sense of purpose than I had felt in a while. Was it possible I had a hint of my father's moxie? I am obliged to believe that optimism is my most dangerous inclination. For now I had an impulse to look at the nude Polaroids I had taken years ago of Madeleine and more recently of Patty Lareine. What a curious desire. To think of obscene Polaroids at just the moment one is feeling encouraged by signs of character in oneself. Let no one say I have a classic personality.

I went upstairs, and sequestered in a file box, was an envelope with the pictures. There were three of Patty and two of Madeleine. All, I fear, had their legs sufficiently separated to show the Luciferean gleam of their nether soul, yes, the labia were well exposed. Now, however, there were ten pieces of glossy paper in the envelope. All the heads had been neatly snipped from the bodies.

Do you know, I believe that was the moment when my father, having used baling wire to fasten the two heads to the links of the anchor chain, had chosen—out where he was in deep water—to drop his grisly assemblage overboard. I know I was immediately laid low by an attack from Hell-Town. It was the most prodigious bombardment I ever received.

"Fuck-face, foul and moldy," shrieked the first voice. "*Sieg heil* to the ghoul, fool," said the second.

"It's Timmy Light-Fingers, smash his yeggs."

"Maim the bloody sandbagger. Open the moon cancer full of pus."

"Hey, Timmy, sniff the rot, burn the snot."

"You're a raider, you're a depredator, you traitor."

"Bring him in—he stole my house."

"You ravisher, you floated across on my bed."

"Disembowel the pikeman. Masticate his prick."

"He and his dad did the job. Crazy kooks. Cockeyed killers."

"You murdered Jessica!" came the howl in my ear.

"Dougy killed Patty!" screamed the harpy in the other ear.

"Why? Why did we kill?" I asked aloud.

"Oh, darling boy, Dad is looking for his cure. That's the cure. Sniff the blood."

"That's him," I said aloud, "but what of me?"

"You're sick as well, you swagman. You're under our spell."

"Go away, you whores!" I shouted.

Standing alone in the rosy-gray air of twilight in that third-floor study, my eyes out to sea, my ears in the sands of Hell-Town, and my feet, for all I knew, on the floor of the bay, I saw in my mind how the heads, blonde hair waving, descended like sea flowers tied to the stem of the chain and the root of the anchor. Down they went through palisades of water to the bottom of the sea, and I believe I knew the moment when the anchor touched, for the voices ceased. Had their cries in my ear been a welcome to the head of Patty Lareine? I stood soaked in my own perspiration.

Now my limbs began to tremble freely of one another. Parts of my body were shivering while the rest was still, an experience I had not had before. It was then I felt an idea coming forward to the center of my attention, pressing into my spirit against all resistance, as if the thought and I were on opposite sides of a door. Then I could hold it off no longer: I had to examine my pistol (Patty's pistol). It was a .22.

How implausible this sounds, but, do you know, for the last five days I had succeeded somehow in avoiding the thought. Now, however, the subpoena was served: I had to examine the .22.

It was where it had always been, there in a cabinet on her side of the bedroom. It was sitting in its case. The lid once raised, the box reeked. Someone had fired it recently and put it back uncleaned. Was it myself? The casing had been ejected from the chamber and there was a round missing from the magazine.

I did not feel guilty. I was angry. The nearer the evidence, the more furious I became. The pistol was particularly infuriating, as if I were a criminal lawyer presented with one more nasty witness inserted without fair notice; yes, I felt innocent and full of anger. How dare they? Whoever *they* were. What was being done to tear my mind from its hinges? How curious that the more likely it would seem to others—including my father—that I had killed at least one of these women, the more certain it seemed to me that I had not.

The telephone was ringing.

I took it for a sign that it was Madeleine.

"Thank God, it's you, darling," she said and began to weep.

That rich and husky voice had dimensions for expressing misery. Her emotion soon opened into those deeps of sorrow that speak of the loss of years of love, and hot vows of fucking in the wrong bed. "Oh, baby," she managed to say, "Oh, darling," and was off again. I could have been listening to the wails of a woman who had just learned she was a widow.

"Darling," she said at last, "I thought you were dead. I had a chill in my heart." She started to wail again. "I was so afraid no one would answer your phone."

"What is it?"

"Tim, don't go out. Lock your door."

I could not remember a time when she had wept so terribly as this. "What's the matter?" I begged.

Slowly it came from her. Phrase by phrase. Every few words were followed by her woe, her fear, her outrage. Now there were moments when I did not know if she failed to speak from horror or fury.

She had found some photographs. That was clear at last. She had been putting fresh laundry in his drawers and came across a locked box she had not seen before. It had enraged her that he kept a locked box in their bedroom. If he had secrets, why didn't he hide them in the cellar? So she smashed the box.

How her terror keened into me. Over the phone, I could hear her trembling.

"Madeleine, no," I said, "speak clearly. You must speak clearly. Who is in these photographs?"

"Patty Lareine," she said. "They're of Patty Lareine. They're nude. They're obscene." She began to choke on her words. "They're worse than the ones you took of me. I don't know if I can bear it. The moment I saw those pictures, I thought you were dead."

"Am I in them?"

"No."

"Then why did you have such a thought?"

Her weeping changed. It was not unlike the whimpering of a young girl who has been thrown from a horse and now must, no matter the shock, sheer panic and bottomless fright, get back on again. So did Madeleine force herself to see the photos in her mind. Then she said, "Darling, he cut the head off every one of them."

"You better get out of that house," I told her.

"I believe he's decided to kill you."

"Madeleine, get out of your place. It's more unsafe for you than for me."

"I'd like to burn his house," she said. Then she began to giggle. That was more upsetting than her grief. "I can't, though. I might burn the neighbors down."

"You would."

"But think of his face when those guns melted."

"Listen to me carefully. Does he have a machete in his collection?"

"Several," she said. "And swords. Only he uses a pair of scissors." She began to giggle once more.

"Do you see any swords missing?"

"I don't know," she said. "I don't keep up with his collection."

"Could you recognize a .22 handgun?"

"Is that a pistol?"

"Yes."

"He's got all kinds of pistols."

I let it go.

"Madeleine, I want you to join me here."

"I don't know if I can move. I ripped up a few gowns he bought for me. It's left me paralyzed."

"Hey," I said, "you can do it. You can make the move."

"No," she said. "Nothing works right now."

"Madeleine, if you won't come, I'll drive down to get you."

"Don't," she said. "With his timing, he'll walk in on us."

"Then pack your bags and get in your car."

"I don't want to drive," she said. "I've been up all night. I haven't slept since you were here."

"Why?"

"Because I love you," she said.

"All right," I said.

"All right, what?"

"I can understand that," I said.

"Sure," she said. "Both of us loving you. That's not hard to under-stand." She actually stirred out of her woe long enough to give one suspicion of a merry laugh. "You're a fiend," she said. "Only a fiend could hit a happy note at a time like this."

"If you don't want to drive," I said, "call a cab. Take it to Province-town."

"Take a cab fifty miles? No," she said, "I won't support the cab companies." Yes, she still had her dependable thrifty streak.

"I need you," I told her. "I think Patty Lareine is dead."

"You think?"

"I know it."

"You saw her?"

"I know it."

"All right," she said after a time, "I'll come. If you need me, I'll come."

"I need you," I said.

"What if he shows up?"

"Let's face him here."

"I don't want to see that man anywhere," she said.

"Maybe *he's* afraid of you too."

"You better believe," said Madeleine, "that he is afraid of me. Before he left the house this morning, I told him not to turn his back. I said, 'If it takes ten years, you filthy horror, I'm going to shoot you from behind.' He believed it. I could see his face. He *would* believe something like that."

"I'd believe it more," I said, "if you knew what a .22 was."

"Oh," she said, "please don't understand me too quickly."

"Who said that?" I asked.

"André Gide."

"André Gide? You never read him."

"Don't tell anybody," she said.

"Take your car. You can do it."

"I'll get there. Maybe I'll call a cab. But I'll get there." She asked for the address and was fortified when I told her my father would be with us.

"There's a man I could live with," she said and hung up.

I calculated that it should take her no more than an hour to pack, and an hour to drive here. Madeleine's habits, however, being likely to remain constant over ten years, I could count on waiting four to five hours before she showed. Again, I wondered whether I should drive out for her and decided I wouldn't. We would be stronger here.

Now I heard the rattle of the dinghy being hauled up the davits, then the heavy tread of my father on the deck. He went around, however, to the front door of the house and let himself in with the key Patty Lareine gave him years ago when he first visited us.

Patty Lareine was dead.

This thought, which kept arriving in my mind like a telegram delivered every fifteen minutes, still had nothing to offer but its integument. It was like the envelope to a telegram that has no message inside. Certainly no emotion. Yes, Madeleine, I said to myself, I could get crazy about you, but not now.

My father came into the kitchen. I took one look at him and poured some bourbon into a glass, and put the water on to boil for coffee. He looked as tired as I had ever seen him. Yet the flush on his cheekbones was still spread across his face. He also looked virtuous.

"You did a good job," I said.

"Pretty good." He squinted at me like an old fisherman. "You know, I was three miles out in the bay before I realized they might be following me with field glasses or worse. Maybe they even had a surveyor's transit. If they get two of those on you, they can take a finding on where you drop it off. Then they send a diver down. Nothing to it. So I realized I better drop my package while I'm moving at medium throttle, and make sure I do it casual on the side of the boat away from shore. That way my body covers what I'm doing. I'm sure it was all for nothing," he said, "and nobody was watching. That's the likelihood. But that's not how I felt then."

The coffee was ready. I handed it to him. He poured it down his throat as if he were an old diesel taking in fuel. "Just at the moment I was about to drop it off," he resumed, "I started to worry if the baling wire would hold. You know, getting those heads onto the chain was the toughest part of the job." He went into detail. Like an obstetrician describing how he got two fingers in to turn the baby's head out of breech, or, yes, like an old fisherman taking you along step by step on how to bait a hook so that the wriggler stays alive, he accompanied his account with motions of his hand. I followed enough of it to realize that the operation had carried him through the socket of one eye and out through a hole he had driven in the skull with a spike. It left me startled again at how little I knew my father. He gave his account with a ruminative relish like a man who works for the Department of Sanitation giving a recital of the worst barrel he has collected in an interesting work career, and it was only when he was done that I could recognize why he had enjoyed the account. There was some kind of cure in process. Do not ask me to certify my statement. But there was a smug complacency in my father's air as if he were a convalescent who was getting better by disregarding doctor's orders.

Then he startled me. "Did you feel anything unusual," he asked, "while I was gone?"

"Why do you ask?"

"I wasn't going to tell you," he said, "but when I dropped the anchor I heard a voice."

"What did it say?"

He shook his head.

"What did you hear?"

"I heard you did it."

"You believe such voices?"

"Considering the circumstances—no. But I'd like to hear you say so."

"I didn't do it," I said. "As far as I know, I didn't do it. I'm beginning to think, however, that I'm responsible in some way for the minds of all the others." When I saw that he did not really follow me, I said, "It's as if I was polluting the pipeline."

"I don't care if you're only half Irish," he said. "You're certainly degenerate enough in your mentality to be all Irish."

"Shove the abuse," I said.

He took another sip from his coffee.

"Tell me about Bolo Green," he said.

"I can't keep up with you," I told him.

Our conversation was taking on the slippery frustrations of a dream. I felt close to some elusive truth and he wanted to talk about Bolo Green.

He certainly did. "All the while," he said, "that I was bringing the boat back, this Bolo Green kept coming into my head. I felt as if Patty was telling me to think about him." He stopped. "Am I being a sentimental son of a bitch about Patty?"

"Maybe you're a little drunk."

"I'm getting a lot drunk," he said, "and I miss her. I tell myself—you want to see how crude I am deep down?—I tell myself, if you put a weight on an old dog and sink him at sea, you're going to miss the dog. Is that crude enough for you?"

"You said it."

"It's gross. But I miss her. I buried her, goddamnit."

"Yes, Dad, you did."

"You didn't have the balls to do it." He stopped. "I'm getting unreasonable, aren't I?"

"What's the good of being a Mick if you can't welcome senility?"

He roared. "I love you!" he cried out.

"I love you."

"Tell me about Bolo."

"What do *you* think?"

"I think he's part queer," said Dougy.

"What's your evidence?"

He shrugged. "Patty. Patty told me on the water."

"Why don't you take a nap," I said. "We may need each other later."

"What are you up to?"

"I want to do a little snooping around town."

"Stay alert," he said.

"Get your rest. If Regency comes around, talk to him nicely. When he's not looking, hit him over the head with a shovel, then tie him up."

"Too bad you ain't serious," my father said.

"Give him a wide berth. He may be able to hold his own against both of us."

I could read my father's thought, but he pinched his lips together and said nothing.

"Get some sleep," I told him, and left.

I had been casual but, truly, I was not in hailing distance of such a state. An outsize stimulation had begun as soon as I said, "I'm responsible for the minds of others." A recognition stirred that I must get into my car and drive around town. The impulse was as powerful as the force that came through my drunkenness on the night I tried to climb the Monument. I knew the same fear, delicate, near to exquisite in my chest, like the shadow of one's finest pride.

I obeyed. I had not spent close to twenty years contemplating the lessons of my climb up the tower for too little—no, with as much marching grace as my bunged-up toe and half-paralyzed shoulder would permit I crossed the street, got into my Porsche and drove slowly with one arm on the wheel down Commercial Street, not knowing what I looked for, nor whether feats would be demanded of me, no, it was something like the excitement, I must suppose, of an African hunter when big animals are near.

The town was quiet. The town bore no relation to my mood. In the center The Brig was half empty, and through the windows of The Bucket of Blood I could see only one pool player contemplating his next shot. He looked as lonely as the waiter Van Gogh once painted standing in the middle of the café at Arles.

I took a turn to the right at Town Hall and parked across the street from the basement entrance to the police station. Regency's car was outside, standing double-parked and empty. The motor was running.

Then came a temptation clear as the mandate to mount the tower. It told me to step out of my car, walk over to his, turn off the motor, take his keys, open his trunk, look inside—speak of creative visualization, I saw the machete in the trunk!—remove it, lock the trunk, put the keys back in the ignition, start the motor, leave his car and stroll back to my Porsche and a good exit, yes, I saw all of this in advance and as vividly as any trip to the burrow I had thought out for myself before I went. Now my first reaction was yes, do it! My second was no.

It was then I understood, as never before, that we live with not one soul but two, our father and our mother—at the least!—the night and the day, if you will; well, this is no exposition of dualities, but two souls I possessed that were equal to two matched horses—badly matched!— if one said yes, the other said no, and the poor driver was nothing but my own person who now cast the deciding vote: Yes, I would do it, I had to. I could not live through the debacle of the Monument one more time.

So I got out of my car. To my misery, the side street was deserted, thereby giving me no excuse to delay, and with an exaggerated hobble (as if a maimed man could do less harm in the eyes of the police) I crossed to his car, my heart beating at such a pitch that fear passed right through vertigo into the delirium of intoxication itself. Have you ever taken an anesthetic through a mask and seen the concentric circles bore in upon your brain as you go under? I saw them now as I took the keys from his car.

"Oh, hullo, Regency," I said. "Hope you don't mind. I need a tire iron from your trunk."

"Oh, yes, I mind," said he and drew his gun and shot me.

That passed. The vision passed. Toes tingling, hand shaking, I got the key into the lock of his trunk.

The machete was there.

In that instant when my heart spun like a cat on a high power line and I thought I would die, I knew some far-off chord of exultation and woe: He exists, or It exists, or *They* are out there. It was confirmation that the life we live with all our wit and zeal is only half our life. The other half belongs to something other.

My first impulse was to run. Instead, I pried the machete from the floor of the trunk—it was stuck to it!—slammed down the rear deck of the police cruiser, forced myself (it was the most demanding measure in the sequence) to get inside his vehicle long enough to start his motor again and only then was I free to cross the street to my own car. Under way, the steering wheel of the Porsche kept oscillating in my good hand until I was obliged to hold it with both.

Five blocks down Bradford Street I pulled under a lamp for a moment and looked at the machete. It was covered with dried blood on the side of the blade that had not been stuck to the rubber mat. All my notions of Regency collided. Never could I have conceived he would be so careless as this.

Of course, if he had used this weapon upon Jessica (and, yes, he must have used it) was it possible that he had not been able to go near the blade since? If one is going to perch on the abyss, it is reassuring to discover that one's fellow maniacs also know fear and trembling.

Awash in my thoughts, I drove through all of town before I came to the simple conclusion that the machete ought to be transferred to my trunk rather than kept beside me in the front seat. I happened to be then at the circle at the end of Commercial Street where the Pilgrims landed and the breakwater now crosses the marsh. There I stopped, lifted my front lid and laid the machete in—its blade was nicked, I noticed—closed the trunk and saw a car stopping behind me.

Wardley got out. He must have put a new beeper on my rear bumper. God, I had not even checked my car.

Now he came toward me. We were all alone by the breakwater and there was just enough moon to see.

"I'd like to talk to you," he said. He had a gun in his hand. It most certainly had a silencer on its muzzle. And, yes, it looked just like my .22. It took little creative visualization to conceive of the head of the soft-nosed bullet resting in its chamber.

Eight

"Wardley," I said, "you look a mess." My voice, however, quivered enough to spoil the suggestion that I was feeling no large respect for his firearm.

"I've been," he said, "on a burial detail."

Even by the uncertain gleam of the moon taking its wan trip through the scud, I could see that he was covered with wet sand up to his hair and eyeglasses.

"Let's take a walk along the rocks," he suggested.

"It'll be difficult," I told him. "I hurt my foot kicking Stoodie."

"Yes," Wardley answered, "he thought you kicked him. He was angry about that."

"I expected him to come over today."

"We won't see Stoodie anymore," said Wardley.

He made a delicate move with the muzzle of his gun as if pointing me to the most comfortable chair in the room. I set out a few steps in front of him.

It was not easy walking. The breakwater extended for a mile across the sand flats, the marshes and the bay, and you had to pick your route over the jetty boulders. They were level enough on top to form a sort of rough path for much of the way, but now and again you had to leap a four- or five-foot gap, or else go down the angle of one big rock and up another. In the dark, with my injuries, we made slow progress. He did not seem to mind. Behind us, a car would occasionally come along

Commercial Street on its way to the circle, and either turn in at the Provincetown Inn or continue past the marshes out to where the highway began, but after we had traversed a few hundred feet of the breakwater, these cars might as well have been a good distance away. Their headlights seemed as removed from us as a ship's running lamps at sea.

The tide had been high but was going out, and so the tops of the boulders were some eight or ten feet above the water. Beneath was the sound of the sea coming out of the marshes and passing through the jetty. Maybe it was the pain in my foot and the heavy throb of my shoulder, but I was resigned. If my life were to end on this endless breakwater, well, there were worse places, and I listened to the unrest of the gulls, cawing at our nocturnal passage. How loud were these transactions at night! I felt as if I could even hear the eelgrass stirring in the inlets and the sponge eating at the oyster shells. The wrack and sea lace began to breathe on the rocks as the swells undulated from our jetty. It was a windless night which, if not for the chill of November, was reminiscent of summer, given the placidity of the water, but no, a late-fall night it had to be: a northern chill lay upon the calm, telling us of those eternities where the realms of magnetism are icy and still.

"Tired?" he asked.

"Are you planning to go all the way across?"

"Yes," he said, "and I warn you, after we cross this, you've got another half mile along the beach." He pointed to our left, perhaps midway between where the breakwater ended and the lighthouse at the point a mile farther to the left out at the tip of the long barrier beach of Cape Cod. For all of that mile of beach to the lighthouse there would be no dwelling and no roads, nothing but sand trails for four-wheel vehicles. They would hardly be stirring on a November night.

Hell-Town had once thrived out there.

"It's quite a walk," I said.

"See if you can make it," he replied.

He was keeping a good number of yards behind me in order not to have to carry his gun in his hand, and whenever I came to a difficult passage (and there were one or two descents where the rocks had settled and were slippery from the outgoing tide) he merely waited until I found my way across, then took it himself.

After a time I felt cheered. Local news is most important in catastrophic times, and my toe, broken or not, nonetheless seemed to be flexing a little better, and my bad left arm was finding a few more movements it could make without pain. Besides, I did not feel totally afraid. Despite what I knew of him in prison, I could not always take Wardley seriously. I had, after all, seen him cry on the day we were kicked out of school. On the other hand, I did not wish to stimulate his trigger finger by any rude act. Old boyhood certainties could prove dangerous.

More than halfway across, I asked for a break. He nodded and sat about ten feet away from me, near enough so that we could talk. Now he held the gun. It was here that he filled me in quickly on some details. He wanted to talk.

In brief: Nissen was dead. Stoodie was dead. Beth had left town with Bolo Green.

"How do you know all this?" I asked.

"I saw Bolo kill Stoodie. And I certainly saw Beth and Bolo off on their trip. Why, I gave them the money. They left in the van you damaged. It's hers."

"Where are they going?"

"Beth was thinking of a visit to her mother and father in Michigan. Apparently they're retired and live in Charlevoix."

"Bolo ought to make a considerable impression on Charlevoix."

"Personable blacks have entrée everywhere but Newport," he answered me solemnly.

"Wasn't Beth concerned about Spider?"

"I told her that he had decamped. She didn't seem too perturbed. She said she would sell their house. I think she's been missing Michigan."

"Does she know that Stoodie is dead?"

"Of course not. Who would inform her?"

I tried to ask the next question with tact. It was as if I had been talking to a stranger and had just told a Polish joke. Now I had to ask, "Are you by any chance Polish?" So with considerable modesty of voice, I inquired, "Do you know who killed Spider?"

"Well, if you want to know, I did."

"You did?"

"It's sordid," said Wardley.

"Was he holding you up for money?"

"Yes."

"May I ask why?"

"Tim, I would think you've been concerned lately about heads. *Chez moi*, it's been *bodies*. You see, Spider and Stoodie were on the burial detail."

I hazarded a guess. "They buried the bodies?" I asked.

"Both women."

"Where? I would like to know."

"Right where we're going."

"Terrific."

We were silent.

"Right in Hell-Town," I said.

He nodded.

"You know about Hell-Town?" I asked.

"Of course. Patty Lareine told me. She's fixed on Hell-Town. It's a pity her remains are so separated."

"From her point of view, yes."

"Where's the head?" asked Wardley.

"At the bottom of the sea. I don't know enough to tell you more than that. I wasn't along."

"I don't think that I'd want to do her such a great favor, anyway," he said, "as to restore her parts."

No reply came to me easily.

"Where are Stoodie and Spider buried?" I asked.

"Close-by. I have them all together. The two women and the two men. They're near enough so they can have a *dansant* should the spirit arise." He was taken by a small convulsion of mirth, but since it came forth soundlessly, I cannot say that either of us expected me to laugh along with him.

Then he raised his pistol and fired a shot in the air. It made the pop I expected—like a small inflated paper bag suddenly broken, no great event.

"Why do that?" I asked.

"Exuberance," he said.

"Oh."

"I'm feeling good. I finished my burials. It was a good piece of work."

"Didn't Bolo help you?"

"Of course not. I sent him off, as I told you, with Beth. He was much too hyper to keep around in the state he was in. I always knew he was strong, but he killed Stoodie with his hands. Just strangled him."

"Where?"

A perverse look seemed to come on his face. I say *seemed* because I could not see too clearly by the moon we had, but I did have the impression that he chose not to answer this question for the pure pleasure of failing to reply.

"Why do you want to know?" he asked at last.

"Curiosity."

"The desire to know is so powerful," he said. "Do you think that if I do kill you, and I'm not saying I will or I won't—to tell the truth, I don't have a clue—do you believe you'll go out into that dark dominion better armed if a few of your questions are satisfied?"

"Yes, I think I do feel that."

"Good. So do I." He gave a sly smile. "It all happened in the Provincetown woods. Stoodie had a little shack off the highway. Just as well it's by itself. We made a racket."

"And you left both men lying there and took Bolo over to visit Beth?"

"Yes."

"And he and she took off. Like that?"

"Well, they began something last night. Apparently she had quite a time with him after you left The Brig. So I encouraged them to travel together."

"But why did Bolo kill Stoodie?"

"Because I primed him." Wardley nodded. "I said that Stoodie had killed Patty Lareine and disposed of her body by feeding it to his dogs."

"Good Lord."

"Stoodie didn't even have a dog," said Wardley, "as far as I know. But you'd think he would. He's the kind of cur should have a beast."

"Poor Stoodie. *Did* he kill Patty Lareine?"

"No."

"Who did?"

"I'll tell you in a while, perhaps." He became so thoughtful that I started to think the muzzle of his gun might be lowering, but no, it wasn't. It kept pointing at me. I would say it was as powerful in its effect as a bright light in one's eyes during interrogation.

"Well," I muttered at last, "let's get going."

"Yes," he said, and stood up.

We began walking.

"Can I ask another question?"

"Of course."

"How did you ever get both men all the way out to Hell-Town?"

"I just put them in the trunk of my car and drove them over to the house I'm renting. It's at Beach Point, by the way. There's no one there now. So it was no great trick to transfer the bodies onto my boat. Not in the dark."

"Weren't they heavy?"

"I'm a little stronger than I look."

"You didn't used to be."

"Tim, I work out now."

"I ought to."

"Perhaps you should."

"You took the bodies out by water to Hell-Town and buried them there?"

"Just the men's bodies. Actually, I should have done all the burials from the beginning. If I hadn't delegated that little task, Spider and Stoodie would never have gained such leverage on me."

"But in any event, after this last burial, you returned in your boat to your house at Beach Point?"

"Yes."

"And the beeper led you to me?"

"No, you threw my beeper away." He gave his shy smile once more. "I just wandered into you."

"That's awesome."

"I love design," he said. "That may be what it's all about."

"Yes," I said.

"Do you possess much faculty of *déjà vu?*" he asked. "I live with it all the time. I wonder if we don't inhabit the same situation more than once. Perhaps we're supposed to do better the second time."

"I don't know," I said.

We kept walking. "I have to admit I was looking for your car," he said. "I just drove around until I saw the Porsche."

"I can't say if that makes me feel better or worse," I replied. Maybe it was the pain, but I felt compelled to exhibit the cheerful wit of a patient being wheeled by his surgeon to the hour of his operation.

We walked in silence. Below us was a great deal of phosphorescence in the water, and I pondered the luminous activity of the plankton but cannot say I had a new thought. We had come to the deepest cleft in the walk, and since I could hardly jump across, I had to take a series of lower boulders on the flank of the cut, and thereby got a mean scrape on my hand from barnacles. When I swore, he sympathized. "It's cruel to march you this far," he said, "but it's essential."

We continued. It took on at last that rhythm which speaks of movement without beginning or end, and so I hardly noticed when we came to the other shore a mile from where we had begun. Now we left the breakwater and trudged along the last arm of the bay beach. It was icy on one's feet to walk down in the moist sand, but slow going where the strand was dry. In the dark, for the moon was now behind a cloud, one had to watch each step. Old boat timbers, stout as bodies, and as silver as the light of lunacy itself, were at every odd place in the sand. One could hear the ebbing of the tide. Every chirp of a sandpiper stirred by us, every scuttling of crabs and whistle of field mice was audible. Our feet crunched upon oyster shells and razor-clam shells, empty quahogs and mussels and whelks—how many sounds could calcium offer when cracking? All the dry kelp and sargassum weed scrunched like peanut shells beneath our feet, and the mourning of the harbor buoy came back to us on the slow expiring of the tide.

Maybe we walked for half an hour. By the water's edge, pink jellyfish and moon jellies lolled in the moonlight like fat ladies in the sun, and the seaweed that is spoken of as mermaid's tresses washed ashore. I lived in the wet phosphorescence of the tide's edge as if the last lights of my life might pass into these cold flashes.

We came at last to our destination. It was a strip of sand, no less and no more remarkable than any other, and he pointed me up a shallow dune through long grass to a beach hollow. If you sat down, you could no longer view the bay. I tried to tell myself that I was on the sands of Hell-Town but I doubted if spirits nested here. There was only a pall upon us. The winds must be astringent on this barrier beach. Spirits, I thought, would prefer to cluster by the sheds floated over a century ago to Commercial Street.

"Patty's body is here?" I said at last.

He nodded. "You can't see where I buried them, can you?"

"Not in this light."

"Not in broad daylight either."

"How do you know where they are?"

"By their relation to these shrubs," he said pointing to a plant or two on the perimeter of the sunken bowl.

"Seems vague."

"Do you see that horseshoe-crab shell on its back?"

I nodded.

"Take a better look. There's a stone I put in it so it wouldn't shift."

I could not really see the stone in this light, but pretended I did.

"Patty Lareine," said Wardley, "is buried beneath that shell, Jessica is four feet to the right, and Spider four feet to the left. Stoodie is still another four feet to the left."

"Do you have a place picked for me?" was what I wished to say—the élan of the brave patient demanded no less—but I did not trust my voice. I was feeling some huskiness of throat. It is absurd, but now, at such proximity to my death, I felt no more terror than before the kickoff of my first high school football game. Certainly I felt less than before my one and only bout in the Golden Gloves. Had life ground my heart down to the manageable emotions? Or was I still on the alert to snatch his pistol?

"Why did you kill Patty Lareine?" I asked.

"Don't be certain it was I," he replied.

"What about Jessica?"

"Oh, no. Laurel had some serious flaws in her character, but I wouldn't kill her." With the hand that did not hold the pistol, he passed sand through his fingers, as if debating the run of his next remarks. "There," he said, "I think I'm going to tell you."

"I wish you would."

"What difference does it make?"

"As I say, I think it does."

"How interesting if your instinct is well-founded."

"Please tell me," I said, as though speaking to an older relative.

He liked this. I don't believe he had heard such a tone in my voice before. "Do you know what a hog you are?" Wardley answered.

"We don't always see that in ourselves," I told him.

"Well, you're a fearfully covetous person."

"I have to admit I don't know why you say that."

"My friend Leonard Pangborn was a silly man in a lot of ways. He claimed to gallivant through many a gay world that in fact he never went near. He was a creature of the closet. How he suffered his homosexuality! It was agonizing for him. He wanted so much to be hetero. He was incredibly pleased that Laurel Oakwode had that affair with him. Did you think of any of that? No. You had to have sex with her right in front of him."

"How do you know all that?"

"Because Jessica, as you call her, told me."

"What are you saying?"

"Yes, darling, she phoned me late that night, Friday night—six nights ago."

"Were you already in Provincetown?"

"Of course."

"What did Jessica say?"

"She was in a total state. After putting them both through all that show business—they're simple people!—you had the gall to drop them back at their own car. 'Get lost,' you snarled at them, 'you're pigs.' How's that for bartender's rectitude, Madden? Scratch one of your kind and out comes a lout. What could they do to answer? They went off by themselves and had a terrible fight. Lonnie reverted. Just like a little boy in a tantrum. I mean, they had this godawful end-of-the-earth fight. He told her that she was a slut. She called him an old aunty. That's got to be the worst word. Poor Lonnie. He gets out of the car, slams the trunk lid and walks away. So she thinks. She waits. She doesn't even hear the pop until it comes through to her that she did hear something. There has definitely been a pop. Like a champagne bottle. She's sitting by herself in the car out near the beach parking lot at Race Point totally deserted and has just been called a slut, and she hears someone opening a champagne bottle. Is Lonnie making a conciliatory gesture? She waits, then she gets out and looks. No Lonnie in sight. Boy, oh boy. On impulse, she lifts the trunk. There he is, dead, the gun in his mouth. The perfect death for one of my ilk. 'Dear friend,' he might as well have said, 'I'd rather have a cock in my mouth, but if one must go out cold tit, then cold tit it will be.' "

All the while that Wardley was telling me this, he kept the gun barrel pointed in my direction like a forefinger.

"Where did he get the .22 with the silencer?" I asked.

"He always carried one. Years ago I bought a rare set of three—I don't believe there are a hundred such sets in the world—and I gave one to Patty Lareine and another to Lonnie. But that's another story. There was a time, believe it or not, when I was very much in love with Lonnie."

"I don't understand why he was carrying a gun on Friday night."

"He always carried that gun. It made him feel like a man, Tim."

"Oh," I said.

"Never occurred to you?"

"If he was so bothered by what I was doing with Jessica, why didn't he plug me?"

"You don't carry a gun," said Wardley, "because you would use it. He couldn't. Oh, I know Lonnie. His fury wished to reach cataclysmic proportions. Kill you, kill Laurel—but, of course, he could do neither. He was queer, dear."

"So he killed himself?"

"I want to be truthful. It isn't all your fault. He was also in terrible financial trouble. Facing a stiff sentence. He threw himself on my mercy just a month ago. Begged me to help. I told him I would try. But, do you know, as much money as I have, it would have made too big a dent. He sensed I wasn't going to come through."

I was beginning to shiver once more. It was as much from fatigue as anything else, but my shoes and the bottoms of my trousers were wet.

"Would you like to make a fire?"

"Yes," I said.

He debated it. "No," he said at last, "I'm afraid it would be too hard to start. Everything is damp."

"Yes."

"I hate smoke."

"Yes."

"I'm sorry," he said.

My hands were playing with the sand. Suddenly he fired a shot. Like that. Pop. It dug in one inch below the heel of my shoe.

"Why did you do that?" I asked.

"Don't try to blind me with a handful of dust."

"You're a good shot."

"I've practiced."

"I can see."

"It didn't come naturally. Nothing graceful has ever come naturally to me. Do you think that's unfair?"

"Maybe."

"It's enough to solicit the devil."

We were silent. I tried not to shiver. It seemed to me that such shivering might irritate him, and then what would he do?

"You didn't tell me the rest," I said. "What did you do when Jessica called?"

"I tried to calm her down. I wasn't so calm myself. Lonnie dead! Finally I told her to wait in the car. I'd pick her up."

"What were you planning?"

"I hadn't begun to think. At times like that, all you tell yourself is, 'What a mess.' I didn't have a clue how to handle it, but all the same, I set out for Race Point. However, the directions given me were treacherous. I found myself in North Truro and all turned around. By the time I located Race Point, Laurel was gone and so was the car. I went back to Beach Point to tell Patty Lareine what I thought of her directions, and she, too, was gone. She didn't come back all night. And I never saw Jessica's face again."

"Patty Lareine was living with you?"

"We'll get to that."

"I'd like to."

"First tell me: Did Patty go to your house?" Wardley asked.

"I don't think so."

"You can't remember?"

"I was too drunk. It's possible she passed through the house."

"Do you know," asked Wardley, "what Patty Lareine used to say about your forgetful spells?"

"No."

"She'd say, 'There's the asshole flying up his asshole again.' "

"She would say that."

"She always spoke of you as an asshole," said Wardley. "When you were our chauffeur in Tampa, she used to refer to you that way when she was alone with me. Last month, she still spoke of you that way. Asshole. Why would she call you that?"

"Maybe it was her word for jerk."

"Patty hated you intensely."

"I don't know why," I said.

"I think I do," said Wardley. "Certain men indulge the female component in themselves by encouraging their women to practice special oral sex."

"Oh, Christ," I said.

"Did you and Patty ever have anything of the sort?"

"Wardley, I don't care to talk about it."

"Heteros are uptight about such matters." He sighed. He rolled his eyes. "I wish we did have a fire. It would be sexier."

"It would certainly be cozier."

"Well, we can't." To my amazement, he yawned. Then I realized he did it like a cat. He was casting off tension. "Patty Lareine used to do it for me," he said. "In fact, that's how she got me to marry her. I'd never had it practiced so well before. Then, after we were married, she stopped. Cold turkey. When I indicated that I'd like our little practice to continue, she said, 'Wardley, I can't. Every time I see your face now, it reminds me of your rear end.' That's why I didn't like it at all when she called you 'asshole.' Tim, did she ever do it with you?"

"I'm not going to reply," I said.

He fired the pistol. From where he sat. He didn't aim. Just pointed it, and pressed the trigger. Only the best shots can do that. I was wearing baggy pants and the bullet went through a billow in the trousers above the knee.

"Next time," he said, "I'm going to shatter your thigh. So please answer my question."

He had gotten to me. No question of that. My courage was now down to the reserve tank. It seemed enough under these conditions to keep a semblance of poise.

"Yes," I said, "I asked her to do it once."

"Asked her or made her?"

"She was ready. She was young and it was a novelty to her. I would say she had never done it before."

"When did this happen?"

"The first time Patty Lareine and I went to bed."

"In Tampa?"

"No," I said. "She never told you?"

"Tell me, and I'll tell you."

"I took a trip with a girl to North Carolina. A girl I had been living

with for two years. We answered an ad and went down to North Carolina to meet a couple who wanted to swap partners for a night. On our
arrival, there was this big old boy and his young bride, Patty Lareine."

"Was that when she was called Patty Erlene?"

"Yes," I said, "Patty Erlene. She was married to one of the local
preachers. He doubled as the high school football coach and was the
town chiropractor as well. In his ad, he had said he was a gynecologist.
As he soon told me, 'It's a decoy. No Yankee girl can resist a swap if she
thinks she's getting an obstetrician.' He was one big gangling old boy,
bald, and bountiful down below, at least from what my girl later told
me. To my surprise, they hit it off. On the other hand, Patty Erlene was
excited that I was a real bartender from New York." I stopped. I had the
uneasiness of having talked too much. I had certainly lost my feeling for
his attention.

"And that first night, she actually did it with you?"

I shouldn't have been wondering about his attention.

"Yes," I said, "that night was like no other we had. We seemed made
for each other." Let him live with that, I thought, after I'm gone.

"She did everything?"

"More or less."

"More?"

"Put it that way."

"Did she ever go as far again in Tampa?"

"No," I lied.

"You're lying," he said.

I didn't want him to fire the gun. It came to me that his good father
Meeks must often have struck Wardley without warning.

"Can you take the truth?" I asked.

"Rich people are always lied to," he said. "So it's my pride that I will
live with the truth no matter how unpalatable."

"All right," I said, "in Tampa it did happen."

"When?" he asked. "On what occasions?"

"When she wanted me to kill you."

It was the largest gamble I had yet taken. But Wardley was a man of
his word. He nodded at the truth of what I had said. "I always thought
so," he said. "Yes, of course," he went on, "that's why she spoke of you
that way."

I did not tell him that after our night in North Carolina, Patty Lareine used to write to me for a while. It was as if once I was back in New York, so did our night back up on her too. She had to keep wiping the memory of it off her mouth. "Asshole," she kept calling me in the letters she wrote. "Dear asshole," she would begin, or "Listen, asshole." It never stopped until the letters did. Which was about the time I'd had a year in prison. In the slammer, I did not take to being called such words and didn't answer, and she stopped writing. We were out of touch. Then, a few years later, standing one evening in a bar in Tampa, I felt a tap on my shoulder, and when I turned, saw a beautiful blonde, very well dressed, who said, "Hello, asshole." I was gazing upon the powerful signature of coincidence.

"I guess she really wanted to kill me," Wardley said.

"You have to face it."

He began to weep. He had been holding it for a long time and it came out. To my surprise, I was moved, but that was only half of me. The other part was locked tight—it had never seemed so dangerous to make a move.

After a few minutes he said, "This is the first time I've cried since my last day at Exeter."

"Is that true?" I said. "I cry from time to time."

"You can afford to," he said. "You have something manly to come back to. I'm more or less self-created."

I let that stand.

"How did you and Patty get together again?" I asked.

"She wrote a letter to me. It was a couple of years after our divorce. I had every right to hate her, she said in this letter, but she did miss me. I told myself, 'She's short of money.' I threw her letter away."

"Wasn't Patty awarded a chunk for the divorce?"

"She had to settle for less. My lawyers would have appealed her to death. She couldn't afford to wait. She never told you?"

"We didn't talk about finances."

"She just paid your way?"

"I wanted to be a writer. I made my contract."

"Did you write well?"

"She kept my thoughts too occupied to write as well as I hoped."

"Maybe you're a bartender," said Wardley.

"Maybe I am."

"You don't know anything of her finances?"

"Are you saying she was broke?"

"She had no instinct for investments. Too much of a redneck to trust good advice. I think she began to see that some mean economic years lay ahead."

"So she started writing to you."

"I held off as long as I could. Then I answered. Did you know she kept another post office box in Truro?" Wardley asked.

"I had no idea."

"We corresponded. After a while she revealed her interest. It was to buy the Paramessides estate. I think it must have reminded her of all she'd lost in Tampa."

"And you played with her desire?"

"I wanted to scourge each of the four chambers of her heart. Of course I played with her. For two years I brought her hopes up and then I took them down again."

"And all the while I used to think her hideous moods were my fault."

"Vanity is your vice," said Wardley. "It's not mine. I kept telling myself that to return to her was to go back to the devil. But I missed her. I kept hoping that I might yet be truly attractive to her." He patted the sand by his feet. "Does that surprise you?"

"She never said anything good about you."

"Nor about you. The most unpleasant aspect of Patty's character is that she had to badmouth everybody. If you want to find true lack of compassion, give me a good Christian every time."

"Maybe it's because she gave such good measure other ways."

"Of course," said Wardley. He coughed from the cold. "Do you know I used to fuck her good?"

"No," I said. "She never told me."

"Well, I did. No dyke could have done her better. There were times when I felt sensational around her."

"What happened when she turned up in Tampa with Bolo Green?"

"I didn't mind," said Wardley. "I thought that was clever of her. If she'd appeared on my doorstep by herself after all those years, I would have been suspicious as hell. This way, we had fun. Bolo swings in both directions. We had three-way scenes."

"It didn't bother you watching Patty with another man?"

"I always say, for sexual naïveté, call on the Irish. How could it bother me? While I was in Patty, Bolo was in me. You haven't lived till you feel that little thrill."

"It didn't bother you?" I repeated. "Patty used to describe you as very jealous."

"That was because I was trying to be a husband. There is no way to feel more vulnerable. But now I was playing Mr. Bountiful. I enjoyed it so much that I finally gave the word to Laurel. Go East, dear woman, and bid on the Paramessides estate. She did. Unfortunately, it all got complicated by her greed. Lonnie Pangborn was talking to me on the phone and happened to mention that Oakwode was back in Santa Barbara. I didn't like that. She was supposed to be dickering with the lawyer in Boston. So I had to wonder if she was calling on some rich California friends to help her buy the estate herself. That way, she could really hold me up. By now, I confess, I wanted it. Patty Lareine needed a castle to play the queen, but I wanted her in position to need me altogether. That's not so exceptional, is it?"

"No," I said.

"Laurel's presence in Santa Barbara, therefore, disturbed me. I proposed to Patty that we pay a surprise visit to the Coast. It was, incidentally, a good opportunity to get rid of Bolo. He was taking up too much time."

Wardley's voice had gone dry. It was as if he had determined to tell the tale no matter how his throat might protest. For the first time I recognized that he was even more weary than myself. Was the muzzle of his handgun pointing just a hair toward the ground?

"Laurel couldn't have tried harder at the dinner in Santa Barbara. Told Patty all sorts of fabulous stuff. What a splendiferous personality Patty had, and so forth. When it was over, I told Pangborn, 'I don't trust your woman. Find some business in Boston and stick with Laurel. Keep an eye on her.' After all, he had recommended her. How could I know I was sending him to his suicide?"

I lit a cigarette. "And you and Patty also came East?"

"Yes. That was when I got the place out at Beach Point. Hadn't been here twelve hours when Lonnie did himself in. And the next time I saw Laurel was when Spider Nissen took me out to his shack to visit her body. Did you ever see headless remains? It looks like a statue when they pull the torso out of the lime."

"Where did this take place?"

"In Stoodie's backyard. He had Laurel in a stout metal garbage can. The old-fashioned kind they used to make before plastic got into everything."

"Were you ill?"

"I was aghast. Think of staring upon such a sight in the company of people as awful as Spider and Stoodie."

"But how did you know them in the first place?"

"Through Bolo Green. I have to tell you. The night after Patty disappeared I decided to look for her in the bars on Commercial Street, and there was Bolo. It took a bit of convincing to get him to believe I no longer knew where Patty was."

"And through him you got to know Spider?"

"No, Spider I met by way of Stoodie. It was Bolo who introduced me to Stoodie. That same night. Bolo and Stoodie, it seems, spent last summer dealing drugs together. That's got to be karma."

He sounded distracted. Now I feared that I had been encouraging him to talk for too long. If he started going in too many directions, the pistol might go off in one.

It was not yet time to fear him, however. He still wanted to get the story out. "Yes, Spider came on quickly. Almost as soon as we met. He had heard about me, he said, and he was all for getting into the largest operations immediately. I was ready to shun him except that Spider was making the most incredible presentation. He said he could control the top narcotics officer in town! If I would be forthcoming with the bread, he was ready to run a prodigious drug operation for me. Yes, he said, the Acting Chief of Police was now under his thumb. You may be certain I asked him how he could prove it. That was when he and Stoodie took me out to Stoodie's place, and brought Laurel forth from the lime."

"How'd you know it was Laurel?"

"The silver nail polish. And the tits. You did notice Laurel's tits?"

"What did you say to Spider's proposition?"

"I didn't say no. I was intrigued. I thought: This peculiar town! How extraordinary to be proprietor of a fabulous hotel, and control a mountain of drugs. I'll be equal to a Renaissance prince."

"It wouldn't have worked."

"Well, it wouldn't, but I played with him. After all, I was half out of my mind. Lonnie's dead, Laurel's dismembered, Patty is missing, and these disreputable sleazos have the body in their possession. So I took Spider seriously enough to ask how the headless lady came to him. He was on pot sufficiently to inform me. I can't believe how trusting certain criminal types are. Spider tells me the narc left the body with him, but was reserving the head for himself."

"Regency?" I asked.

"That's the name."

"Did Regency kill Jessica?"

"I don't know. He certainly wanted her body disposed of. How arrogant these drug enforcement people are. I'm sure he had eighteen ways to incriminate Spider, so he assumed he could use him."

"Why not? If the body were produced, Regency could say that Spider and Stoodie had done it. They had no true leverage over him."

"Of course," said Wardley. "Gall backed up by powers. But I couldn't think properly. Being without Patty had me too disturbed. Yet when I got back to Beach Point after this dreadful visit to Stoodie's shack, there was Patty Lareine. Waiting for me. Not a word about where she'd been."

Again he began to cry. It caught me by surprise. He worked, however, to choke down his misery. Like a child forbidden to whimper, he said, "She no longer wanted the Paramessides estate. Now that Lonnie was a suicide, she had decided the deal was spooked. Besides, she was in love. She had decided to tell me the real truth, she said. She wanted to go away with a man. She had been in love with him for months. He wanted to live with her, but had remained loyal to his wife. Now at last he was ready to take off. Did she mind, I asked, telling me who it was? A good man, she said, a strong man, a man without money. What about myself, I asked her. What about Bolo? Was it Bolo? No, she told me, Bolo had been a sad mistake. She had only been trying to drive this other man out of her heart, but she had failed. How do you think I felt?" Wardley asked me now.

"Ashes."

"Ashes. I had not been playing the game I thought I was playing. I realized all over again that I adored her so much I was ready to take whatever she would offer. Even if it was no more than her big toe." He began inhaling very rapidly, as if there was no time to take a deep breath.

" 'All right,' I said to her, 'go out of my life.' I was hoping to clutch some dignity. I felt like a nude standing before a mad artist. 'Just go,' I said. 'It's all right.' 'No,' she said, 'it's not all right. I need money.' Tim, she named a sum on the order of magnitude of what I would have paid for renovations on the Paramessides estate. 'Don't be insane,' I told her. 'I won't give you a cent.' 'Wardley,' she said, 'I reckon you owe me two million and change.'

"I couldn't believe how hideous it was. You know, when I first met her, she was only a stewardess and not at all polished. You have no idea how she developed under my tutelage. She was so bright. She seized so many of the little tricks of making her way in my world. I thought she'd be wild to have a hotel for her palace. She certainly encouraged me all the while to think so. But do you know, *au fond*, she didn't give two spits for high society. Boy, she let me have it. She told me that the two million I was ready to allot to fix up the Paramessides estate had to be squirreled off now into other ventures. With that mysterious friend of hers! She would have had me investing in the cocaine trade."

"She informed you of all that?"

"No, but she said enough. I could see the rest. At the end she said, 'Wardley, I warn you. Just give me the money. Or, this time, you *will* get killed. I have the man to do it now. All the worms will run out of you.' "

He rubbed his face. His nose must have felt as harsh as a salt mine. " 'All right,' I said, 'I'll write a check,' and I went into the bedroom. I took out my .22, popped on the silencer, walked back into the living room and shot her. It was the calmest thing I ever did in my life. I picked up the phone to call the police. I was going to turn myself in. But some spirit of survival must have come right out of Patty and into me. I bundled her up, put her in the car, called Spider to meet me at Stoodie's, and asked them to bury her and Laurel. I would pay them well, I said. What do you think Spider replied?"

"What?"

" 'Take off,' he said, 'and leave the details to me.' "

"The rest is a nightmare?" I asked.

"All of it."

"Why did you tell me you wanted the head of Patty Lareine?"

"Because that was the day I found out that Spider had already performed the act of decapitating her. He buried the body, but he told me he was keeping the head. He giggled when he told me. Spider said he was ready to take a photograph of me holding her head. I could see where Spider's mind was moving. Right into the Hilby millions. They think my money is there to make raids on. As if it were not part of me. I think you can see now why I shot him. What substance do I have other than my money?" He laid the gun on the ground beside him.

"Then, just at this moment, Stoodie had the bad luck to come back with Bolo. I was still standing over Spider's body. Thank God I managed to convince Bolo that Stoodie was the fellow he'd been looking for."

Wardley put his face in his hands. The gun was on the sand beside him, but some instinct told me not to move. When Wardley looked up, his expression—at least as I could see it—was far away.

"You may not believe this," he said, "but Patty was my romantic hope. I don't mean for me. If she'd found true love, I would have been best man at the nuptials. She had such possibilities. I adored the idea that she and I would create this extraordinary place on the very tip of Cape Cod where only the most insanely special people could get reservations. Just the most perfect mix of true celebrity and true society. Oh, how they'd have gone for Patty and me as co-hosts." He gave the weariest sigh. "She never took it seriously. She *gulled* me. Planning all the time to make her fortune in cocaine. Tim, she was crass. And I had no acumen. People like me are a trial to the world if they lose their acumen."

Now he picked up his gun. "I came here thinking I would shoot you. There's a peculiar pleasure in shooting people. It's much more intoxicating than you'd think. So I've been trying to find a good reason to off you. But I'm not certain I can. I can't get angry enough." He sighed. "Maybe I should turn myself in."

"Should you?"

"No," he said, "that's not a viable alternative. During my divorce trial, I suffered abominably. I couldn't live through such ridicule again."

"Yes," I said.

He lay on his side, curled up, brought the gun barrel near his mouth and said, "I guess you're in luck." He put the muzzle in his mouth.

But I think he now felt how vulnerable it would be to lie out here exposed.

"Will you cover me with sand," he asked, "afterward?"

"Yes."

I cannot explain what I did next, but I stood up and came near. Whereupon he took the gun out of his mouth and pointed it at me.

"Trick or treat," he said.

Then he lowered the barrel. "Sit beside me," he said.

I did.

"Put your arm around me," he said.

I obeyed.

"Do you like me a little?"

"Wardley, I do like you a little."

"I hope so," he said, and put the gun to his head and fired into his mind.

For a weapon with a silencer, it made a loud sound. Maybe a door to his spirit was blown ajar.

We sat together for a long time. There would never be another classmate I would mourn so well.

When the chill became intolerable, I rose at last and tried to dig a grave, but the shingle was too cold for my fingers. I could do no more than leave him in a shallow trench covered by a few inches of sand. Then I made a vow to come back with a shovel tomorrow, and started down the beach for the walk to the jetty.

Once I came to the rocks, it took longer. My foot, for all its earlier flexibility, now ached as badly as an exposed tooth, and my shoulder gave the most startling twinges on each mean twist of an unsuspecting nerve.

Yet pain provides its own palliative. Battered by a hundred experiences too large for me, I felt calm, and began at last to think of the death of Patty with something like a commencement of grief. Yes, that might be the antidote to pain—sorrow itself.

I had lost a wife I never comprehended, and with her had departed the vitality of her invincible confidence and the horrid equations of her unfathomable mind.

I began to think of the day before Patty left me—was it now twenty-nine or thirty days ago? We had gone on a drive to look for October foliage that would be prettier than our own scrub pines. There were hardwood trees still in abundance around Orleans at the elbow of the bent arm of the Cape. Coming around a turn, I saw a maple with orange-red plumage against a full blue sky, the leaves quivering and ready, tipped between their last red and the later shadows of the brown oncoming fall. Looking at the tree, I murmured, "Oh, you sweet bitch," and do not know what I meant, but Patty, sitting beside me, said, "I'm going to leave you someday." (It was the only warning she gave.)

"I don't know that it matters," I said. "I don't feel near anymore. It's as if I don't even have half a half of you."

She nodded.

There was always a touch of hyena in her catlike sumptuousness—a hard, untouchable calculation of the will at the corners of her mouth. No matter her strength, she was always full of pity for herself, and now she whispered to me, "I feel so trapped. I'm so terribly trapped."

"What do you want?" I asked.

"I don't know," she said. "It's always out of my reach." And then, in the limited degree to which she could feel sympathy for others, she touched my hand. "Once, I thought I had it," she said, and I squeezed her hand back. For even as I had told Wardley, we had our romantic point of reference. It was the night we met and fornicated like fire dancers and copulated into cornucopias of each other, one night—yes— when we were as happy as Christopher Columbus, for we each discovered America, our country forever divided into two halves. We danced in the pleasure of our complimentary charms, and slept as sweetly as two sugar tits nestled side by side.

In the morning Big Stoop, her husband, put on one of his other hats, and we all went to church, Madeleine and Patty, Big Stoop and I. He conducted the service. He was one of our fundamental American mad-men: he could orgy on Saturday and baptize on Sunday. Our Father's House has many mansions but I'm sure Big Stoop saw Saturday night as the outhouse. I never understood their marriage. He was the football coach and she was the cheerleader, and he got her in trouble and they married. The baby came out stillborn. That was her last attempt at procreation. By the time we met, they had had several returns on their ad. ("No golden showers . . . must be married.") Yes, with talent enough, I could write a book about Big Stoop and the compartments of his American mind, but in this year I will not try to describe him further except to tell you of the sermon, for that I do remember, and had a recollection here, making my way across the rocks, of sitting in a plain white church, no larger than a one-room schoolhouse and no grander than a Hell-Town shed. His voice was near me now that Patty was gone.

"Last night I had a dream," he said, and Patty, sitting on the other side of Madeleine from me, squeezed my hand and whispered up my ear like a high school girl, "*Your* wife—that was *his* dream," but Big Stoop never felt her presence. He went on: "Brethren, it was more than a dream, it was a vision of the end of time. The skies rolled back and Jesus came again on the clouds of glory to gather His children to Him. And it was awful to see, Brethren, the sinners that screamed and cried and begged for mercy, falling on their faces before Him. The Bible says that there will be two women grinding corn—one will be taken and one will be left. There will be two in the bed"—Patty Erlene gave me a stiff jolt to the ribs with her elbow—"one will be taken and one left. Mothers will wail as their babies are lifted from their breast to be with Jesus and they are left behind because they would not give up their sins." Patty Erlene's fingernails were cutting into my palm but I did not know if it was to suppress her giggling or from a pinch of childish fright.

"The Bible says," said Big Stoop, "that there will not be one sin allowed in heaven. You can't be a Christian sitting in the Church on Sunday morning and then stay out of Church on Sunday night because you want to go fishing. Brethren, the Devil wants you to say, 'Well, it won't hurt to miss this one night.' "

"It sure didn't," whispered Patty Erlene with her breath in my ear, while Madeleine, offended to her core by such carrying-on, sat in disapproval, cold as congealed grease, on my other side.

"The next thing you know," said his voice, "you're going to the movie houses, and then you're taking a drink, and then *you are on your way* to Hellfire and damnation—where the fire is not quenched and the worm dieth not."

"You're a hell-cat," whispered Patty Erlene, "and so am I."

"Come, Brethren," said Big Stoop, "before the clouds roll back and it's too late to call for mercy. Come to Jesus tonight. Give up your sins. Give your heart to Jesus. Come and kneel. Patty Erlene, come to the piano. Sing number 256 with us, and let Jesus speak to your heart."

Patty Erlene played the piano in bang-it-out style, and the congregation sang:

Just as I am without a plea
But that Thy blood was shed for me,
And that Thou biddest come to Thee,
Oh, Lamb of God, I come—I come.

Afterward we went back to Big Stoop's house for the Sunday dinner his spinster sister had cooked. It was pot roast done to a gray dead turn, and potatoes, rescued cold and early from the boiling, served with wilted turnip greens. I had rarely met people who had so much vitality on Saturday night as Big Stoop and Patty Erlene, but that Sunday dinner was the other side of the moon. We ate in silence, and all shook hands when we left. A couple of hours later came the automobile accident with Madeleine. It was almost five years before I was to see Patty Erlene again and that was in Tampa where she, after a divorce from Big Stoop, and her stint as an airline stewardess, had met Wardley on a flight and become Mrs. Meeks Wardley Hilby III.

The power of recollection can lift you above pain, and so I concluded my walk on the jetty in no worse condition than when I began. The tide was out and the sand flats carried the smell of the marsh. Under the moon, Irish moss and sea colander waved in tidal pools gifted with silver. I was surprised to find my Porsche where I had left it. Death might be in one universe, but parked automobiles were in another.

Only as I was turning the key in the ignition did it occur to me that the four to five hours I had allowed for Madeleine to arrive must certainly have expired by now. If not for that, I do not know if I would have gone back to my house (Patty's house) to face Regency—no, I might have stopped at The Widow's Walk where it all began and become so drunk I would remember nothing by morning. Instead, I lit another cigarette, set the car down Bradford Street for home and was back before the fag had to be dinched in the ashtray.

Across the street from my door, a police cruiser was parked behind my father's car. It was Regency's. That I was ready to expect, but Madeleine had not arrived.

I didn't know what to do. It seemed crucial to see her first, to arm myself indeed with those mutilated photographs she had found in the locked box, but then it occurred to me that I had not even told her to bring them. Of course she would, but would she? It was not her gift nor her vice to exploit her horrors and woes for practical purposes.

In Madeleine's absence, however, I thought I might as well make certain that my father was all right (although I certainly expected he was), so I walked as silently as I could around the house to the kitchen window and there, on either side of the table, Dougy and Alvin Luther were visible, each appearing to be quite comfortable with a drink in his hand. Indeed, Regency's holster and gun were slung on another chair. I would have sworn by his composure that he had not yet discovered the loss of the machete. But then, it was also possible that he had had no occasion to open his trunk lid.

As I watched they began to laugh, and curiosity overcame me. I thought I would take the chance that Madeleine, not having arrived for five hours, would not get here in the next five minutes. (Although my heart began to race in rebellion against such a gamble.) Nevertheless, I went around the house again, let myself in by the trap door to the cellar and walked to the area beneath the kitchen. It had become my retreat at many a party when I became too bored with guests lapping at my booze (Patty's booze). Thereby I knew that you could hear below all that was said in the kitchen above.

Regency was talking. He was reminiscing, no less, about old days on narcotics in Chicago and told my father of a tough partner he had, a black man named Randy Reagan. "Do you believe the name?" I heard Regency say. "Of course everybody called him Ronnie Reagan. The real Ronnie was only governor in California then, but everybody had heard his name. So Ronnie Reagan became my partner."

"I once had a waiter worked in my bar named Humphrey Hoover," said my father. "He used to say, 'Count the salt shakers that's missing, and multiply by five hundred. That's the receipts for the night.' "

They laughed. Humphrey Hoover! Another of my father's arts. He could keep a man like Regency in his chair for an evening. Now Alvin Luther went on with his story. Ronnie Reagan, it seems, had set up a cocaine bust. But the accomplice was a rat, and when Ronnie came through the door, he received for his pains a sawed-off shotgun blast in his face. They gave him operations to restore the missing half of his physiognomy. "I was feeling sorry for the son of a bitch," said Regency, "so I brought a pup bulldog up to the hospital. But when I got to the room, the doctor was there putting in this plastic fucking eye."

"Oh, no," said my father.

"Yeah," said Regency, "a plastic fucking eye. I had to wait while he installed it. Then, the moment I'm alone with Ronnie I drop the bull pup right on the bed. A tear comes into his real eye. Ronnie says—the poor bastard—he says, 'Will I scare the pup?'

" 'No,' I tell him, 'the pup loves you already.' If peeing all over the blankets is love, the pup loves him already.

" 'How do you think I look?' asks Ronnie Reagan. 'I want the truth.' The poor bastard! His ear is also gone.

" 'Well,' I says, 'it's all right. You never was an orchid.' ' "

They laughed. They would go on, story for story, until I came in. So I left the cellar to return outside, and encountered Madeleine at the front door. She had been registering her nerve to ring the bell.

I made no effort to kiss her. It would have been a mistake.

She clutched me instead, and laid her head on my shoulder until the quivering stilled. "I'm sorry I took so long," she said. "I turned back twice."

"It's all right."

"I brought the pictures," she said.

"Let's go to my car. I have a flashlight there."

By its light, I had one more surprise. The photos were no more or less obscene than my Polaroids, but they were not of Patty Lareine. It was Jessica's head that the scissors had cut from the body. I looked again. No, Madeleine could not tell the difference. Jessica's body looked young, and her face was blurred. It was a natural error. But it offered further light on Alvin Luther Regency. It was one thing to take a beaver shot of one's wife or steady girl, but quite another to convince a lady who had been in your bed for no more than a week. Prowess is prowess, I thought glumly, and debated whether to tell Madeleine who the model was. I did not wish, however, to disturb her further so I kept silent. I could not decide whether the introduction of another woman in her husband's love life would halve her disruption or double it.

She quivered again. I made the decision to take her inside.

"We'll have to be quiet," I said. "He's here."

"Then I can't go in."

"He won't know. I'll put you in my room and you can lock the door."

"It's her room too, isn't it?"

"I'll take you to my study."

We managed to ascend the stairs silently. After we were on the third floor, I guided her to a chair by the window. "Do you want a light?" I asked.

"I'd rather sit in the dark. The view is beautiful through the window." I suppose it was the first time she had ever seen the sand flats of the bay when the moon was on them.

"What are you going to do down there?" she asked.

"I don't know. I've got to have it out with him."

"That's crazy."

"Not with my father present. It's our advantage, really."

"Tim, let's just go away."

"Maybe we will. But I need the answers to a couple of questions first."

"For peace of mind?"

"To keep from going crazy," I nearly said aloud.

"Hold my hands," she said. "Let's just sit here for a moment."

We did. I think her thoughts may have passed into me on the intertwining of our fingers, for I found myself remembering the early days when we met, I, a bartender much in demand (for in New York, good young bartenders build a reputation among restaurant proprietors not unanalogous to good young professional athletes) and she, a saucy hostess, in a Mafia midtown restaurant. Her uncle, a man much respected, got her the job, but she made it her own—how many sports and dudes passing through her purlieu tried to get a piece of her, but we had a perfect romance for a year. She was Italian and a one-man girl and I adored her. She loved silences. She loved sitting in a dim room for hours while the velvets of her loving heart passed over to me. I might have stayed with her forever, but I was young and got bored. She rarely read a book. She knew the name of every famous author who had ever lived but she rarely read a book. She was as smart and shiny as satin, but we never went anywhere except into each other, and that was enough for her, but not for me.

Now I might be going back to Madeleine, and my heart lifted like a wave. A wave at night, be it said. Patty Lareine at her best used to give me emotions that were close to sunlight, but I was approaching forty, and the moon and the mist were nearer to my sentiments.

I relinquished her hands and kissed Madeleine lightly on the lips. It brought back how nice was her mouth and how much like a rose. A faint sound, husky and sensual as the earth itself, stirred in her throat. It was marvelous, or would be so soon as I was not full of thinking of what awaited me below.

"I'll leave you a gun. Just in case," I said, and took Wardley's .22 from my pocket.

"I have one," she said. "I brought my own," and from the flap of her coat she withdrew a little over-and-under Derringer. Two shots. Two .32 holes. Then I thought of Regency's Magnum.

"We're an arsenal," I said, and there was enough light in the room to see her smile. A good line, well delivered, was half, I sometimes thought, of what you needed to keep her happy.

So I went downstairs with a piece, after all.

I did not like the idea, however, of talking to Regency with the bulges of the handgun poking out of my pants or shirt—there was really no place to conceal it. I compromised by leaving it on a shelf above the telephone within easy reach of the kitchen door. Then I strolled in on both men.

"Hey, we never heard you open the outside door," said my father.

Regency and I said hello with eyes averted, and I made myself a drink to coat the double barrels of my fatigue. I threw the first bourbon down neat and poured another before I put the ice in the glass.

"Which leg are you filling?" asked Regency. He was drunk, and when I finally did reach his eyes I could see that he was not nearly so calm as he had appeared by his posture when seen through the kitchen window, or as I had supposed by the sound of his voice heard through the kitchen floor—no, he had the ability of many a big powerful man to stow whole packets of unrest in various parts of his body. He could sit unmoving like a big beast in a chair, but if he had had a tail, it would have been whipping the rungs. Only his eyes, glazed by the last hundred hours of lurid unmanageables and preternaturally bright, gave any clue to what he was sitting on.

"Madden," he said, "your father is a prince."

"Ho, ho," said my father, "you'd think we were getting along."

"Dougy, you're the best," said Regency. "I'll flatten anyone who disagrees. What do you say, Tim?"

"Well," I said, tipping my glass, "cheers."

"Cheers," said Regency, tipping his.

There was a pause. He said, "I told your father. I'm in need of a long vacation."

"Are we drinking to your retirement?"

"I'm resigning," he said. "This town brings out everything that's worst in me."

"They should never have assigned you here."

"Right."

"Florida is where you belong," I said. "Miami."

"Who," said Regency, "put the hair up your ass?"

"All the tongues in town," I told him. "It's common knowledge you're a narc."

His eyelids fell heavily. I do not wish to exaggerate, but it is as if he had to turn a mattress over. "That obvious, huh?" he asked.

"There's a job profile to being a narc," said my father equably. "You can't conceal it."

"I told those chowderheads who appointed me, it was bad enough pretending to be a State Trooper, but this was the pits. Portuguese are stupid, stubborn people except for one thing. You can't bullshit them. Acting Chief of Police!" If there had been a cuspidor, he would have spit into it. "Yeah, I'm going," he said, "and, Madden, don't say 'Three cheers.' " He burped and said "Excuse me" to my father for the indelicacy, then looked morose. "I've got an ex-Marine over me," he said. "Can you imagine a Green Beret in a chain of command under a Marine? It's like putting the steak on the fire and the skillet on top of the steak."

My father thought that was funny. Maybe he laughed to ameliorate everyone's mood, but it did tickle him.

"I got one regret, Madden," said Regency, "it's that we never did get to talk a little about our philosophies. It would have been good to get shit-face."

"You're practically there right now," I said.

"Never. Do you know how much I can drink? Tell him, Dougy."

"He says he's halfway through his second fifth," said my father.

"And if you put a Mickey in my glass, I'd drink right through that too. I burn the stuff faster than it can touch me."

"You have a lot to burn," I said.

"Philosophy," he said. "I'll give you a sample. You think I'm a crude, unlettered son of a bitch. Well, I am, and proud of it. You know why? A cop is a human creature born stupid and raised in stupidity. But he desires to become bright. You know why? It is God's wish. Every time a stupid guy gets a little intelligence, the devil's in shock."

"I always thought," I said, "that a man becomes a cop to be shielded from his own criminality."

The remark was too smart-ass for the occasion. I knew it as it left my lips.

"Fuck you," said Regency.

"Hey . . ." I said.

"Fuck you. I'm trying to talk philosophy and you make quips."

"That's twice," I said, holding up a finger. He was about to say it again and restrained himself. My father's mouth, however, was tight. He was not pleased with me. I could see where it would be a disadvantage to have him there. Regency would not be divided so much as myself. Alone with Alvin, I would not have cared if he said "Fuck you" all night long.

"What is the power of a dirty soul?" asked Regency.

"Tell me," I said.

"Do you believe in karma?"

"Yes," I said. "Most of the time."

"So do I," he said. He reached across and shook my hand. For a moment I think he debated whether to crunch my fingers, and then gave me the charity of releasing them. "So do I," he repeated. "It's an Asian idea, but what the hell, there's cross-fertilization in war, right? There ought to be. All that slaughter. At least, let's get a couple of new cards in the deck, right?"

"What's your logic?"

"I got one," he said. "It's as big as a battering ram. If a lot of people die unnecessarily in a war, a lot of innocent American kids"—he held up a hand to forestall any argument—"and a lot of innocent Vietnamese, I'll give you that, the question becomes: What's their redress? What's their redress in the scheme of things?"

"Karma," said my father, beating him to the punch. If my father didn't know how to wear a drunk down, who did?

"That's right. Karma," he said. "You see, I am not an ordinary cop."

"What are you," I asked, "a social butterfly?"

My father happened to like that one. We all laughed, Regency the least.

"The average cop puts down cheap hoods," he said. "I don't. I respect them."

"For what?" asked my father.

"For having the moxie to get born. Contemplate my argument: Think about it. The strength of a rotten, dirty soul is that no matter how foul it is, it has succeeded in being reborn. Answer that one."

"What about gay people being reborn?" I asked.

I had him there. His prejudices had to bow to his logic. "Them, too," he said, but it wearied him of the argument.

"Yeah," he said, looking at his tumbler, "I've decided to resign. In fact, I have. I left them a note. I'm taking a long leave of absence for personal reasons. They'll read it and send it to the Marine in Washington. The grunt who's over me. They took this grunt and ran him through a computer. Now he thinks only in BASIC! What do you think he'll say?"

"He'll say your personal reasons translate into psychological reasons," I said.

"Fucking aye. Up his Mrs. Grundy, I say."

"When are you leaving?"

"Tonight, tomorrow, next week."

"Why not tonight?"

"I have to turn in the cruiser. It's town-owned."

"You can't turn it in tonight?"

"I can do anything I want. I think I want a rest. I've been working for eight years without a real vacation."

"Are you feeling sorry for yourself?"

"Me?" I had made the mistake of jolting him. He looked at my father and myself as if measuring us for the first time. "Fellow, get it straight," he said. "I have nothing to complain about. I have the kind of life God wants you to have."

"What kind is that?" asked my father. I think he was genuinely curious.

"Action," said Regency. "I've had all the action I wanted. Life gives a man two balls. I've used them. Let me tell you. It's a rare day when I don't bang two women. I don't sleep well at night if I haven't gotten my second bang in. Do you read me? There's two sides to one's nature. They both got to express themselves before I can sleep."

"What are those two sides?" asked my father.

"Dougy, I'll tell you. They are my enforcer and my maniac. Those are my two names for myself."

"Which one is talking now?" I asked.

"The enforcer." He laughed to himself. "You had to be wondering if I'd say the maniac. But you haven't seen *him* yet. I'm merely enforcing this conversation with two *so-called* good men."

He had gone too far. I could take his insults, but there was no reason for my father to suffer them.

"When you turn in your police cruiser," I said, "be careful to wash out the mats in your trunk. The bloodstains from the machete are all over it."

It came to him like a bullet from a thousand yards away. By the time the idea reached, its force was gone, and the shot fell at his feet.

"Oh, yeah," he said, "the machete."

Then he struck himself across the face with more force than I had ever seen a man give to a blow against his own person. If someone else had done it, the act would have been comic, but in his case, the sound shattered the air in the kitchen.

"Would you believe it?" he said. "This sobers me up." He seized the edge of the kitchen table in his hands and gave it a squeeze. "I'm trying," he said, "to be a gentleman about all this and leave town quietly, Madden, without impinging on you and without you encroaching on me."

"Is that why you're here?" I asked. "To leave quietly?"

"I want to see the lay of the land."

"No," I said, "you want the answers to some questions."

"Maybe you haven't got it wrong for once. I thought it might be more courteous to pay a visit than pull you in for an interrogation."

"That's all you need," I said. "If you bring me in, you have to enter me on the books. Then I don't answer a single question. I just get a lawyer. When I finish telling him what I know, he'll ask the State to investigate you. Regency, do me a favor. Treat me with the same courtesy you'd give a Portugee. Don't try these bullshit threats."

"Hear, hear," said my father, "he's laying it out for you, Alvin."

"What do you know," said Regency. "Your son is not incompetent with a problem."

I glared at him. When our eyes locked, I felt like a small craft cutting too near the bow of a ship.

"Let's talk," he said. "We got more in common than we're opposed. Isn't that true?" he asked my father.

"Talk," said my father.

Regency's expression was bent by the last remark as much, I thought, as if we were brothers at odds looking for good marks from our father. The insight meant much. For I recognized then how jealous I was of Regency now that he was around Dougy. It was as if he, not I, were the good, strong and unmanageable son that Big Mac wanted to straighten out. God, I was as bad about my father as most girls are about their mothers.

Now all three of us stayed silent. There are chess games where half of the time allotted a player is spent on one move. He is studying how to go on. So I was silent.

Finally I decided that his confusion had to be deeper than mine.

Therefore I said, "Correct me if I'm wrong, but you want answers to these questions. One, where is Stoodie? Two, where is Spider?"

"Check," he said.

"Where is Wardley?"

"Ditto."

"Where is Jessica?"

"I'll buy that."

"And where is Patty?"

"You got it all," he said. "Those are my questions."

If he had had a tail, he would have thumped it hard at the mention of Jessica's name and twice as hard at Patty's.

"Well," he said, "let's have the answers."

I wondered if he was wired. Then I realized it didn't matter. He was not there to act as a police officer. The .357 Magnum in the holster on the chair was what I wanted to keep my eyes on, rather than the remote possibility that he was recording what I said. After all, he was here with me to look for his own sanity.

"What are the answers?" he repeated.

"Both women are dead," I told him, as if he might not know.

"Dead?" His surprise lacked all conviction.

"I found their heads in the same place my marijuana is kept." I waited.

He really didn't have the conviction that to pretend astonishment would serve any purpose.

"What happened to those heads?" he asked.

"You put them there, didn't you?"

"I never put both heads there," he said. To my astonishment, he began without warning to groan. Like a wounded animal. "I've been in hell," he said. "I can't believe it. I've been in hell."

"I'll bet you have," whispered my father.

"It doesn't matter anymore," Regency said.

"Why did you sever Jessica's head?" my father asked.

He hesitated. "I can't tell you."

"I believe you want to," said my father.

"Let's slow up," said Regency. "I'll tell you what you want to know, provided you inform me about what I want to know. *Quid pro quo.*"

"It won't work," I said. "You have to trust me."

"Where's your stack of Bibles?" he asked.

"It won't work," I repeated. "Every time I tell you something, you're going to ask another question. After I tell it all, there won't be any reason for you to give anything back."

"Turn it around," he said. "If I talk first, what's in it for you to tell me?"

"Your Magnum," I said.

"You think I'd off you in cold blood?"

"No," I said, "I think you'd lose your temper."

My father nodded. "That's logical," he murmured.

"All right," Regency said. "But, go first. Give me one piece of news I don't have."

"Stoodie is dead."

"Who did it?"

"Wardley."

"Where is Wardley?"

"You have a reflex," I said. "You ask questions. I'll tell you when the time comes. Keep your part of the bargain."

"I'd like to meet this Wardley," said Regency. "Every time I take a step, he's underfoot."

"You'll meet him," I said. Only after the words were out of my mouth did I realize how spooked they were.

"I'd like to. I'd give him a fistful of teeth."

I began to laugh. I couldn't help it. That may, however, have been the best reaction. Regency poured himself a drink and swallowed it. I realized it was the first liquor he had tasted since I mentioned the machete.

"All right," he said, "I'll tell you my story. It's a good one." He looked at my father. "Dougy," he said, "I don't respect many people. I respect you. From the moment I came in here. The last guy I met who was your equal was my colonel in the Green Berets."

"Make it a general," said Dougy.

"We'll get there," said Regency. "But I want to make it clear. There's rough stuff ahead."

"I would think so," said Dougy.

"You're going to lose sympathy with me."

"Because you hated my son?"

"Hated. That's past tense."

My father shrugged. "You seem to respect him now."

"I don't. I half respect him. I used to think he was dirt. Now I don't."

"Why?" I asked.

"I'll tell it my way," he said.

"All right."

"Get it straight. I did a lot. Tim, I was trying to drive you off your nut."

"You nearly succeeded."

"I had a right to."

"Why?" asked Dougy.

"My wife, Madeleine, when I first met her, was a rescue case. Your son drove her into depravity. She was a cokehead. I could have arrested her. Your son put her in orgies, cracked her up in his car, destroyed her womb and took off on her a year later. I inherited a woman who had such a habit she was obliged to deal for the stuff in order to feed her own nose. You try living with a female who can't have your son. So, get it straight, Madden, I hated your guts."

"Well, you stole my wife in turn," I said quietly.

"I tried to. Maybe she stole me. I got caught between two women, your wife and mine."

"Jessica, too," I said.

"I make no apologies. When your wife took off, she was not only leaving you, she was leaving me, buster. I got my habit. Love has noth-ing to do with it. I tool two women a night. I've even made it with some of Stoodie's disease-bags—to give you an idea of the force of the principle," he said with some verbal pride. "Jessica was a surrogate for Patty, no more."

"Then you and Madeleine . . . every night you went home?"

"Of course." He belted more bourbon. "It's simple. Let's not get side-tracked. What I want to say is that I hated you, and I have a simple mentality. So I took Jessica's head and put it next to your marijuana. Then I told you to go to your stash."

"Didn't you think I might associate you?"

"I figured it would open your ass. I thought you would die in your own shit. That's the word."

"Did you put the blood on the front seat of my car?"

"I did."

"Whose was it?"

He didn't reply.

"Jessica's?"

"Yes."

I was about to ask, "How did you do it?" but I could see his eyes going in and out of focus as if the scene were still thrusting itself upon his mind and he kept forcing it back. I wondered if he had used her head for such a purpose but I put the thought away before I could start to visualize it.

"Why," asked my father, "didn't you do a test next day for the blood on the seat of the car?"

Regency smiled like a cat. "Nobody would ever believe," he said, "that I put the blood there if I was too dumb to test it, and let you wash it off. How could they ever accuse me of entrapment then?" He nodded. "I woke up that morning worried that I would be accused of entrapping you. It sounds stupid now, but that's how I was thinking then."

"You were losing the best part of your case against Tim."

"I didn't want to arrest him. I wanted to drive him nuts."

"Did you kill Jessica?" I asked. "Or did Patty?"

"We'll come to that. It's not the point. The point is that I was crazy about Patty, but all she'd talk about is you, and how much she hated you, and how you used up her life. All I could see is that you had half her guts, so what was she bellyaching about? Then I got it. She fucking well had to destroy a man. Because when I wouldn't lift a finger against you, she almost destroyed me. She took off. So I got the picture then. I was supposed to do a job on you. Forsake my police vows and do a job."

"It wasn't a small one," said Dougy.

"Fucking aye. It was *brilliant*." He shook his head. "The details were brilliant. I told Patty to take the gun that was used on Jessica and put it back in its case uncleaned. The smell alone should have given you a heart attack. There you were, all passed out, and she stopped by the bed and put the gun away."

"How did you ever find my Polaroids that night? Patty didn't know where they were."

He looked blank.

"What kind of Polaroids?" he asked.

I believed him. My heart fell into a small hole lined with cold lead. "I found some Polaroids with the heads cut off—" I started to tell him.

"Patty says you do crazy things when you're drunk. Maybe you sliced those heads off yourself."

I didn't wish to live with the thought, but how could I confute him?

"Well, if you were to cut up a photo," I asked, "why would you do it?"

"I wouldn't. Only a creep would do that."

"But you did. You cut up Jessica's photos."

He took a little more bourbon. A paroxysm seized his throat. He spat forth the bourbon.

"It's true," he said. "I cut up Jessica's photos."

"When?" I asked.

"Yesterday."

"Why?"

I thought he was going to have a fit. "So I would stop seeing her last expression," he managed to say. "I want to get her last expression out of my system."

His jaws were grinding, his eyes bulged and his neck muscles knotted. But he pushed out the question, "How did Patty die?"

Before I could answer he gave a fearful groan, stood up, went over to the door and began to butt his head against the doorjamb. I could feel the kitchen shake.

My father approached from behind, seized him around the chest and tried to pull him away. He threw my father off. My father was seventy. Nonetheless, I could not believe it.

It calmed Regency, however. "I'm sorry," he said.

"So be it," said my father, giving farewell to some last illusion that strength remains intact.

I was afraid of Regency again. As if I were the accused and he the aggrieved husband of the victim, I said softly, "I had nothing to do with Patty's death."

"I will pull you apart with my hands," he said, "if you are telling a lie."

"I didn't know she was dead until I saw her head in the burrow."

"I didn't either," he said, and began to weep.

He must not have cried since he was ten years old. The sounds that came out were like the pounding of a machine when one of the legs comes loose from the floor. I felt like a towel boy in a whorehouse comparing my grief to his. How he had loved my wife!

Yet I knew I could ask him anything now. Weeping, he was helpless. He had lost his rudder. He would wallow in questions.

"Did you remove Jessica's head from the burrow?"

He rolled his eyes. No.

I had an inspiration. "Did Patty?"

He nodded.

I was going to ask why, but he could hardly speak. I didn't know how to continue.

My father stepped in. "Did Patty think," he asked, "that no matter what my son deserved, you couldn't drop the head on him?"

Regency hesitated. Then he nodded.

How would I ever know if that was the reason or whether she had removed it to confuse me further? His nod did not convince me. In any case, he nodded. I also wondered if Patty had some notion of black-mailing Wardley with the head, but I would never find out.

"Patty asked you to keep the head?" my father went on.

He nodded.

"You hid it for her?"

He nodded.

"And then Patty left you?"

He nodded. "Gone," he managed to say. "She left me with the head."

"So you decided to put that back where it had been?"

Regency nodded.

"And now you also found," said my father in a most gentle voice, "Patty's head. It had been placed there too."

Regency put his hands to the back of his head and used them to bend his neck. He nodded.

"Was that the most terrible sight you ever saw?"

"Yes."

"How did you keep yourself together?"

"I did," said Regency, "until now." He began to weep again. He made a sound like a horse screaming.

I thought of the time when we smoked marijuana in his office. He could only have discovered Patty's head a few hours before, yet he had concealed his agitation. Such prodigies of will were not easy to watch as they came apart now. Was this how a man looked just before he had a stroke?

My father said, "Do you know who put Patty next to Jessica?"

He nodded.

"Was it Nissen?"

He nodded. He shrugged. Maybe he didn't know.

"Yes, it had to be," said my father.

I agreed. It had to be Spider. I had only to contemplate how implicated Spider must have felt himself. Of course, he would have wanted to implicate me. Yes, he and Stoodie had wanted to catch me with the heads. Who would believe I was innocent if I was found with two heads?

"Did you kill Jessica?" I asked Regency.

He shrugged.

"It was Patty?"

He shook his head. Then he nodded.

"It was Patty?"

He nodded.

I wondered if I did not know the story. Of this much I could be certain: Patty and Regency, not Wardley, had been there to meet Jessica at Race Point, and probably it was Patty who drove the car with Lonnie's body back to The Widow's Walk. Then all three must have gone off together in the police cruiser. Somewhere in the woods they stopped and there Patty shot Jessica. Patty shot Jessica.

I could not say why so much as that she had her reasons. Who could measure Patty's rage when it came to reasons? Jessica had tried to purchase the Paramessides estate for herself. Jessica had had a fling with Alvin Luther. In extreme circumstances it would take no more than one reason to violate Patty's temper. Yes, I could see her jamming a gun barrel into Jessica's mendacious lips. And if Ms. Pond had chosen at that moment to appeal for help to Regency and if Regency had made a move to take the gun away, yes, that would have been enough to kick a trigger. Patty, like me, had lived for years on such an edge. With anger such as ours, murder—most terrifying to say—could prove the cure for all the rest.

Regency sat in his chair the way a fighter sits in his corner after he has taken a terrible beating in the last round.

"Why did you sever Jessica's head?" I asked, but having asked, was obliged to pay the price: in my mind, I saw the sweep of the machete blade.

He made a gurgling sound in his throat. His mouth was distended at the corner. I began to think that indeed he was having a stroke. Then his voice came out hoarse and full of reverence. "I wanted," he said, "to finalize Patty's fate with mine."

He fell off his chair onto the floor. His limbs began to thrash.

Madeleine came into the kitchen. She was holding the Derringer in her hand but I do not think she was aware of that. I suppose she had held it all the while she was up in the study.

She looked older and more Italian than before. Her face showed something of the mute fright a stone wall may feel when it is about to be pulled down. She was further away than any of us from the promise of tears. "I can't leave him," she said to me. "He's ill, and I think he may die."

Regency's fit was finished now but for his right heel. It beat against the floor in an ongoing convulsion, a lashing of that tail he did not have.

It took all of my father and myself to carry him upstairs, and then it was a near thing. We almost toppled more than once. I laid him on the king-size bed that Patty and I had occupied upon a time. What the devil, he had been ready to die for her, not I.

Epilogue

Regency lay there day after day and Madeleine nursed him as if he were
a dying god. It is incredible what you can get away with in Provincetown. She called the police station in the morning to tell them that he
had had a breakdown and she was taking him on a long trip. Would
they arrange the papers for a leave of absence? Since I had found the wit
to wash the trunk of his cruiser before dawn and park it at Town Hall
with the keys under the seat, there was nothing to connect my house to
his absence. Madeleine made a point of calling his office each day for
four days and chatted with the Sergeant about his condition and the
poor weather in Barnstable, and how she had had the phone turned off
so he wouldn't be disturbed. Indeed, she did have her phone service
disconnected. Then, on the fifth day, Regency made the mistake of
recovering to a degree, and we had some horrible scenes.

He lay in bed and cursed us all. He spoke of how he would bust us.
He would have me taken down for my marijuana patch. He was also
going to accuse me of the murder of Jessica. My father, he declared, was
a closet sodomite. He, Regency, was leaving for Africa. He would be a
professional soldier. He was also stopping in El Salvador. He would
send me a postcard. It would be a photo of himself holding a machete.
Ha, ha. He sat there in bed, his muscles bulging out of his T-shirt, his
mouth twisted from the stroke, his voice coming to him by way of new
arrangements in his brain, and he picked up the phone and slammed it
down when he discovered the line was dead. (I had been quick to cut

it.) We gave him tranquilizers and he went through the pills like a bull breaks a fence.

Only Madeleine could control him. I saw a side of her I had never witnessed before. She would soothe him, she would lay a hand on his forehead and calm him, and when all else failed, she would upbraid him into silence. "Keep quiet," she would say, "you are paying for your sins."

"Are you going to stay with me?" he would ask.

"I will stay with you."

"I hate you," he told her.

"I know that."

"You're a filthy brunette. Do you know how dirty brunettes are?"

"You need a bath yourself."

"You disgust me."

"Take this pill and be silent."

"It's designed to injure my testicles."

"Good for you."

"I haven't had a hard-on in three days. Maybe I'll never have one again."

"Never fear."

"Where's Madden?"

"I'm here," I said. I was always there. She tended him alone at night, but my father or I was always on guard in the hall holding his Magnum.

Very few calls came on the downstairs phone. No one who was left connected me to much. Regency, as far as anyone knew, was on the road. Beth was gone, and Spider as well, so people, if they thought of them, assumed they were on a trip. After all, the van was also gone. Stoodie's family, being afraid of him, were probably happy not to hear. No one I knew missed Bolo, and Patty was assumed to be traveling in some part or another of the wide world. So was Wardley. In a few months Wardley's relatives might consider how long he had been away without a word and declare him a missing person: after seven years, the nearest of kin, just in case, could pick up his estate. In a few months I might declare Patty missing, or then again, not open my mouth. I thought I would let events decide that for me.

Jessica Pond's son, Lonnie Oakwode, could yet prove to be a problem. But then, how could he connect me to her? I did worry about my tattoo and Harpo, but not too much. Having informed on me once, he would not do it again, and the tattoo I would alter as soon as I could.

It was Regency. If our security depended on Alvin Luther, then we had none. He inhabited every crossroads. Nor did I like the way he kept to his bed. It indicated to me no more than that he was waiting until he could find a story for himself. In any event, he did not leave his bed.

Within it, however, he had a fearful mouth. To Madeleine, in our hearing, he said, "I made you come sixteen times in one night."

"Yes," she said, "and none were any good."

"That," he said hopefully, "is because you got no womb."

She shot him that afternoon. Any one of us could have done it, but it happened to be Madeleine. My father and I had already discussed it in the hallway. "There's no way out," Dougy said. "It has to be done."

"He's sick," I said.

"He may be sick, but he's no victim." Dougy looked at me. "I have to do it. I understand him. He's my kind of guy."

"If you change your mind," I said, "I can manage it." I could. My damnable faculty of being able to visualize what I might soon see was becoming more palpable. In my mind, I discharged Regency's Magnum into his chest. My arm flew up in the air from the kick of the handgun. His face contorted. I saw the maniac. Regency looked like a wild boar. Then he died, and as he did, his face took on an austere look, and his chin became as wooden and set as the good jaw of George Washington.

Do you know, that was the last expression he offered before he died? I came in after the double blast of Madeleine's little Derringer, and he was expiring on what had been my marriage bed. It seems the last thing he said before she pulled the trigger was "I liked Patty Lareine. She was big time and I belong there."

"Good luck," said Madeleine.

"I thought you were big time when I met you," he said, "but you were small potatoes."

"Bet on it," said Madeleine and pulled the trigger.

It was nothing remarkable to go out on, but she had come to her own conclusion that he must be executed. Crazy people in serious places had to be executed. That much you learned with your Mafia milk.

A year later, when she would talk about it, she told me, "I just waited for him to say the word that would get my blood to rise." Do not call an Italian queen small potatoes.

His body was taken out to sea by my father that night. Regency was buried with a cement block tied by separate wires to his waist, his armpits and his knees. By now, of course, my father was practiced at such a course. On the first morning after Alvin Luther had his attack and lay unconscious, Dougy insisted on being taken out in my boat to Wardley's cemetery on Hell-Town beach, and there had me find the graves. I did. That night while I kept guard over our fallen narc, my father put in six hours of the most sordid labor. Near the dawn, on the rising of the tide, he took out all five bodies to the deep water and sank them well. Doubtless I am in danger of writing an Irish comedy, so I will not describe the gusto with which Dougy now made his preparations to take Alvin Luther to the watery rest, except to say his comment when done was "Maybe I been in the wrong occupation all this time." Maybe he was.

Madeleine and I went out to Colorado for a while, and now we inhabit Key West. I try to write, and we live on the money that comes from her work as a hostess in a local restaurant and mine as a part-time bartender in a hole across the street from her place. Once in a while we wait for a knock on the door, but I am not so sure it will ever come. There was a flurry about the disappearance of Laurel Oakwode and pictures of her son in the papers. He said he would not rest until he found his mother, but his face in the photographs lacked, I thought, the kind of character you need for such a search, and the feature story hinted that the local people in Santa Barbara were ready to assume that Laurel, sharing a financial peccadillo or two with Lonnie Pangborn, might have found a wealthy Singapore businessman or someone of that ilk. Despite the shirred blood in the car trunk, Pangborn's end was officially called a suicide.

One piece appeared in the Miami *Herald* about the disappearance of Meeks Wardley Hilby III, and a reporter actually tracked me down to Key West and asked if I thought Patty and Wardley might be together again. I told him they were both out of my life but dwelling in Europe, or Tahiti, or somewhere between. I suppose that story can always flare up again.

No one ever seemed to want to know what happened to Regency. It is hard to believe, but there were almost no official inquiries to Madeleine. A man from the Drug Enforcement Administration in Washington telephoned her once and she told him she and Regency had been driving down to Mexico, but Alvin disappeared on her in Laredo, so she never crossed the border. (Earlier, on our way to Colorado, we had even taken the long detour to Laredo to provide her with a motel receipt that she could show official eyes if her story was ever questioned.) I do not think, however, that anyone on the official side of the drug business was wholly unhappy to lose him. There, for now, it rests. I asked Madeleine once about Alvin's brother, but the occasion on which the photograph of those nephews was taken, happened to be the only time she met his family—one brother.

Since we had little money, we thought of selling our respective houses, but neither was in our name. I guess they will be taken eventually for taxes.

My father is still alive. The other day I received a letter from him. It said: "Keep your fingers nice and crossed, but the chirpy birds, to their big surprise, now say I got remission. It's as big as absolution to them."

Well, Douglas Madden's son, Timothy Madden, has his own theory. I suspect my father's present state of physiological grace has something to do with all the heads and bodies he plumbed and weighted and carried out to sea.

No wonder that cancer is so expensive to cure.

And I? Well, I am so compromised by so many acts that I must try to write my way out of the internal prison of my nerves, my guilts and my deep-rooted spiritual debts. Yet I would take the chance again. In truth, it is not all bad. Madeleine and I sleep for hours with our arms around each other. I live within the fold of her deed, not uncomfortable and not insecure, deeply attached to her and aware that all my present stability of mind rests on the firm foundation of a mortal crime.

Let no one say, however, that we escape from Hell-Town wholly unscathed. One fine summer sunset in Key West when winds from the equator were blowing across the Caribbean and the air conditioning had given out, I could not sleep for thinking of the photographs of Madeleine and Patty that I beheaded with a pair of scissors. For it came to me then to remember that I had done it after sunset (in some dreadful act of amateur voodoo, I suppose, to keep Patty from leaving me) yes, did it just before we set out for the séance which Harpo conducted. If you remember, Nissen began to scream because he had a vision of Patty in her final state.

What can I tell you? The last news I had from Provincetown was by way of a friendly floater who passed through Key West and told me Harpo went mad. It seems he gave another séance some time ago and claimed to glimpse six bodies at the bottom of the sea. From these depths, two headless women spoke to him. Poor Harpo was committed, and from what I hear, is only to be released a little later this year.

Comedy:
    bad people and things, marriages, drinking
    parties, gaming, swindling, and mischievous
    servants, braggart squires, intrigues, youthful
    indiscretion, stingy old age, procuring, and the
    like as they occur daily among the common
    people.

Tragedy:
    death-blows, desperations, infanticide and
    parricide, fire, incest, war, insurrection, wailing,
    howling, sighing.

—Martin Opitz von Boberfeld
(1597–1639)

While Provincetown is a real place, and is most certainly located on Cape Cod, a few names and places have been changed and a couple of houses are invented, as well as one important job. There is not now, and so far as I know, has never been an Acting Chief of Police in Provincetown. The police force in my novel bears, incidentally, no relation to the real one in town. This is in preface to remarking that all the characters are products of my imagination and all the situations are fictional. Any resemblance to living people is entirely coincidental.

I'd like to acknowledge John Updike's gracious permission to reprint the excerpt from his "One's Neighbor's Wife" in *People One Knows,* Lord John Press, California, 1980. Its use in the novel is, of necessity, anachronistic. In addition, I'd like to thank my old friend Roger Donoghue, who first told me the anecdote from which the title is taken.

N. M.